Cynewulf, Charles William Kent

Elene

An Old English Poem

Cynewulf, Charles William Kent

Elene
An Old English Poem

ISBN/EAN: 9783337401092

Printed in Europe, USA, Canada, Australia, Japan

Cover: Foto ©Andreas Hilbeck / pixelio.de

More available books at **www.hansebooks.com**

EDITED WITH INTRODUCTION, LATIN ORIGINAL, NOTES, AND
COMPLETE GLOSSARY

BY

CHARLES W. KENT, M.A.(U. of Va.), Ph.D.(*Leipsic*)

PROFESSOR OF ENGLISH AND MODERN LANGUAGES
IN THE UNIVERSITY OF TENNESSEE

— —oo♦oo— —

BOSTON, U.S.A., AND LONDON
PUBLISHED BY GINN & COMPANY
1889

TYPOGRAPHY BY J. S. CUSHING & CO., BOSTON.

PRESSWORK BY GINN & CO., BOSTON.

TO

THOSE SCHOLARS

TO WHOM AMERICA OWES THE REVIVAL OF THE

STUDY OF

𝕺𝖑𝖉 𝕰𝖓𝖌𝖑𝖎𝖘𝖍

THIS LITTLE VOLUME IS DEDICATED

AS A MARK OF THE AUTHOR'S HIGH ESTEEM, AND A

PLEDGE OF HIS HUMBLE SUPPORT

PREFACE.

IT was at first intended that this edition should be the joint work of Dr. Henry Johnson, of Bowdoin College, Maine, and the present editor. Those who miss the scholarly criticism and excellent taste of Dr. Johnson cannot more sincerely regret that his duties and engagements threw the burden of editing upon me, than I have regretted the loss of his aid and advice. His sympathy and interest, I am fortunate in being able to say, I have retained.

Because I do not know how to divide my knowledge in order to ascribe to its proper source each of its parts, I gratefully and cheerfully acknowledge my general indebtedness to my esteemed instructors, Drs. Napier, Zupitza, and Wülker. Without their influence and encouragement my study of Old English would have been meagre indeed, and without their instruction perhaps this work would never have been attempted.

In attributing, then, all that is good in this edition to them, I assume all responsibility for its errors and deficiencies.

To Professor Wülker I am furthermore indebted for renewed expressions of interest in this edition, and to Professor Garnett, of the University of Virginia, and Dr.

Baskervill, of Vanderbilt University, I owe sincere thanks for appreciated kindnesses.

The text of this edition is that of Zupitza's Second Edition, carefully compared with Wülker's Edition and Zupitza's Third Edition, in which the results of Napier's collation are contained.

The introduction and the notes have been prepared as helps for students, and in nowise to furnish scholars with an *apparatus criticus*. The glossary has been made more complete than is usual in English editions of Old English poems, and it is hoped that it may prove of especial use to students.

I do not deprecate unfavorable criticism; if the book deserve it, in the interest of scholarship, let it not be withheld; but I do beg those to whom the errors seem too numerous, to attribute them not to carelessness, but to my inexperience in text-editing, and the necessity I have been under of being my own proof-reader.

                                        CHARLES W. KENT.
UNIVERSITY OF TENNESSEE,
     June 3, 1889.

INTRODUCTION.

MANUSCRIPT.

THAT a manuscript in letters that resembled the Latin letters, but in a language unknown to the Italian scholars, was preserved in the Cathedral Library in Vercelli, was known early in this century. It was even conjectured that this was an Old English manuscript; but this was not ascertained with certainty until 1822, when Dr. Fr. Blume visited, among others, the library of Vercelli, and not only called the attention of scholars to it, but also made a copy of the poetical parts. Blume published the results of this famous visit to Vercelli, in 1824.

Kemble intended to examine the manuscript for himself (1834) and publish the results, but was prevented by a protracted stay in Germany and the obstruction of the mountain passes. He returned to England to find that the Record-Commission had employed Dr. Blume to copy the manuscript, and engaged Mr. Thorpe to extract and print the poems.

The poems were first published in Appendix B to Mr. Cooper's Report for 1836. From one of the few copies of this Report issued, Jacob Grimm published his "Andreas und Elene," 1840, and later (1843 and 1856) Kemble published "The Poetry of the Codex Vercellensis."

The manuscript, according to Wülker, who has twice examined the Codex carefully, consists of twenty *lagen* ("quires"), with one added folio. Each one of these *lagen* is marked with numbers and with letters in this wise. For example: Lage II. begins 10ᵃ. which is marked at the top II.; it closes on 18ᵇ where at the bottom B stands. Lage III. ends 24ᵇ; here we find C at the bottom, etc. This system of marking shows us at once that the manuscript exists to-day very much as it left the copyist's hands. There are some leaves missing which were clearly cut out before the copying was

completed, because they cause no break; other leaves have been
cut out since.

Wülker is of the opinion that the copy was made by two,
probably three, copyists. This copy was probably made about
the beginning of the eleventh century.

The most puzzling question connected with the Codex Vercellensis is this, — How comes it to be in Vercelli? There are several
theories to account for this. The Italian scholar Gazzera was of
the opinion [1] that Johannes Scotus Erigena, who sojourned a while
in Vercelli, was the medium through which it reached Vercelli.
Scotus died in 875. The manuscript cannot be so old. Wülker
says (*Grundriss*, p. 237): "Ich kann nur *eine* Erklärung, die mir
aber auch genügend zu sein scheint, finden. Wie mir in Vercelli
mitgeteilt wurde, befand sich dort ziemlich frühe ein Hospiz für
angelsächsische Pilger, welche nach Rom wollten. Vercelli liegt ja
auch für jeden, der über den Mont Cenis, den kleinen oder grossen
St. Bernard wollte (dies waren im frühern Mittelalter die Strassen,
welche für einen Angelsachsen in Betracht kamen), geradezu auf
dem Wege nach Rom. Hier mag bei dem Hospiz auch eine kleine
Bibliothek gewesen sein und aus dieser dann später die Handschrift
in den Besitz der Dombibliothek übergegangen sein."

This is a reasonable conjecture; but it is based upon no direct,
or even strong, circumstantial evidence. Wülker mentions, in a
foot-note on pp. 485, 486, of the *Grundriss*, the opinion of a certain
critic in the *Quarterly Review*, vol. lxxv. (December, 1844, and
March, 1845), that Guala Bicchiere gave this manuscript, along
with other collections, to this library.

Pauli in his "History of England," iii. 512, accepts this as true,
and in 1866 (in the *Gött. Gel. Anz.*, p. 1412), says: "Es ist längst
bekannt dass das Buch erst im Jahre 1218 mit dem Kardinal Guala
nach Sant Andrea zu Vercelli kam." Wülker characterizes this
opinion as a supposition which has much to oppose it.

In the University of California Library Bulletin No. 10, Cook
has examined with acumen and pains this question. After quoting
the words of the critic and Pauli, he says : —

"The facts upon which the Quarterly Reviewer and Pauli seem
to have based their inferences are these, —

---

[1] This view of Gazzera is found in No. 12 of the *Serapeum*, published by
Naumann, Leipzig, 1857.

"1. Cardinal Guala was in England from 1216 to 1218.

"2. While in England he had in his possession the priory of St. Andrew at Chester (*Quarterly Review*) or at Chesterton in Cambridgeshire (Pauli).

"3. After his return to Italy he founded the Collegiate Church of St. Andrew, at Vercelli, and bestowed upon it relics of English saints.

"4. The income from his English benefices perhaps enabled him to establish and endow the church at Vercelli.

"5. The plan and many of the details of the church are Early English.

"6. One of the chief poems of the Vercelli book is 'St. Andrew.'"

After a careful examination of these and other grounds of inferences, Cook says:—

"The facts not hitherto adduced in support of the hypothesis, and which seem to be as conclusive as circumstantial evidence can well be, are: Guala was a learned man, zealous for learning and religion, and the owner of perhaps the finest private library possessed at that time in Western Europe. The funds for the establishment of the monastery and the purchase of his books must have come largely from England — and why not certain books, also? He must have been open-minded, and appreciative of the good he found in foreign parts, and especially anxious to testify his appreciation of English art; then why not of English letters? His spirit of good-will toward England was to some extent reciprocated there, and he sought to perpetuate it by selecting as Abbot an ecclesiastic who, though French, should have English connections and sympathies and a stake in English prosperity. The wisdom of his course is attested by the renown of the monastery school, and the fact that it immediately attracted one of the greatest Englishmen of the Middle Ages, who remained a firm friend after his departure and perhaps gained other friends for its head. Guala must have thought oftenest of St. Martin and St. Andrew, patrons of France and North Britain respectively, especially revered by the two foreign nations in which his lot was cast, and which he afterwards honored on his return to his native country and his native town. Several circumstances must have conspired to deepen the impression thus made, particularly with reference to St. Andrew. We need not be surprised, then, at his immediate commemoration of that saint (by founding the monastery of St. Andrew in 1219), nor should we be surprised if a book once belonging to him commemorated both St. Martin and St. Andrew. By evincing a special interest in the Vercelli book, he would have been honoring another saint (St. Helena) peculiarly dear to the English heart. Finally, his library did contain one or more books in English chirography, was bequeathed to this monastery, and, with whatever augmentations it had received, was a notable one at the beginning of the fifteenth century."

This chain of circumstances, constructed upon evidence adduced and compared by Cook, may not be flawless, but it represents at present not only the most plausible, but by far the best substantiated theory to account for the presence of this famous book in Vercelli.

"Elene" is found in the Vercelli book in folios 121ᵃ–133ᵇ, and is complete.

AUTHOR.

KEMBLE first discovered that the runes in "The Riddles," "Crist," "Juliana," and "Elene," gave the name *Cynewulf* [ᚻᚱᚾᛏᛗᛈᚾᚱᚠ], and recognized in this the name of the author of these poems.

Much has been written about this author, and, upon small foundations of fact, many imposing structures of his life have been erected. As a matter of fact, very little is known about him except that the authorship of the works already mentioned — which bear, as it were, his signature — entitle him to our respect and grateful memory. It is generally agreed that he lived in the eighth century. Ten Brink puts the date of his birth between 720 and 730. Ten Brink and Rieger have attempted to show that he was by birth a Northumbrian. This they will establish by proving that the proper form of the name is *Cynewulf*, not *Cynewulf*. Their proof is in no wise conclusive; and, as the manuscript is West-Saxon, and there is no linguistic testimony to a Northumbrian origin, the presumption is that he was a West-Saxon. His youth was hopeful and full of joy (1264), and hunting was one of its greatest pleasures (1266); the bow and his caparisoned horse were his beloved companions (1260). To him, too,

were well known the festive mead-halls, where the assembled lis-
teners had applauded his song and rewarded him with golden
gifts (1259'); but even in the midst of these distractions, frequent
thoughts of the cross and all it portended had entered his mind
(1252); but it was not until he became an old man (1247) that,
after much study of books, he fathomed its real mystery (1255).
Scholars once thought that there was evidence in the words "þurh
lēohtne hād" (1246) that he entered the ranks of the clericals:
but there seems no justification of this interpretation, and no evidence, except an austere monastic asceticism, that he was in any
way connected with the church. He complains of the burdens of
his life in his old age, and asserts that all the joy of living has
passed out of his life with the vanishing days.

"The Riddles" belong, no doubt, to the youthful period of his
life; and it is altogether probable that the "unwise words formerly
spoken" (1285) may refer to these worldly poems. "Elene," from
internal evidence as well as by poetical worth, is no doubt his last
work, while "Crist" and "Juliana" belong between "The Riddles"
and "Elene." These are the only works that can be declared to
be Cynewulf's.

Among others ascribed to him, *very probable* seem the last part
of "Guðlac," and "Phœnix"; *possible*, "The Harrowing of Hell,"
"Andreas" and "Ruthwell Cross"; *very improbable*, "Bi manna
cræftum," "Bi manna wyrdum," "Bi manna mode," "Bi manna
lease," "Old English Physiology" (designated a Fragment by
Thorpe), "The Wanderer," "The Seafarer," "The Ruin."

THEME, PLAN, AND LITERARY MERIT OF THE POEM.

CYNEWULF tells us that this work of his was the joint result of
his reading and reflection, that the material was collected, and that
its present shape cost him much thought — perhaps many a sleep-
less night (1237 ff.). The question arises, at once, Where had he
found his material?

Source. — It has been generally accepted that the source of this
poem is the "Vita Quiriaci" in the *Acta Sanctorum* of the 4th of

May.   It has been thought by some that Cynewulf may have used
the Greek original direct, and not through a Latin medium; while
Glöde, in "Anglia," ix.,[2] attempts to show that the source of "Elene"
must have possessed some other form than that given in this work.
Glöde's argument, while ingenious and suggestive, is by no means
convincing.

Treatment of Original. — Comparing in outline the text of this
poem with its source, we find these peculiarities : —

The few lines relating to Constantine's fear of the opposing hosts,
and the appearance of the angel to allay this terror, are expanded
to some forty odd (57–98).   The vivid description of the battle is
the author's work (110 ff.).   Constantine's return home and his
inquiry about the cross are described much more fully (148 ff).
There is no notice in the text of the visit of Eusebius, from whom
Constantine is said to have received baptism; but, on the other
hand, Silvester is said to have performed this act (198 ff.).   We
have no mention, in this part of the poem, that Constantine built
churches and destroyed idols' temples (193 ff.).

The simple mention, in the original, that Helena was sent to seek
the cross is expanded into a description of Constantine's investigation of the Scriptures and consequent command (195 ff.); while no
mention is made in the poem of Helena's careful study of the
Scriptures.   The splendid description of the journey of Helena is
the poet's own conception (220 ff.).

After Helena arrives in Jerusalem and begins to hold assemblies
of the learned Jews, there is a marked parallelism between text
and original; so in divisions IIII., V., VI., VII., VIII., IX., X., *i.e.*
277–894.   In these, however, Judas's prayer — a most remarkable
production — is greatly expanded (726 ff.).   A like expansion is
found in the Devil's speech (899–934) and Judas's rejoinder (940–
953), as well as in Helena's gratification (953–967).

The description of the spread of the news concerning the discovery of the cross, and the effect of this news, the announcement
of this discovery to Constantine, his order to erect a church upon
the site, and Helena's execution of this order, as well as the ark in
which the cross was to be kept, are barely mentioned in the original (968–1033).

The baptism of Judas, his elevation to the bishopric, and Helena's
delight, are drawn from the original (1033–1067), as are also the

discovery of the nails (1067–1147), the use made of the nails (1147–1197), Helena's injunction, etc. (1197–1236). From 1237 to the end is, of course, independent of any basis.

In general it may be said, that, though Cynewulf has followed his source with fidelity, he has rarely limited himself to a literal translation — and never, except for a few clauses or sentences. Now and then there is a striking parallelism between the text and the original, though freedom in expression, and, more frequently, expansion of the thought, are characteristics of the poem. In several places there have been noted interpolations; and these belong to the chief beauties of the poem. Perhaps the appreciative reader would most praise the description of the battle and the description of Helena's journey, both of which Cynewulf himself draws.

The *motif* of this Christian legend is the discovery of the cross; and the whole action of the poem proper leads to this end. The *dramatis personæ* are chiefly Helena and Cyriacus; in less important rôles, Constantine, the Devil, and the wise men among the Jews, and Constantine's counsellors. The Huns, Goths and Franks, Jews and Romans, complete the list of personages.

Constantine's vision of the cross, after having experienced the terrors of imminent danger, is the type of Helena's vision of the true cross, after braving the dangers of the deep, hostile peoples, and conspiring enemies. From one vision to another we are led without much clogging of dramatic action, save that due to the peculiarities of Old English style, in describing effects of events by corresponding states of mind, in adding predicate after predicate to personalities, etc. On the whole, however, little time is lost, few words wasted, in picturing fully Helena's journeyings, her pleadings, her stratagem, and her success. One cannot help feeling that the climax has been reached with the discovery of the cross.

The historical account of Judas sounds like an author's postscript to tell the reader what became of a certain character; while Helena's anxiety about the nails may contribute to the perfection of her saintly character, but in nowise to the unity and harmony of the poem.

Division XV., the most entertaining portion for some reasons, is a kind of author's appendix, filled with autobiographical notes and a salutary "exhortation in conclusion," and forms no part of the poem proper.

METRICAL INTRODUCTION.

THE essential element of Old English verse is the regular recurrence of accented syllables. The marked characteristics of Old English verse are that it is stichic and alliterative. The so-called "long-verse" consists of two hemistichs, which are separated by cæsura and united by alliteration. In each of these hemistichs there are two accented syllables; and at least one of these accented syllables in the first hemistich must be used in alliteration with one of the accented syllables in the second hemistich. All words beginning with vowels may be used in alliteration, as may all words with the same initial consonants; except that *sc*, *sp*, and *st* are always taken together, — and hence may be used only with *sc*, *sp*, *st*, respectively, — and that *j* and *g* may be so used.

Of the *four* accented syllables in a long-verse, 1, 2, and 3 may show alliteration.

> *w*intra for *w*orulde, þæs þe *w*ealdend god   4

So may 1, 2, and 4, —

> rincas under roderum, wæron *R*ômware   46

So may 2, 3, and 4, —

> heht þû *w*igena *w*eard þâ *w*isestan   153

So may 1 and 3, —

> sôð fæstra léoht; þâ wæs *s*yxte geâr   7

So may 2 and 3, —

> þâ wearð on slæpe *s*ylfum ætýwed   69

So may 1 and 3, 2 and 4, —

> ârenned *w*earð, cyninga *w*uldor   5

It was once thought that 1, 2, 3, and 4 might all be used in alliteration; but this is questionable. Compare

> sægdon sígeröfum, swâ fram *S*iluéstre   190

There are, then, in each long-verse, two or three alliterative syllables. As a rule, in Old English the first hemistich contained two, and the second one, such syllables. The twofold alliteration is, however, more used in " Elene." The proportion is as follows : [1] —

In every hundred verses there are, —

Verses with two alliterative syllables . . . . . 52.
Verses with three alliterative syllables . . . . . 48.

Where there is a relative diminution of the threefold alliteration, as in " Elene," " Juliana," etc., there seems to be a corresponding increase in the number of cases in which the hemistichs, either of the same long-verse or of successive long-verses, are bound together by assonance or rime.

In " Elene " the vowels are naturally much used in alliteration. The consonants are used in the following order of frequency : —

$$w, s, h, f, g, l, m.$$

The anacrusis of the first hemistich consists of from one to three syllables, generally of one only; the anacrusis of the second hemistich is most frequently dissyllabic.

The first hemistich closes generally with a syllable or with syllables (from one to five) unstressed; and the second hemistich closes generally with one unstressed syllable, but occasionally with two or three. Now and then an accumulation of syllables occurs, giving us such unwieldy verses as " Elene," 582–585.

Rime. — It is very difficult — indeed, well-nigh impossible — to determine just when we are dealing with intended rime and when this rime is purely accidental. It is true that in some cases — as, for instance, in the 114th and 115th lines, and in 1237 ff. — there can be little doubt that the author purposely used rime; but there are other cases, and these are numerous, where this seems doubtful or improbable. There has been no attempt made to determine this question in the examples of rime given below. While these results have been obtained by a careful investigation of the text, it is not unlikely that there are other occurrences which the independent investigator would desire to see included, and some here recorded he would probably reject.

---

[1] These figures are taken from Fritzsche, "Andreas und Cynewulf." (See Bibliography.)

Masculine[1] rimes are perfect when the riming vowels are identical, and are followed by the same consonants or consonant combinations.

Perfect Masculine Rimes. —

     lixtan : wælhlencan   23ᵇ 24ᵃ
     hornboran : friccan   54
     ende : sammode   60
     gebrec : geþrec   114
     handgeswing : hergagring   115
     hildenædran : onsendan   119ᵇ 120ᵇ
     bordhrêðan : dufan   122
     flugon : burgon   134
     stênan : nêosan   151ᵇ 152ᵇ
     ôðŷwde : generede   163
     meahton : cûðon   166ᵇ 167ᵇ
     gefrugnon : wêron   172ᵃ 173ᵃ
     wêron : môston   174ᵇ 175ᵇ
     hergum : witum   180
     dryhtnes : nihtes   198
     weorðan : gehyrwan   220ᵇ 221ᵇ
     stôdon : wrǣcon   232
     ordum : byrnwîgendum   235
     scriþan : brimþissan   237ᵇ 238ᵃ
     snyrgan : plegean   244ᵇ 245ᵇ
     plegean : wǣgflotan   245ᵇ 246ᵃ
     bliðe : collenferhðe   246ᵇ 247ᵃ
     bôcum : geârdagum   290
     unclǣnum : gâstum   301ᵃ 302ᵃ
     þŷstrum : inwitþancum   307ᵇ 308ᵇ
     ongunnon : lifdon   311
     ord : word   393ᵃ 394ᵃ
     cûðon : cunnon   398ᵇ 399ᵇ
     gangað : âsêcað   406ᵇ 407ᵃ
     frignan : rêran   443
     hâlgan : sendan   457
     bisǣton : sôhton   473ᵇ 474ᵃ
     ealra : bearna   475ᵇ 476ᵇ
     êlêrendra : betera   506
     gefremmað : geswicaþ   515ᵇ 516ᵇ

---

[1] See Introduction to Cook's "Judith," pp. xlix. ff.

friccan : bodan 550ᵇ 551ᵃ
wǣron : éodon 556ᵇ 557ᵇ
-ongan : négan 558ᵇ 559ᵇ
lufan : heardran 564ᵇ 565ᵇ
geséðan : beniðan : wénan 582ᵃ 583ᵇ 584ᵇ
ûreccan : rim ne can 635
dareðlâcendra : byrgenna 651ᵃ 652ᵇ
can : cann 683ᵇ 684ᵇ
sceolu : heolstorhofu 763ᵇ 764ᵃ
þrówian : þolian 769ᵇ 770ᵃ
méðum : mânweorcum 812
delfan : turfhagan 829ᵇ 830ᵃ
sceoldon : hŷrdon 838ᵇ 839ᵇ
féðegestas : æðelingas 845ᵇ 846ᵃ
ferhðsefan : ongan 850
feorhnere : cynne 898
wyrdeð : strûdeð 904ᵇ 905ᵇ
can : siððan 925ᵇ 926ᵇ
halfa : glædra 955ᵇ 956ᵇ
hellesceaþan : bryttan 957ᵇ 958ᵇ
gehwæðres : sigebéames 964ᵇ 965ᵇ
gefrége : folesceare 968
wealdend : nergend 1085ᵃ 1086ᵃ
féollon : gespon 1134ᵇ 1135ᵃ
géoce : þancode 1139
ongan : sécan : 1156ᵇ 1157ᵇ
sélost : déorlicost 1158ᵇ 1159ᵃ
cûðe : ferhðe 1168ᵇ 1169ᵃ
sécað : winnað 1180ᵇ 1181ᵇ
geweorðod : god 1193ᵇ 1194ᵇ
fûs : hûs 1237
riht : miht 1241ᵃ 1242ᵃ
onwrâh : fâh 1243
færeð : gewurðeþ 1274ᵇ 1275ᵇ

When the first riming syllables are perfect masculine rimes, and the following syllables are identical, we have perfect feminine rimes.

Perfect feminine rimes are the following : —

ymbsittendra : burgwigendra 34
dynede : elynede 50

wǣre : nǣre   171
andsweredon : leornedon   396ᵇ 397ᵇ
healdan : wealdan   449ᵇ 450ᵃ
sweartestan : wyrrestan   931ᵇ 932ᵃ
nearwe : gearwe   1240
gepeaht : þeaht   1241ᵇ 1242ᵇ
âsǣled : gewǣled   1244

Rimes that vary from these are called "imperfect." These may be of various kinds, —

1. The consonants of the riming syllables may be identical, and the preceding vowels similar but not identical.

gescyrded : lindwered   141ᵇ 142ᵃ
þus : ûs   400
wis : is   592ᵃ 593ᵇ
sefa : wâ   627ᵇ 628ᵇ
hyge : geswerige   685ᵇ 686ᵃ
gode : ânmôde   1117ᵇ 1118ᵃ
sêleste : wiste   1202ᵇ 1203ᵇ

2. The consonants of the riming syllables may be identical, and the preceding vowels dissimilar.

âgêfon : gecýðan   587ᵇ 588ᵇ
dëað : bið   606
brâd : geswiðrod   917ᵇ 918ᵇ
þreodude : reodode   1239
âmæt : begeat   1248

3. The vowels may be identical, and the following consonants dissimilar. This is "assonance."

fôr : gôl   51ᵇ 52ᵇ
boda : þingode   77
ǣrdæge : wǣpenþræce   105ᵇ 106ᵇ
sungon : hergum   109ᵇ 110ᵃ
âhôf : stôd   112ᵇ 113ᵇ
geolorand : gemang   118
hafen : galen 123ᵇ 124ᵇ
ôð : forð   139
þræce : dæge   185
lagofæsten : hæfdon   249
ǣelêawe : geþrêade   321

ꝼǽre : getǽhte 601
cwicne : scyldigne 691ᵃ 692ᵃ
séað : léas 693
fǽst : wæs 883ᵃ 884ᵇ
gode : sceolde 1048ᵇ 1049ᵇ
wǽf : lǽs 1238
gebunden : geðrungen 1245
onlâg : hâd 1246
ontýnde : gerýmde 1249

4. Two syllables may rime, perfectly or imperfectly, but one of them be followed by another syllable while the other is not.

god : scéawode 345
þin : þine 928ᵇ 929ᵇ
stânhleoðum : some 653
gâst : fæste 936ᵇ 937ᵃ
onféng : swengas 238ᵇ 239ᵇ

Besides these, attention must be called to

cræftige : cræftige 314ᵇ 315ᵇ

and to the imperfect feminine rime, —

boden : samnodan 18ᵇ 19ᵇ

Moreover, there are several cases of rime within a single hemistich. This occurs usually in formulas or fixed expressions.

mærðum ond nihtum 15
wordum ond bordum 25
beorhte ond léohte 92
yldra oððe gingra 159
bordum ond ordum 235
werum ond wifum 236 1222
side ond wide 272
engla ond elda 476
sume hyder, sume þyder 548
óð ende forð 590
frôdra ond gôdra 637
heofon ond eorðan 728
nu ic wât, þæt ðû eart 815
bord ond ord 1187

BIBLIOGRAPHY.

EDITIONS.

1836. Appendix B to Mr. Cooper's Report (on Rymer's Fœdera. Edited by Benjamin Thorpe).

1840. Andreas und Elene herausgegeben von Jacob Grimm. Cassel.

1856. The Poetry of the Codex Vercellensis, with an English Translation. Part II. By J. M. Kemble. London.

1858. Bibliothek der angelsächischen Poesie herausgegeben von Christ. Grein. II. Band. Göttingen.

1877. Cynewulf's Elene. Mit einem Glossar herausgegeben von Julius Zupitza. Berlin.

1883. Second edition of the same.

1888. Bibliothek der angelsächischen Poesie begründet von Christ. Grein. Neubearbeitet, etc., von Richard Paul Wülker, Bd. ii. Leipzig.

1888. Third edition of Zupitza's " Elene."

TRANSLATIONS.

1856. Translation into English in Kemble's Edition of the Codex Vercellensis. (See above.)

1859. Dichtungen der Angelsachsen stabreimend übersetzt von C. W. M. Grein. Zweiter Band. Göttingen, 1859.

1863. (Zweite Ausgabe, Cassel und Göttingen, 1863, pp. 104 ff.)

1888. A Literal Translation of Cynewulf's Elene by Richard Francis Weymouth. London.

MANUSCRIPT, COLLATIONS, TEXTUAL CRITICISM, AND REVIEWS.

The results of Prof. P. Knöll's manuscript collation are incorporated in Zupitza's first, second, and third editions.

The results of Professor Wülker's examinations, in 1881 and 1884, are embodied in Wülker's edition of Grein's " Bibliothek " (see above). Zupitza's second edition contains the fruit of the 1881 collation; and the third edition, those of both 1881 and 1884. Napier's recent collation has been used by Zupitza in his third edition.

Christ. Grien : Zur Textkritik der angelsächsischen Dichter, in Pfeiffer's *Germania*. Bd. x., S. 424 f.

Einleitung in das Studium des Angelsächsischen, von K. Körner. ii. Heilbronn, 1880.

Sievers in den Gött. gel. anz : vom 9ten aug. 1880. S. 997 ff.

The following reviews of Zupitza's editions of "Elene" : —

Sievers, in *d. Anglia*, i., 573 ff.

Körner, in *d. Englischen Studien*, ii., 252 ff.

Ten Brink, in *Anzeiger für Deutsches Altertum*. v.

Varnhagen, in *d. Deutschen Litteraturzeitung*, 1884, 426 ff.

Kluge, in *Litteraturblatt*, 1884, S. 138 f.

Cardinal Guala and the Vercelli Book. University of California Library Bulletin, No. 10. By A. S. Cook. Sacramento, 1888.

Zöpfl. Forschungen über das Recht der salischen Franken. Berlin, 1876.

Anglosaxonum poetae atque scriptores prosaici, quorum partim integra opera, partim loca selecta collegit, correxit, edidit Ludovicus Ettmüllerus. Quedlinburgii et Lipsiae, 1850. pp. 156 ff.

LANGUAGE.

1884. Joseph Schürman : Darstellung der Syntax in Cynewulf's Elene. (Münster Diss.) Paderborn.

1885. R. Rössger : Über den syntaktischen Gebrauch des Genitivs in Cynewulf's Elene, Crist, und Juliana. *Anglia*, Bd. viii., Heft. 3.

1888. Hermann Leiding : Die Sprache der Cynewulfschen dichtungen Crist. Juliana, und Elene. Marburg.

1888. F. Holthausen : Deutsche Litteraturzeitung sp. 1114 ff.

METRE.

E. Sievers : Zur Rhytmik des germanischen alliterations verses in d. Beiträgen von Paul und Braune. x., 209 ff., 453 ff.; xii., 454 ff.

Philipp Frucht : Metrisches und sprachliches zu Cynewulf's Elene, Juliana, und Crist. (Greiswald. Diss.) 1887.

G. Jansen : Beiträge zur Synonymik und Poetik allgemein als echt anerkannter Dichtungen Cynewulf's. (Münster Doktorschrift.) 1883.

SOURCE.

Otto Glöde: Cynewulf's Elene und ihre quelle (Rostocker Diss.), 1885; und dessen Untersuchungen über die quelle von Cynewulf's Elene in *der Anglia*, ix., 271 ff.

Wolfgang Golther, im *Litteraturblatt*, 1887, sp. 261 ff.

Acta sanctorum maii collecta, digesta, illustrata a G. Henschenio et D. Papebrochio. Tomus i. Antverpiae, 1680. pp. 445[b] ff.

Mombritii : Vitae sanctorum. Mediolani, 1479. Tomus i., fol. ccxii.

Jacobi Gretseri : Opera omnia. Tomus ii. Ratisbonae, 1734. pp. 417 ff.

Legends of the Holy Rood. Edited by R. Morris. London, 1871. E. E. Text Society, No. 46.

Heilagra manna sogur. Edited by C. R. Unger. Christiania, 1877. i., pp. 301 ff.

AUTHOR.

1840. Kemble: On Anglo-Saxon Runes, in *Archaeologia*, vol. xxviii., pp. 360–363.

Grimm's Andreas und Elene, S. l., lii., and S. 167–170.

1842. Wright: Biographia Brittanica Literaria. i.. pp. 501 ff.

Thorpe's Codex Exoniensis, pp. v.–xi., 501–502.

1843. Kemble's Codex Vercellensis, pp. vii.–x.

1844. Thorpe: The Homilies of the Anglo-Saxon Church, vol. i., p. 622.

1847. Ettmüller's Handbuch. pp. 132 f.

1850. Ettmüller's Scopas and Boceras p. x. f.

1853. Dietrich : Über Crist, in Haupt's *Zeitschrift*, ix., S. 193–214.

1857. Henrici Leonis, Quae de se ipso Cynewulfus, sive Cenevulfus, sive Coenevulfus, poeta Anglo-Saxonicus tradiderit. Hallesches Universitäts Programm.

1859. Dietrich, in Ebert's *Jahrbuch*, vol. i., pp. 241–246.

Dietrich : Die Rätsel des Exeterbuches. In Haupt's *Zeitschrift*, ii., S. 448–490, 232–252.

1859. Francisci Dietrichi : Commentatio de Kynewulfi poetae aetate, aenigmatum fragmento e codice Lugdunensi edito illustrata. Marburg.

1865. Francisci Dietrich : Disputatio de Cruce Ruthwellensi. Marburg.

1865. Christ. Grein: Das Reimlied des Exeterbuches. In Pfeiffer's *Germania*, Bd. x., S. 305–307.

1867. Morley: English Writers, i., pp. 323 and 325.

1869. Rieger: Über Cynewulf. In Zacher's *Zeitschrift für deutsche Philologie*, i., 215–226, 313–334.

1871. Henry Sweet: Sketch of the History of Anglo-Saxon Poetry. In " Warton's History," vol. ii., pp. 16–19.

1873. Hammerich's Epick-Kristelige Oldquad und die deutsche Übersetzung. 1874. pp. 75–104.

1877. Ten Brink's Geschichte der englischen Litteratur, i., S. 61–75.

1878. Richard Wülker, in *der Anglia*, i., S. 483–507.
Charitius: Die angelsächsischen Gedichte von Guðlac, in *der Anglia*, ii., S. 265–308.

1879. Fritzsche: Das angelsächsische Gedicht Andreas und Cynewulf, in *der Anglia*, ii., S. 441–500.
Ten Brink, in Haupt's *Zeitschrift*, xxiv., und *Anzeiger*, S. 53–70.

1880. Christ. Grein, in seiner kurzgefassten angelsächsischen Grammatik, S. 11–15.

1883. Ten Brink's Early English Literature, pp. 386–389.
Theodor Müller: Angelsächsische Grammatik, pp. 16, 26 ff.
Lefevre: Das altenglische Gedicht von Guðlac. In *der Anglia*, vi., S. 181–240.
Otto D'Ham: Der gegenwärtige Stand der Cynewulf-Frage. (Tübinger Doktorschrift.)

1884. J. Earle: Anglo-Saxon Literature, chap. xi.

1885. Friedrich Ramhorst: Das altenglische Gedicht vom Heiligen Andreas. (Berliner Doktorschrift.)

1887. Sarrazin: Beowulf und Kynewulf. *Anglia*, ix., 3.

1888. H. Morley: English Writers, ii., chaps. viii. and ix.

BIBLIOGRAPHICAL.[1]

1885. Wülker: Grundriss zur Geschichte der Angelsächsischen Literatur, pp. 147, 148, 174, 175, 514.

1888. Zupitza: Cynewulf's Elene, third edition. pp. vii., viii.

---

[1] From these sources most of the bibliography of this edition has been compiled.

ELENE.

I.

Þa wæs âgangen gêara hwyrftum
tuhund ond þrêo geteled rîmes,
swylce .xxx. êac, þinggemearces,
wintra for worulde, þæs þe wealdend god
5 âcenned wearð, cyninga wuldor,
in middangeard þurh mennisc hêo,
sôðfæstra lêoht; þâ wæs syxte gêar
Constantînes câserdômes,
þæt hê Rômwara in rîce wearð
10 âhæfen, hildfruma, tô heretêman.
Wæs se lindhwata lêodgebyrga
eorlum ârfæst. Æðelinges wêox
rîce under roderum. Hê wæs riht cyning
gûðweard gumena. Hine god trymede
15 mærðum ond mihtum, þæt hê manegum wearð
geond middangeard mannum tô hrôðer,
werþeodum tô wræce, syððan wæpen âhôf
wið hettendum. Him wæs hild boden,
wîges wôma. Werod samnodan,
20 Hûna lêode ond Hrêðgotan,
fôron fyrdhwate Francan ond Hûgas
wêron hwate weras . . . . .

(1–41ᵃ) Anno ducentesimo tricesimo tertio post passionem domini nostri Jesu Christi regnante venerabili dei cultore, magno viro, Con-

gearwe tô gûðe : gâras lîxtan
wriðene wælhleucan : wordum ond bordum
25 hôfon herecumbol. Þa wêron heardingas
sweotole gesamnod † ond eal geador.
Fôr folca gedryht. Fyrdlêoð ágôl
wulf on wealde, wælrûne ne máð :
ûrigfeðera earn sang âhôf
30 lâðum on lâste. Lungre scynde
ofer burgenta beaduþrêata mêst
hergum tô hilde, swylce Hûna cyning
~ymbsittendra âwer meahte
âbannan tô beadwe burgwîgendra.
35 Fôr fyrda mêst, fêðan trymedon
ćoredcestum, þæt on ælfylce
deareðlâcende on Dânûbie
stærcedfyrhðe stæðe wîcedon,
ymb þæs wæteres wylm, werodes breahtme.
40 woldon Rômwara rîce geþringan,
hergum âhýðan. Þêr wearð Hûna cyme
cûð ceasterwarum. Þâ se câsere heht
ongeân gramum gûðgelêcan
under earhfære ofstum myclum
45 bannan tô beadwe, beran ût Þræce
rincas under roderum. Wêron Rômware
secgas sigerôfe, sôna gegearwod
wêpnum tô wîgge, ſêah hie werod lêsse
hæfdon tô hilde, þonne Huna cining
50 ridon ymb rôfne. Þonne rand dynede
campwudu clynede ; cyning þrêate fôr,
herge, tô hilde. Hrefen uppe gôl

stantino in sexto anno regni eius gens multa barbarorum congregata
est super Danubium parati ad bellum contra Romaniam.

(41ᵇ–56) Nunciatum est autem regi Constantino, tunc congregans et
ipse multitudinem exercitus profectus est obviam et invenit eos, qui
vindicaverunt Romaniae partes et erant secus Danubium.

wan ond wælfel. Werod wæs on tyhte,
hleopon hornboran, hreopan friccan.
55 Mearh moldan træd. Mægen samnode,
cafe, tô cease. Cyning wæs âfyrhted,
egsan geâclad, siððan elþeodige.
Hûna ond Hreða here, sceawedon.
 ðæt þe on Rômwara rîces ende
60 ymb þæs wæteres stæð werod samnode,
mægen unrîme. Môdsorge wæg
Rômwara cyning, rîces ne wênde
for werodleste : hæfde wîgena tô lŷt,
eaxlgestealna, wið ofermægene
65 hrôrra tô hilde. Here wîcode,
eorlas, ymb æðeling egstreame neah
on neaweste nihtlangne fyrst,
þæs þe hîc feonda gefær fyrmest gesegon.
Þâ wearð on slæpe sylfum ætŷwed
70 þâm câsere, þær he on corðre swæf,
sigerôfum gesegen swefnes wôma.
Þûhte him wlitescŷne on weres hâde
hwît ond hîwbeorht hæleða nâthwylc
geŷwed ænlicra, þonne he ær oððe sîð
75 gesege under swegle. He of slæpe onbrægd
eofurcumble beþeaht. Him se âr hraðe,
wlitig wuldres boda, wið þingode
ond be naman nemde (nihthelm tôglâd):
' Constantînus, heht þe cyning engla,
80 wyrda wealdend, wære beodan,
duguða dryhten. Ne ondræd þû ðe,
ðeah þe elþeodige egesan hwôpan,
heardre hilde. Þû tô heofenum beseoh

(56ᵇ-98) Videns autem quia multitudo esset innumerabilis, contrista-
tus est et timuit usque ad mortem. Ea vero nocte veniens vir splendi-
dissimus suscitavit eum et dixit: "Constantine, noli timere, sed respice

    on wuldres weard : þǽr ðû wraðe findest,
85 sigores tâcen'. Hê wæs sôna gearu
    þurh þæs hâlgan hǽs, hreðerlocan onspéon,
    ûp lôcade, swâ him se âr âbéad,
    fǽle friðowebba. Geseah hê frætwum beorht
    wliti wuldres trêo ofer wolcna hrôf
90 golde geglenged : gimmas lixtan.
    Wæs se blâca bêam bôcstafum âwriten
    beorhte and léohte : · mid þŷs bêacne ðû
    on þâm frêcnan fære fêond oferswîðesð,
    geletest lâð werod': Þâ þæt léoht gewât,
95 ûp sîðode ond se âr somed
    on clǽnra gemang. Cyning wæs þŷ blîðra
    ond þê sorgléasra, secga aldor,
    on fyrhðsefan þurh þâ fǽgeran gesyhð.

II.

    HEHT þâ onlíce æðelinga hlêo,
100 beorna bêaggifa, swâ hê þæt bêacen geseah,
    heria hildfruma, þæt him on heofonum ǽr
    geîewed wearð, ofstum myclum,
    Constantinus, Cristes rôde,
    tîrêadig cyning, tâcen gewyrcan.
105 Heht þâ on ûhtan mid ǽrdæge
    wîgend wreccan ond wǽpenþræce,
    hebban heorucumbul ond þæt hâlige trêo
    him beforan ferian, on fêonda gemang

---

sursum in coelum, et vide;" et intendens in coelum vidit signum Crucis
Christi, ex lumine claro constitutum, et desuper litteris scriptum titu-
lum; 'IN HOC VINCE.' (99) Viso autem signo hoc Rex Constantinus
fecit similitudinem Crucis quam viderat in coelo: et surgens impe-
tum fecit contra Barbaros, et fecit antecedere signum Crucis; et veniens cum suo exercitu super barbaros, coepit caedere eos proxima luce;

beran bêacen godes.   Býman sungon
110 hlûde for hergum.   hrefn weorces gefeah,
ûrigfeðra earn sîð behéold,
wælhrêowra wîg, wulf sang âhôf,
holtes gehlêða.   Hildegesa stôd.
Þêr wæs borda gebrec ond beorna geþrec,
115 heard handgeswing ond herga gring,
syððan hêo earhfære êrest mêtton.
On þæt fêge folc flâna scûras,
gâras ofer geoloraud on gramra gemang
hetend heorugrimme, hildenêdran
120 þurh fingra geweald forð onsendan.
Stôpon stîðhîdige, stundum wrêcon,
brêcon bordhrêðan, bil in dufan,
þrungon þræchearde.   Þâ wæs þûf hafen,
segn, for sweotum, sigelêoð galen.
125 Gylden grîma, gâras lixtan
on herefelda.   Hêðene grungon,
fêollon friðelêase.   Flugon instæpes
Hûna lêode, swâ þæt hâlige trêo
ârêran heht Rômwara cyning
130 heaðofremmende.   Wurdon heardingas
wîde tôwrecene.   Sume wîg fornam,
sume unsôfte aldor generedon
on þâm heresîðe, sume healfcwice
flugon on fæsten ond feore burgon
135 æfter stânclifum, stede weardedon
ymb Danûbie, sume drenc fornam
on lagostrêame lifes æt ende.
Þâ wæs môdigra mægen on luste,
êhton elǀéoda ôð þæt æfen forð
140 fram dæges orde : daroðæsc flugon,
hildenêdran.   Hêap wæs gescyrded,

et timuerunt barbari, et dederunt fugam per ripas Danubii, et mortua

láðra lindwered. Lýthwôn beewom
Húna herges hâm eft þanou.
þâ wæs gesýne, þæt sige forgeaf
145 Constantíno cyning ælmihtig
æt þâm dægweorce, dômweorðunga,
ríce under rodernm, þurh his rôde trêo.
Gewât þâ heriga helm hâm eft þanon
húðe hrêmig (hild wæs gesceâden),
150 wigge geweorðod. Côm þâ wîgena hlêo
þegna þrêate þrýðbord stênan,
beadurôf cyning, burga nêosan.
Heht þâ wigena weard þâ wîsestan
snûde tô sionoðe, þâ þe snyttro cræft
155 þurh fyrngewrito gefrigen hæfdon,
hêoldon higeþancum hæleða rêdas.
Ðâ þæs fricggan ongan folces aldor,
sigerôf cyning, ofer sîd weorod,
wêre þær ænig yldra oððe gingra,
160 þê him tô sôðe secggan meahte,
galdrum cýðan, hwæt se god wêre,
blædes brytta, · þe þis his bêacen wæs,
þê mê swâ lêoht ôðýwde ond mîne lêode generede,
tâcna torhtost, ond mê tîr forgeaf.
165 wigspêd wið wrâðum, þurh þæt wlitige trêo'.
hio him andsware ænige ne meahton
âgifan tôgênes nê ful geare cûðon
sweotole gesecggan be þâm sigebêacne.
Ðâ þâ wîsestan wordum cwêðon
170 for þâm heremægene, þæt hit heofoncyninges

est non minima multitudo; et dedit Deus in illa die victoriam Regi
Constantino per virtutem sanctae Crucis. (148) 2. Veniens autem Rex
Constantinus in suam civitatem, convocavit omnes Sacerdotes omnium
deorum vel idolorum: et quaerebat ab eis cujus vel quid esset hoc
signum Crucis, et not poterant dicere ei. Responderunt autem quidam
ex ipsis et dixerunt: "Hoc signum coelestis Dei est." (172ᵇ) Audi-

tácen wǽre ond þæs twéo nǽre.
þá þæt gefrugnon, þá þurh fulwihte
lærde wǽron, him wæs leoht sefa,
ferhð geféonde, þéah hira féa wǽron,
175 ðæt hie for þám cásere cýðan móston
godspelles gife, hú se gásta helm
in þrýnesse þrymme geweorðad
ácenned wearð, cyninga wuldor,
ond hú on galgan wearð godes ágen bearn
180 áhangen for hergum heardum wítum,
álýsde léoda bearn of locan déoða,
geómre gástas, ond him gife scalde
þurh þá ilcan gesceaft, þé him geýwed wearð
sylfum on gesyhðe sigores tácne
185 wið þéoda þrǽce, ond hú ðý þriddan dæge
of byrgenne beorna wuldor,
of déaðe, árás, dryhten ealra
hæleða cynnes, ond tó heofonum ástáh.
Þus gléawlíce gástgerýnum
190 sægdon sigerófum, swá fram Siluestre
lǽrde wǽron. Æt þám se léodfruma
fulwihte onféng ond þæt forð gehéold
on his dagana tíd dryhtne tó willan.

---

entes autem hoc pauci Christiani, qui erant eodem tempore, venerunt
ad Regem, et evangelizaverunt ei mysterium Trinitatis et adventum
Filii Dei, quemadmodum natus est et crucifixus et tertia die resurrexit.
Mittens autem Rex Constantinus ad Eusebium Episcopum urbis Romae,
fecit eum venire ad se, et catechizavit eum fidem Christianorum et
omnia ministeria, et baptizavit eum in nomine Domini nostri Jesu
Christi, et confirmatus est in fide Christi. Jussit autem aedificari
ubique ecclesias, templa vero idolorum destrui.

III.

    Ðᴀ wæs on sǽlum sinces brytta,
195 nîðheard cyning. Wæs him nîwe gefêa
befolen in fyrhðe. Wæs him frôfra mǽst
ond hyhta hihst heofonrîces weard.
Ongan þá dryhtnes ǽ dæges ond nihtes
þurh gâstes gife georne cýðan
200 ond hinc, sôðlice, sylfne getengde
goldwine gumena in godes þêowdôm
æscrôf, unslâw. Þá se æðeling fand,
lêodgebyrga, þurh lârsmiðas
gûðheard, gârþrîst on godes bôcum,
205 hwǽr âhangen wæs heriges beorhtme
on rôde trêo rodora waldend
æfstum þurh inwit, swâ se ealda fêond
forlǽrde ligesearwum lêode, fortyhte
Iûdêa cyn, þæt hîe god sylfne
210 âhêngon, herga fruman: þæs hîe in hýnðum sculon
tô wîdan feore wergðu drêogan.
Þá wæs Crîstes lof þâm câsere
on firhðsefan † forð gemyndig
ymb þæt mǽre trêo ond þá his môdor hêt
215 fêran foldwege folca þrêate
tô Iûdêum, georne sêcan
wigena þrêate, hwǽr se wuldres bêam
hâlig under hrûsan hýded wǽre,
æðelcyninges rôd. Elene ne wolde
220 þæs sîðfates sǽne weorðan

    (194 ff.) Erat autem beatus Constantinus perfectus in fide, et fervens
Spiritu sancto exercebatur in sanctis Evangeliis Christi. Cum didi-
cisset autem a sanctis Evangeliis ubi esset Dominus crucifixus, misit
suam matrem Helenam ut exquireret sanctum lignum Crucis Domini,
et in eodem loco aedificaret ecclesiam. Gratia autem Spiritus sancti

nê ðæs wilgifan word gehyrwan,
hiere sylfre suna, ac wæs sôna gearu
wíf on willsîð, swâ hire weoruda helm,
byrnwîggendra, beboden hæfde.
225　Ongan þâ ôfstlîce eorla mengu
tô flote fŷsan.　Fearoðhengestas
ymb geofenes stæð gearwe stôdon,
sælde sæmearas, sunde getenge.
Ðâ wæs orcnæwe idese sîðfæt,
230　siððan wæges welm werode gesôhte.
Þær wlanc manig æt wendelsæ
on stæðe stôdon.　Stundum wræcon
ofer mearcpaðu, mægen æfter ôðrum,
ond þâ gehlôdon hildesercum,
235　bordum ond ordum, byrnwigendum,
werum ond wífum wæghengestas.
Lêton þâ ofer fîfelwæg fâmige scrîðan
bronte brimþisan.　Bord oft onfêng
ofer earhgeblond ŷða swengas.
240　Sæ swinsade.　Ne hŷrde ic sîð nê ær
on êgstrêame idese lædan,
on merestræte, mægen fægerre.
Þær meahte gesîon, sê ðone sîð behêold,
brecan ofer bæðweg brimwudu, snyrgan
245　under swellingum, sæmearh plegean,
wadan wægflotan.　Wigan wæron blîðe
collenferhðe : cwên sîðes gefeah.
Syþþan tô hŷðe hringedstefnan
ofer lagofæsten geliden hæfdon
250　on Crêca land, cêolas lêton

requievit in beatissima matre Constantini Imperatoris Helena ; haec
autem in omnibus Scripturis se exercebat, et nimiam in Domino nostro
Jesu Christo possedit dilectionem : postmodum et salutare sanctae Crucis lignum exquisivit.　Cum legisset autem intente adventum humani-
tatis Salvatoris nostri Jesu Christi et crucis ejus assumptionem et a

æt sǽfearoðe sunde bewrecene,
ald ýðhofu, onerum fæste
on brime bidan beorna geþinges,
hwonne héo sio gúðewén gumena þréate
255 ofer eastwegas eft gesóhte.
Þǽr wæs on eorle éðgesýne
brogden byrne ond bill gecost,
geatolic gúðscrúd, grimhelm manig,
ǽnlic eoforcumbul. Wǽron æsewigan,
260 secggas ymb sigecwén, siðes gefýsde.
Fyrdrincas frome fóron on luste
on Créca land, cáseres bodan,
hilderincas hyrstum gewerede.
Þǽr wæs gesýne sinegim locen
265 on þám hereþréate, hláfordes gifu.
Wæs séo éadhréðige Elene gemyndig
þríste on geþance þéodnes willan,
georn on móde, þæt hio Iúdéa
ofer herefeldas héape gecoste
270 lindwigendra land gesóhte,
secga þréate; swá hit siððan gelamp
ymb lýtel fæc, þæt ðæt léodmægen,
gúðrófe hæleþ, tó Hierusalem
cwómon in þá ceastre corðra mǽste,
275 eorlas æscrófe, mid þá æðelan ewén.

mortuis resurrectionem non est moras passa donec victoriae Christi
invenit lignum, ubi dominicum et sanctum fixum est corpus. Invenit
autem illud hoc modo. Vicesima et octava die secundi mensis in
sanctam civitatem Hierusalem introivit una cum exercitu magno,

IIII.

Heut ðà gebêodan burgsittendum
þàm snoterestum sìde oud wide
geoud Iûdêas, gumena gehwylcum,
meðelhêgende on gemòt cuman,
280   þà ðe dêoplicost dryhtnes gerŷno
þurh rihte æ reccan cûðon.
Ðà wæs gesamnod of sìdwegum
mægen unlŷtel, þà ðe Moyses æ
reccan cûðon.   Þær on rìme wæs
285   þreo .iii. þæra lêoda
àlesen tô làre.   Ongan þà lêoflic wìf
weras Ebrêa wordum nêgan :
‘ ic þæt gearolìce ongiten hæbbe
þurg witgena wordgerŷno
290   on godes bôcum, þæt gê geàrdagum
wyrðe wæron wuldorcyninge,
dryhtne dŷre ond dædhwæte.
Hwæt, gê þære snyttro † unwìslìce,
wràðe, wiðwurpon, þà gê wergdou þaue,
295   þe êow of wergðe þurh his wuldres miht,
fram ligewale, lŷsan þôhte,
of hæftnêde.   Gê mid horu spêowdon
on þæs andwlitan, þe êow êagena lêoht,

et congregavit in ea congregationem magnam de impiissima gente
Judaeorum. Non solum autem eos qui in ea erant civitate, sed et eos
qui in circuitu erant castellis, possessionibus vel civitatibus Judaeos
congregari praecepit. Erat autem Hierosolyma deserta tempore illo,
ut vix invenirentur omnes Judaei tria millia virorum. . . . [1](Post haec
congregavit multitudinem magnam de impiissima Judaeorum gente,)
quos convocans beatissima Helena dixit ad eos. Cognovi de sanctis
libris propheticis, quia fuistis dilecti Dei ; sed quia repellentes omnem
sapientiam, eum qui volebat de maledicto vos redimere maledixistis,
et eum qui per sputum oculos vestros illuminavit immundis potius

---

[1] An interpolation from Ruffinus.

fram blindnesse bôte gefremede
300 edníowunga þurh þæt æðele spâld
ond fram unclênum oft generede
dêofla gâstum. Gê tô dêape þone
dêman ongunnon, sê ðe of dêaðe sylf
worn âwehte on wera corþre
305 in þæt ðrre líf êowres cynnes.
Swâ gê môdblinde mengan ongunnon
lige wið sôðe, lêoht wið þýstrum,
ðfst wið âre, inwitþancum
wrôht webbedan. Êow sêo wergðu forðan
310 scêðpeð scyldfullum. Gê þâ scíran miht
dêman ongunnon ond gedwolan lifdon,
þêostrum geþancum, ôð þysne dæg.
Gangaþ nû snûde, snyttro geþencaþ
weras wîsfæste, wordes cræftige,
315 þâ ðe êowre ðe æðelum † cræftige
on ferhðsefan fyrmest hæbben,
þâ mê sôðlîce secgan cunnon,
andsware cýðan for êowic forð
tâcna gehwylces, þe ic him tô sêce'.
320 Êodan þâ on gerûm rêonigmôde
eorlas ðclêawe, egesan geþrêade,
gehðum geômre, georne sôhton
þâ wîsestan wordgerýno.
þæt hîo þðre cwêne oneweðan meahton
325 swâ tiles, swâ trâges, swâ hîo him tô sôhte.
Hîo þâ on þrêate .iii. manna

sputis injuriastis, et eum qui mortuos vestros vivificabat in mortem tradidistis, et lucem tenebras existimastis et veritatem mendacium, pervenit in vos maledictum quod est in lege vestra scriptum. Nunc autem eligite ex vobis viros, qui diligenter sciunt legem vestram, ut respondeant mihi de quibus interrogavero eos. Qui abeuntes cum timore, et multas quaestiones inter semetipsos facientes, invenerunt legis doctores numero mille, et adduxerunt eos ad Helenam, testi-

fundon ferhðgléawra, þâ þe fyrngemynd
mid Iûdêum gearwast cûðon.
Þrungon þâ on þréate, þær on þrymme bâd
330　in cynestôle câscres mǽg,
geatolîc gûðcwên golde gehyrsted.
Elene maþelode ond for eorlum sprǽc :
'gehŷrað, higegléawe, hâlige rûne,
word ond wîsdôm.　Hwæt, gê wîtgena
335　lâre onfêngon, hû se liffruma
in cildes hâd cenned wurde,
mihta wealdend.　Be þâm Moyses sang
ond þæt *word* gecwǽð, weard Israhêla :
" ðow âcenned bið cniht on dêgle
340　mihtum mǽre, swâ þæs môdor ne bið
wæstmum géacnod þurh weres frige ".
Be ðâm Dâuid cyning dryhtléoð âgôl,
frôd fyrnweota, fæder Salomônes,
ond þæt word gecwæþ, wigona baldor :
345　" ic frymþa god fore scéawode,
sigora dryhten.　Hê on gesyhðe wæs,
mægena wealdend, mîn on þâ swîðran,
þrymmes hyrde.　Þanon ic ne wen*de*
ǽfre tô aldre onsîon mîne ".
350　Swâ hit eft be ðow Essâias
wîtga for weorodum wordum mǽlde
déophycggende þurh dryhtnes gâst :
" ic ûp âhof eaforan ging*e*
ond bearn cende, þâm ic blǽd forgeaf,
355　hâlige higefrôfre : ac hîe hyrwdon *mê*,

---

monium perhibentes eis, quod legis scientiam multam haberent.
Helena autem dixit ad eos, Audite mea verba, auribus percipite meos
sermones.　Non enim intellexerunt patres vestri neque vos in ser-
monibus Prophetarum, quemadmodum de adventu Christi propheta-
verunt, quia prius dictum est, "Puer nascetur et mater ejus virum non
agnoscet:" et Isaias vobis dixit, "Filios genui et exaltavi, ipsi autem

féodon þurh féondscipe, náhton foreþancas.
wîsdômes gewitt, ond þâ wéregan néat.
þé man daga gehwâm drîfeð ond þirsceð,
ongitaþ hira gôddénd, nales gnyrnwrécum
360 feogað frŷnd hiera, þé him fódder gifeð.
Ond mê Israhéla ǽfre ne woldon
folc oncnâwan, þéah ic feala for him
æfter woruldstundum wundra gefremede ".

V.

Hwæt, wê þæt gehŷrdon þurh hâlige béc,
365 þæt éow dryhten geaf dôm unscyndne,
meotod, mihta spéd, Moyse sægde,
hû gé heofoncyninge hŷran sceoldon,
lâre léstan. Éow þæs lungre âþréat,
ond gé þâm ryhte wiðroten hæfdon,
370 onscunedon þone scíran scippend eallra,
dryhtna dryhten, ond gedwolan fylgdon
ofer riht godes. Nû gé raþe gangaþ
ond findaþ gén, þâ þe fyrngewritu
þurh snyttro cræft sélest cunnen,
375 ǽriht éower, þæt mê andsware
þurh sídne sefan secgan cunnen '.
Éodan ðâ mid mengo módewánige
collenferhðe, swâ him sío cwén béad,

---

spreverunt me : cognovit bos possessorem suum et asinus praesepe
Domini sui, Israel autem me non cognovit, et populus meus me non
intellexit:" et omnis Scriptura de ipso locuta est. Qui sciebatis legem
errastis, nunc autem eligite ex vobis qui diligenter noverint scientiam
legis, ut ad interrogationes meas dent responsum : et militibus jussit
ut custodirent eos cum summa diligentia.
Consilio autem facto inter se elegerunt optimos legis doctores viros
numero quingentos, et venientes steterunt in conspectu Helenae : quae

fundon þá .d. For|snotterra
380 álesen léodmǽga, |á ðe leornungcræft
þurh módgemynd, mǽste hæfdon
on sefan snyttro. Héo tó salore eft
ymb lýtel fæc laðode wǽron,
ceastre weardas. Hío sio ewén ongan
385 wordum genégan (wlát ofer ealle):
'oft gé dyslíce dǽd gefremedon,
wérge wræcmæcggas, ond gewritu herwdon,
fædera láre, nǽfre furður, þonne nú,
ðá gé blindnesse bóte forségon
390 ond gé wiðsócon sóðe ond rihte,
|æt in Bethleme bearn wealdendes,
cyning ánboren, cenned wǽre,
æðelinga ord. Þéah gé þá ǽ cúðon,
wîtgena word, gé ne woldon þá,
395 synwyrcende, sóð oncnáwan'.
Híe þá ánmóde andsweredon:
'hwæt, wé elréisce ǽ leornedon,
þá on fyrndagum fæderas cúðon,
æt godes earce, né wé ᵹeare cunnon,
400 þurh hwæt ðú ðus hearde, hléefdige, ús
eorre wurde. Wé ðæt ǽbylgð nyton,
þé wé gefremedon on þysse folescere,
þéoden bealwa wið þec ǽfre'.
Elene maðelade ond for eorlum spræc
405 undearninga, ides reordode

hlúde for herigum : ' gê nû hraðe gangað,
sundor âsêcaþ, þâ ðe snyttro mid êow
mægn ond môdcræft mæste hæbben,
þæt mê þinga gehwylc þrîste gecŷðan
410　untrâglîce, þê ic him tô sêce '.
Êodon þâ fram rûne, swâ him sîo rîce cwên
bald in burgum beboden hæfde,
geômormôde georne smêadon, ,
sôhton searoþancum, hwæt sîo syn wære,
415　þê hîe on þâm folce gefremed hæfdon
wið þâm câsere, þê him sîo cwên wite.
Þâ þær for eorlum ân reordode
gidda gearosnotor (ðâm wæs Iûdas nama),
wordes cræftig : ' ic wât geare,
420　þæt hîo wile sêcan be ðâm sigebêame,
on ðâm þrôwode þêoda waldend
eallra gnyrna lêas, godes âgen bearn,
þone † unscyldigne cofota gehwylces
þurh hete hêngon on hêanne bêam
425　in fyrndagum fæderas ûsse.
Þæt wæs þrêalic geþôht. Nû is þearf mycel,
þæt wê fæstlîce ferhð staðelien,
þæt wê ðæs morðres meldan ne weorðen,
hwær þæt hâlige trîo beheled wurde
430　æfter wîgþræce, þŷ læs tôworpen sîen
frôd fyrngewritu ond þâ fæderlîcan
lâre forlêten. Ne bið lang ofer ðæt,
þæt Israhêla æðelu môten

---

meliores legis doctores. Qui cum irent dicebant intra se, pro qua causa
putas hunc laborem facit nobis Regina. Unus ex eis, nomine Judas,
dixit : " Ego scio, quia quaestionem vult facere ligni, in quod Christum
suspenderunt patres nostri : videte ergo nemo ei confiteatur : nam vere
destruentur paternae traditiones, et lex ad nihilum redigetur. Zach-
aeus autem avus meus praenunciavit patri meo, et pater meus cum
moreretur adnuntiavit mihi, dicens :

ofer middangeard má rícsian,
435 æcræft eorla, gif ðis ýppe bið;
swá þá þæt ilce giô mín yldra fæder
sigeróf sægde (þám wæs Sachíus nama),
fród fyrnwiota, fædere mínum,
. . . . caferan
440 (wende hine of worulde) ond þæt word gecwæð:
"gif þé þæt gelimpe on lífdagum,
þæt ðú gehýre ymb þæt hálige tréo
fróde frignan ond geflitu réran
be ðám sigebéame, on þám sóðcyning
445 áhangen wæs, heofonríces weard,
eallre sybbe bearn, þonne þú snúde gecýð,
mín swæs sunu, ær þec swylt nime.
Ne mæg æfre ofer þæt Ebréa þéod,
rédþeahtende, ríce healdan,
450 duguðum wealdan, ac þára dóm leofað
ond hira dryhtscipe . . . .
in woruld weorulda willum gefylled,
ðé þone áhangnan cyning heriaþ ond lofiað".

VI.

Þa ic fromlíce fædere mínum,
455 ealdum æwitan, ágeaf andsware:
"hú wolde þæt geweorðan on woruldríce,
þæt on þone hálgan handa sendan
tô feorhlege fæderas ússe
þurh wráð gewitt, gif híe wiston ær,

"Vide, fili, cum quaestio facta fuerit de ligno, in quod Christum suspenderunt patres nostri, manifesta illud antequam crucieris: jam enim amplius Hebraeorum genus non regnabit, sed regnum eorum erit qui adorant Crucifixum, ipse autem regnabit in seculum seculi." Ego vero dixi ei; "Pater, si ergo sciebant patres nostri quia ipse esset

460 þæt hê Crist wêre, cyning on roderum,
sôð sunu meotudes, sâwla nergend?"
ðâ mê yldra mîn âgeaf andsware,
frôd on fyrhðe fæder reordode :
" ongit, guma ginga, godes hêahmægen,
465 nergendes naman. Sê is niða gehwâm
unâsecgendlic. Þone sylf ne mæg
on moldwege man âspyrigean.
Næfre ic þâ geþeahte, þe þêos þêod ongan,
sêcan wolde, ac ic symle mec
470 âscêd þâra scylda, nales sceame worhte
gâste mînum. Ic him georne oft
þæs unrihtes andsæc fremede,
þonne ûðweotan æht bisêton,
on sefan sôhton. hû hîe sunu meotudes
475 âhêngon. helm wera, hlâford eallra,
engla ond elda, æðelust bearna.
Ne mealhton him swâ disige dêað ôðfæstan
weras wonsêlige, swâ hîe wêndon êr,
sârum settan, þêah hê sume hwîle
480 on galgan his gâst onsende,
sigebearn godes. Þâ siððan wæs
of rôde âhæfen rodera wealdend,
eallra þrymma þrym, þrêo niht siððan
in byrgenne bîdende wæs
485 under þêosterlocan ond þâ þỹ þriddan dæg,
ealles lêohtes lêoht. lifgende ârâs,

Christus, quare manus suas injecerunt in eum ?" Dixit autem mihi:
"Audi me, fili, et cognosce ejus inenarrabile nomen, quia numquam
consiliatus sum neque conveni cum eis, sed multoties contradicebam
illis ; sed quia arguebat seniores et Pontifices nostros, ideo condemnaverunt eum crucifigi, putantes mortificare immortalem: quem et de-
ponentes de ligno sepelierunt. Ipse autem sepultus post tertium
diem surrexit, et manifestavit se suis discipulis: unde credidit
Stephanus frater tuus, et coepit docere in nomine ejus: et consilio

ðeoden engla, ond his þegnum hine,
sôð sigora frêa. seolfne geŷwde
beorht on blêde.　Þonne brôðor þin
490　onfêng æfter fyrste fulwihtes bæð,
lêohtne gelêafan.　Þâ for lufan dryhtnes
Stephanus wæs stânum worpod,
ne geald hê yfel yfele, ac his ealdfêondum
þingode þrohtherd, bæd þrymcyning,
495　þæt hê him þâ wêadæd tô wræce ne sette,
þæt hîe for æfstum unscyldigne,
synna lêasne, Sawles lârum
feore berêddon, swâ hê þurh fêondscipe
tô cwale monige Crîstes folces
500　dêmde, tô dêaþe.　Swâ þeah him dryhten eft
miltse gefremede, þæt hê manegum wearð
folca tô frôfre, syððan him frymða god,
niða nergend, naman oncyrde,
ond hê syððan wæs sanctus Paulus
505　be naman hâten, ond him nænig wæs
ælêrendra ôðer betera
under swegles hlêo syðþan æfre,
þâra þe wîf oððe wer on woruld cendan,
þêah hê Stephanus stânum lehte
510　âbrêotan on beorge. brôðor þînne,
nû ðû meaht gehŷran, hæleð mîn se lêofa,
hû ârfæst is ealles wealdend,
þêah wê æbylgð wið hine oft gewyrcen,

---

facto Pharisaei cum Saducaeis condemnaverunt eum ut lapidaretur;
et tollens eum multitudo lapidaverunt eum.　Sed beatus ille cum
traderet animam, expandit manus suas ad coelum, et orabat dicens:
"Domine ne statuas illis hoc peccatum."　Audi me, fili, et doceo te de
Christo et de pietate ejus: quia et Paulus, qui ante templum sedebat
et exercebat artem scenographiae; erat persequens eos qui in Christo
credebant, qui concitavit populum adversus fratrem suum Stephanum;
et pietate ductus super eum Dominus, unum de sanctis suis fecit eum.

synna wunde, gif wê sôna eft
515 þâra bealudǽda bôte gefremmaþ
ond þæs unrihtes eft geswîcaþ.
Forðan ic, sôðlîce, ond mîn swǽs fæder
syðþan gelŷfdon . . . . ,
þæt geþrôwade eallra þrymma god,
520 lîfes lâttîow, lâðlic wîte
for oferþearfe ilda cynnes.
Forðan ic þê lǽre þurh lêoðrûne,
hyse lêofesta, þæt ðû hospcwide,
æfst nê eofulsǽc ǽfre ne fremme,
525 grimne geagncwide, wið godes bearne. *
Þonne ðû geearnast, þæt þê bið êce lîf,
sêlust sigelêana, seald in heofonum ".
Ðus mec fæder mîn on fyrndagum
unweaxenne wordum lǽrde,
530 septe sôðcwidum (þâm wæs Sŷmon nama),
guma gehðum frôd.   Nû gê geare cunnon,
hwæt êow þæs on sefan sêlest þince
tô gecŷðanne, gif ðêos cwên ûsic
frigneð ymb ðæt trêo, nû gê fyrhðsefan
535 ond môdgeþanc mînne cunnon '.
Him þâ tôgênes þâ glêawestan
on wera þrêate wordum mǽldon :
' næfre wê hŷrdon hæleð ǽnigne
on þysse þêode, bûtan þec nûðâ,
540 þegn ôðerne, þyslic cŷðan
ymb swâ dŷgle wyrd.   Dô, swâ þê þynce,
fyrngidda frôd, gif ðû frugnen sîc
on wera corðre.   Wisdômes beðearf,

Propter quod ego et patres mei credidimus in eum, quia vere filius Dei
est. Et nunc, fili, noli blasphemare eum, neque eos qui in eum credunt :
et habebis vitam aeternam.
      Haec mihi contestatus est pater meus Simon, Ecce omnia audistis :
quid vobis placet, si interrogaverit nos de ligno Crucis ? " Ceteri autem

worda wærlicra ond witan snyttro,
545 sê ðære æðelan sceal andwyrde âgifan
for þyslicne þrêat on meþle '.

VII.

WEOXan word cwidum : weras þeahtedon
on healfa gehwæne, sume hyder, sume þyder,
þrydedon ond þôhton. Þâ cwom þegna héap
550 tô þâm heremeðle. Hrêopon friccan,
câseres bodan : ' êow þêos cwên l-þaþ,
secgas, tô salore, þæt gê seonoðdômas
rihte reccen. Is êow rêdes þearf
on meðelstede, môdes snyttro '.
555 Hêo wæron gearwe, geômormôde
lêodgebyrgean, þâ hie laðod wæron
þurh heard gebann, tô hofe êodon
cýðan cræftes miht. Þâ sio cwên ongan
weras ebresce wordum nêgan
560 fricggan fyrhðwêrige ymb fyrngewritu,
hû on worulde êr wîtgan snugon,
gâsthâlige guman, be godes bearne,
hwær se þêoden geþrôwade,
sôð sunu meotudes, for sâwla lufan.
565 Hêo wæron stearce, stâne heardran,
noldon þæt gerýne rihte cýðan
nê hire andsware ænige secgan.
torngeniðlan, þæs hio him tô sôhte,
ac hio worda gehwæs wiðersæc fremedon

570 fæste on fyrhðe, þæt héo frignan ongan,
cwæðon, þæt hío on aldre ówiht swylces
nè ær né sið æfre hýrdon.

Elene maþelade ond him yrre oncwæð:
'• ic éow tó sóðe secgan wille,

575 ond þæs in life lige ne wyrðeð.
gif gé þissum léase leng gefylgað
mid fæcne gelice, |é mé fore standaþ,
þæt éow in beorge bǽlfýr fornimeð,
hâttost heaðowelma, ond éower hrâ bryttað,

580 lâcende lig, |æt éow |æt léas scual
âwended weorðan tó woruldgedâle.
Ne magon gé ðâ word geséðan, † |e gé hwîle nû on
unriht
wrigon under womma scéatum. Ne magon gé þâ
wyrd bemîðan,
bedyrnan þâ déopan mihte'. Dâ wurdon híe déaðes
on wénan,

585 âdes ond endelifes, ond þǽr þâ ǽnne betǽhton
giddum gearusnottorne (þâm wæs Iûdas nama
cenned for cnéomâgum) — þone híe þǽre cwéne âgêfon,
sægdon hine sundorwîsne: 'hé þé mæg sóð gecýðan,
onwréon wyrda geryno, swâ ðû hine wordum frignest,

590 fériht from orde óð ende forð.
Hé is for eorðan æðeles cynnes,
wordcræftes wis ond witgan sunu,
bald on meðle. Him gebyrde is,
þæt hé génewidas gléawe hæbbe,

595 cræft in bréostum. Hé gecýðeð þé
for wera mengo wîsdómes gife

þurh þâ myclan miht, swâ þîn môd lufaþ'.
Hio on sybbe forlêt sêcan gehwylcne
âgenne eard ond þone êcne genam
600 Iûdas tô gisle ond þâ georne bæd,
þæt hê be ðære rôde riht getæhte,
þâ êr in legere wæs lange bedyrned,
ond hine seolfne sundor âcîgde.
Elene maþelode tô þâm ânhagan,
605 tîrêadig cwên : 'þê synt tû gearu,
swâ lîf. swâ dêað, swâ þê lêofre bið
tô gecêosanne. Cŷð ricene nû.
hwæt ðû þæs tô þinge þafian wille'.
Iûdas hire ongên þingode (ne meahte hê þâ gehðu
bebûgan,
610 oncyrran † rex geniðlan. Hê wæs on þære cwêne
gewealdum):
'hû mæg þæm geweorðan, þe on wêstenne
mêðe ond meteleâs môrland trydeð.
hungre gehæfted, ond him hlâf ond stân
on gesihðe bû samod geweorðað
615 streac ond hnesce, þæt hê þone stân nime
wið hungres hlêo, hlâfes ne gîme,
gewende tô wædle ond þâ wiste wiðsæce,
beteran wiðhycge, þonne hê bêga beneah?'

VIII.

Him þâ sêo êadige andwyrde âgeaf
620 Elene for eorlum undearnunga :

Judam solum. Et convocans eum, dixit ad illum : "Vita et mors propositae sunt tibi : elige tibi quod vis, vitam an mortem." Judas dixit : "Et quis in solitudine constitutus, panibus sibi appositis, lapides manducat ?" Beata autem Helena dixit : "Si ergo in coelo et in terra vis vivere, dic mihi ubi absconditum est lignum pretiosae Crucis."

'gif ðû in heofonrîce habban wille
eard mid englum ond on corðan lif,
sigorlêan in swegle, saga ricene mê,
hwǽr sêo rôd wunige radorcyninges
625 hâlig under hrûsan, þê gê hwîle nû
þurh morðres mân mannum dyrndun'.
Jûdas maðelade (him wæs geômor sefa,
hât æt heortan ond gehwæðres wâ,
gê hê heofonrîces hyht swâ môde
630 ond þis andwearde ânforlête
rîce under roderum, gê hê ðâ rôde tæhte):
' hû mæg ic þæt findan, þæt swâ fyrn gewearð
wintra gangum? Is nû worn sceacen,
.cc. oððe mâ geteled rîme.
635 Ic ne mæg âreccan, nû ic þæt rîm ne can.
Is nû feale siðþan forðgewitenra
frôdra ond gôdra, þê ûs fore wǽron,
glêawra gumena. Ic on geogoðe wearð
on sîðdagum syððan âcenned,
640 cnihtgeong hæleð. Ic ne can, þæt ic nât,
findan on fyrhðe, þæt swâ fyrn gewearð'.
Elene maðelade him on andsware :
' hû is þæt geworden on þysse werþêode,
þæt gê swâ monigfeald on gemynd witon,
645 alra tâcna gehwylc, swâ Trôiâna
þurh gefeoht fremedon? Þæt wæs fær mycel,
open ealdgewin, þonne þêos æðele gewyrd,
geâra gongum. Gê þæt geare cunnon
êdre gereccan, hwæt þǽr eallra wæs

Judas dixit : "Quemadmodum habetur in gestis, sunt jam anni
ducenti plus minusve : et nos, cum simus juniores, quomodo possumus
haec nosse?" Beata Helena dixit : "Quomodo ante tantas generationes in Ilio et Troade factum est bellum, et omnes nunc commemorantur
qui ibi sunt mortui : et monumenta eorum et loca scriptura tradit."
Judas dixit : Vere, Domina : quia conscripta sunt : nos autem non

650 on manrîme morðorslehtes,
 dareðlácendra dèadra gefeallen
 under bordhagan. Gê ʃâ byrgenna
 under stânhleoðum ond ʃâ stôwe swâ some
 ond ʃâ wintergerîm on gewritu setton'.
655 Iûdas maðelade (gnornsorge wæg):
 'wê ʃæs hereweorces, hlæfdige mîn,
 _ for nŷdʃearfe neaŋ myndgiaʃ
 ond ʃâ wîggʃræce on gewritu setton,
 ] ôoda gebæru, ond ʃis næfre
660 ʃurh æniges mannes mûð gehŷrdon
 hæleðum cyðan, bûtan hêr nûðâ':
 Him sêo æðele cwên âgeaf andsware :
 'wiðsæcest ðû tô swîðe sôðe ond rihte
 ymb ʃæt lifes trêow ond nû lŷtle êr
665 sægdest sôðlice be ʃâm sigebêame
 lêodum ʃinum ond nû on lige cyrrest'.
 Iûdas hire ongên ʃingode, cwæð, ʃæt hê ʃæt on gehðu
 gespræce
 ond twêon swîðost, wênde him trâge hnâgre.
 Him onewæð hraðe câseres mæg :
670 'hwæt, wê ðæt hŷrdon ʃurh hâlige bêc
 hæleðum cyðan, ʃæt âhangen wæs
 on Caluarie cyninges frêobearn,
 godes gâstsunu. Þû scealt geagninga
 wîsdôm onwrêon, swâ gewritu secgaʃ,
675 æfter stedewange hwær sêo stôw sîe
 Caluarie, êr ʃee cwealm nime,
 swilt, for synnum, ʃæt ic hîe syððan mæge

habemus haec conscripta. Beata Helena dixit: "Quid est quod paulo
ante confessus es a te ipso, quia sunt gesta ? " Judas dixit: "In dubio
locutus sum." Beata Helena dixit: "Ego quidem habeo beatam
vocem Evangeliorum, in quo loco crucifixus est ipse Dominus: tan-
tum ostende mihi, qui vocatur Calvariae locus; et ego faciam mundari
locum; forsitan inveniam desiderium meum." Judas dixit: "Neque

geclǣnsian Crîste tô willan,
hæleðum tô helpe, þæt mê hâlig god
680 gefylle, frêa mihtig, feores ingeþanc,
weoruda wuldorgeofa, willan mînne,
gâsta gêocend'. Hire Iûdas oncwæð
stîðhycgende : ' ic þâ stôwe ne can
nê þæs wanges wiht nê þâ wîsan cann'.
685 Elene maðelode þurh corne hyge :
' ic þæt geswerige þurh sunu meotodes,
þone âhangnan god, þæt ðû hungre scealt
for cnêomâgum cwylmed weorðan,
bûtan þû forlǣte þâ lêasunga
690 ond mê sweotollîce sôð gecýðe'.
Heht þâ swâ cwicne corðre lǣdan,
scûfan scyldigne (scealcas ne gǣldon)
in drŷgne sêað, þǣr hê duguða lêas
sîomode in sorgum .vii. nihta fyrst
695 under hearmlocan hungre geþrêatod,
clommum beclungen, ond þâ cleopigan ongan
sârum besyleed on þone seofeðan dæg
mêðe ond metelêas (mægen wæs geswiðrod):
' ic êow healsie þurh heofona god,
700 þæt gê mê of ðyssum earfeðum ûp forlǣten
hêanne fram hungres genîðlan. Ic þæt hâlige trêo
lustum cýðe, nû ic hit leng ne mæg
helan for hungre. Is þes hæft tô ðan strang,
þrêanŷd þæs þearl ond þes þroht tô ðæs heard
705 dôgorrîmum. Ic âdrêogan ne mæg
nê leng helan be ðâm lîfes trêo,
þêah ic ǣr mid dysige þurhdrifen wǣre
ond ðæt sôð tô late seolf gecnêowe'.

locum novi; quia nec eram tunc." Beata Helena dixit: " Per Crucifixum fame te interficiam, nisi dixeris veritatem." Et cum haec dixisset, jussit eum mitti in lacum siccum, usque in septem dies, sic
ut custodiretur a custodibus. Cum transissent autem septem dies,

VIIII.

Þâ ðæt gehŷrde, sîo þêr hæleðum scéad,
710 bcornes gebûro, hîo bebéad hraðe,
þæt hine man of nearwe ond of nŷdcleofan,
fram þâm engan hofe, ûp forlête.
Hîc ðæt ofstlîce cfncdon sôna
ond hine mid ârum ûp gelêddon
715 of carcerne, swâ him séo cwên bebéad. ·
Stôpon þâ tô þêre stôwe stiðhycgende
on þâ dûne ûp, ðê dryhten êr
âhangen wæs, heofourîces weard,
godbearn, on galgan, ond hwæðre geare nyste
720 hungre gehŷned, hwêr sîo hâlige rôd
721.2 þurh *fěondes* scaru foldan getŷned
lange legere fæst léodum dyrne
wunode wælreste. Word stunde âhôf
725 elnes oncŷðig ond on chrisc spræc :
'dryhten hêlend, þû ðe âhst dôma geweald
ond þû geworhtest þurh þînes wuldres miht
heofon ond corðan ond holmþræce,
sês sîdne fæðm, samod calle gesceaft
730 ond þâ âmête mundum þînum
calne ymbhwyrft ond ûprador
ond þû sylf sitest, sigora waldend,
ofer þâm æðclestan engelcynne,
þe geond lyft farað léohte bewundene,

---

clamavit Judas de lacu, dicens, "Obsecro vos, educite me, et ego ostendam vobis crucem Christi."

Cum ascendisset autem de lacu, perrexit usque ad locum, nesciens certius ubi jacebat Crux Christi, levavitque vocem suam ad Dominum Hebraica lingua et dixit: "Deus, Deus, qui fecisti coelum et terram, qui palmo metisti coelum et pugno terram mensurasti; qui sedes super currum Cherubin, et ipsa sunt volantia in acris cursibus luce immensa,

735 mycle mægenþrymme. Ne mæg þær manna gecynd
of corðwegum ûp geferan
in lichoman mid þâ lêohtan gedryht,
wuldres âras. Þû geworhtest þâ
ond tô þegnunge þînre gesettest,
740 hâlig ond heofonlic. Þâra ou hâde sint
in sindrêame syx genemned,
þâ ymbscalde synt mid syxum êac
fiðrum, gefrætwad, fægere scînaþ.
Þâra sint .IIII., þe ou flihte â
745 þâ þegnunge þrymme beweotigaþ
fore onsŷne êces dêman,
singallice singaþ in wuldre
hêdrum stefnum heofoncininges lof,
wôða wlitegaste, ond þâs word eweðaþ
750 clênum stefnum (þâm is ceruphîn nama):
'hâlig is se hâlga hêahengla god,
weoroda wealdend. Is ðæs wuldres ful
heofun ond eorðe ond eall hêahmægeu
tîre getâenod'. Syndon tû on þâm,
755 sigorcynn, on swegle, þe man sêraphîn
be naman hâteð. Hîe sceolon neorxnawang
ond lifes trêo lêgene sweorde
hâlig healdan. Heardecg ewacaþ,
beofaþ, brogdenmæl ond blêom wrixleð
760 grâpum gryrefæst. Þæs ðû, god dryhten,
wealdest wîdan fyrhð, ond þû womfulle
scyldwyrcende sceaðan of radorum

ubi humana natura transire non potest; quia tu es qui fecisti ea ad
ministerium tuum: sex animalia, quae habent senas alas; quattuor
quidem ex ipsis quae volant, ministrantia et incessabili voce claman-
tia, "Sanctus, Sanctus, Sanctus," Cherubin vocantur; duo autem
ex his posuisti in Paradiso custodire lignum vitae, quae vocantur
Seraphin. Tu autem dominaris omnium, quia tua factura sumus,
qui incredibiles Angelos profundo tartaro tradidisti; et ipsi sunt sub

âwurpe wonhŷdige.　Þâ sîo wêrge secolu
under heolstorhofu hrêosan sceolde
765　in wîta forwyrd.　Þær hîe in wylme nû
drêogaþ dêaðewale in dracan faðme
þeostrum forþylmed.　Hê þinum wiðsôc
aldordôme, þæs hê in ermðum sceal,
calra fûla fûl, fâh þrôwian,
770　þeownêd þolian.　Þær hê þîn ne mæg
word âwcorpan, is in wîtum fæst,
calre synne fruma, sûsle gebunden.
Gif þîn willa sîe, wealdend engla,
þæt rîcsie, sê ðe on rôde wæs
775　ond þurh Mârian in middangeard
âcenned wearð in cildes hâd,
þeoden engla (gif hê þîn nære
sunu synna lêas, næfre hê sôðra swâ feala
in woruldrîce wundra gefremede
780　dôgorgerîmum.　Nô ðû of dêaðe hine
swâ þrymlîce, þeoda wealdend,
âweahte for weorodum, gif hê in wuldre þîn
þurh ðâ beorhtan bearn ne wære),
gedô nû, fæder engla, forð bêacen þîn.
785　swâ ðû gehŷrdest þone hâlgan wer,
Moyses, on meðle, þâ ðû, milita god,
geŷwdest þâm eorle on þâ æðelan tîd
under beorhhliðe bân Iosephes,
swâ ic þê, weroda wealdend, gif hit sîe willa þîn,
790　þurg þæt beorhte gesceap biddan wille,

---

fundo abyssi a draconum foetore cruciandi, et tuo praecepto contra-
dicere non possunt.　Et nunc, Domine, si tua voluntas est regnare
filium Mariae, qui missus est a te (nisi autem fuisset ex te, non
tantas virtutes fecisset; nisi vero tuus puer esset, non suscitares eum
a mortuis) fac nobis, Domine, prodigium hoc; et sicut exaudisti
famulum tuum Moysen, et ostendisti ei ossa patris nostri Joseph;
ita et nunc, si est voluntas tua, ostende nobis occultum thesaurum:

þæt mé þæt goldhord, gásta scyppend,
geopenie, þæt yldum wæs
lange behýded. Forlét nû, lífes fruma,
of ðâm wangstede wynsumne ûp
795 under radores ryne réc ástigan
lyftlácende. Ic gelýfe þé sél
ond þý fæstlícor ferhð staðelige,
hyht untwéondne, on þone âhangnan Crîst,
þæt hé síe sóðlíce sâwla nergend,
800 éce, ælmihtig, Israhela cining,
walde wîdan ferhð wuldres on heofenum,
â bûtan ende, écra gestealda'.

X.

Dâ of ðǽre stówe stéam ûp árâs,
swylce réc, under radorum. Þǽr ârǽred wearð
805 beornes bréostsefa. Hé mid bǽm handum
éadig ond ǽgléaw ûpweard plegade.
Iûdas maþelode gléaw in geþance :
'nû ic þurh sóð hafu seolf gecnâwen
on heardum hige, þæt ðu hǽlend eart
810 middangeardes. Sîe ðé, mægena god,
þrymsittendum þanc bûtan ende,
þæs ðû mé swâ méðum ond swâ mânweorcum
þurh þîn wuldor inwrige wyrda geryno.
Nû ic þé, bearn godes, biddan wille,
815 weoroda willgifa, nû ic wât, þæt ðû eart

---

et fac ab eodem loco fumum odoris aromatum et suavitatis ascendere :
ut et ego credam crucifixo Christo, quia ipse est Rex Israel, et nunc
et in secula seculorum."

Haec cum orasset Judas, statim commotus est locus, et multitudo
fumi et aromatum odoris suavitatis ascendit de loco : ita ut admira-
tus Judas plauderet ambabus manibus suis, et diceret : " In veritate,

gecýðed ond ácennod allra cyninga þrym,
þæt ðû mâ ne síe mînra gylta,
þâra þe ic gefremede nalles fêam siðum,
metud, gemyndig. Lêt mee, mihta god,

820 on rîmtale rîces þînes
mid hâligra hlýte wunigan
in þêre beorhtan byrig, þêr is brôðor mîn
gewcorðod in wuldre, þæs hê wêre wið þec,
Stephanus, hêold, þêah hê stângreopum

825 worþod wêre. Hê hafað wîgges lêan,
blêd bûtan blinne. Sint in bôcum his
wundor, þâ hê worhte, on gewritum, cýðed'.
Ongan þâ wilfægen æfter þâm wuldres trêo
elnes ânhýdig corðan delfan

830 under turfhagan, þæt hê on .xx.
fôtmêlum feor funde bchelede,
under nêolum niðer næsse gehýdde
in þêostorcofan — hê ðêr .iii. mêtte
in þâm rêonian hofe rôda ætsomne

835 grêote begranene, swâ hîo geârdagum
ârlêasra sccolu corðan be|eahton,
Iûdêa cynn. Hîe wið godes bearne
nîð âhôfun, swâ hîe nô sceoldon,
þêr hîe leahtra fruman lârum ne hýrdon.

840 Þâ wæs môdgemynd myclum geblissod,
hige onhyrded þurh þæt hâlige trêo,
inbryrded brêostsefa, syððan bêacen gesch
hâlig under brûsan. Hê mid handum befêng
wuldres wynbêam ond mid weorode âhôf

Christe, tu es Salvator mundi; gratias tibi ago, Domine, qui cum sim
indignus, non me fraudasti dono gratiae tuae. Deprecor te, Domine
Jesu Christe, memor esto mei et dele peccata mea, et adnumera me
cum fratre meo Stephano, qui scriptus est in Actibus duodecim Apos-
tolorum tuorum." Haec cum dixisset, accipiens fossorium prae-
cinxit se viriliter, et coepit fodere. Cum autem fodisset passus viginti,

845 of foldgræfe. Fêðegestas
ċodon, æðelingas, in on þâ ceastre.
Âsetton þâ on gesyhðe sigebêamas .III.
corlas ânhŷdige fore Elenan cnêo
collenferhðe. Cwên weorces gefeah
850 on ferhðsefan ond þâ frignan ongan,
on hwylcum þâra bêama bearn wealdendes,
hæleða hyhtgifa, hangen wêre.
'Hwæt, wê þæt hŷrdon þurh hâlige bêc
tâcnum cŷðan, þæt twêgen mid him
855 geþrôwedon, ond hê wæs þridda sylf
on rôde trêo. Rodor eal gesweare
on þâ slîðan tîd. Saga, gif ðû cunne,
on hwylcre þyssa þrêora þêoden engla
geþrôwode, þrymmes hyrde'.
860 Ne mealte hire Iûdas (nê ful gere wiste)
sweotole gecŷþan be ðâm sigebêame,
on hwylcne se hêlend âhafen wære,
sigebearn godes, êr hê âsettan heht
on þone middel þêre mêran byrig
865 bêamas mid bearhtme ond gebîdan þêr,
ôð ðæt him gecŷðde cyning ælmihtig
wundor fôr weorodum be ðâm wuldres trêo.
Gesêton sigerôfe, sang âhôfon,
rêdþeahtende, ymb þâ rôda þrêo
870 ôð þâ nigoðan tîd, hæfdon nêowne gefêan
mêrðum gemêted. Þâ þêr menigo cwom,
folc unlŷtel, ond gefærenne man
brôhton on bêre beorna þrêate

invenit tres cruces absconditas, quas ejiciens attulit in civitatem.
Interrogabat autem beatissima Helena, quae esset crux Christi : "sci-
mus autem quia ceterae duae latronum sunt, qui cum eo crucifixi
sunt." Et ponentes eas in media civitate expectabant gloriam Christi.
Et circa horam nonam ferebatur mortuus juvenis in grabato : Judas
autem gaudio repletus dixit : "Nunc cognosces, Domina, dilectissimum

on néaweste (wæs þâ nigoðe tid),
875 gingne gâstléasne. Þâ ðær Iûdas wæs
on môdsefan miclum geblissod.
Heht þâ âsettan sâwlléasne,
life belidenes lîc, on eorðan,
unlifgendes, ond ûp âhôf,
880 rihtes wêmend, þâra rôda twâ
fyrhðgléaw on fæðme ofer þæt fæge hûs,
déophycgende. Hit wæs dêad, swâ ær,
lîc legere fæst: leomu côlodon
þréanédum beþeaht. Þâ sîo þridde wæs
885 âhafen hâlig. Hrâ wæs on anbîde,
ôð ðæt him uppan æðelinges wæs
rôd ârêred, rodorcyninges bêam,
sigebêacen sôð. Hê sôna ârâs
gâste gegearwod, geador bû samod
890 lîc ond sâwl. Þær wæs lof hafen
fæger mid þŷ folce. Fæder weorðodon
ond þone sôðan sunn wealdendes
wordum heredon. Sîe him wuldor ond þanc
â bûtan ende callrâ gesceafta.

XI.

895 Dᴀ wæs þâm folce on ferhðsefan
ingemynde, swâ him â scyle,
wundor, þâ þe worhte weoroda dryhten
tô feorhnere fira cynne,

---

lignum et virtutem ejus." Et tenens grabatum Judas, fecit deponi
mortuum, et posuit super eum singulas cruces, et non surrexit: im-
posita autem tertia cruce Dominica super mortuum, statim surrexit
qui mortuus fuerat juvenis, et omnes, qui aderant, glorificabant
Dominum.

Sed omnium bonorum semper invidus diabolus cum furore voci-

lifes láttïow. Þá þǽr ligesynnig
900 on lyft ástáh lácende féond.
Ongan þá hléoðrian helledéofol,
eatol ǽclǽca, yfela gemyndig :
'hwǽt is þis, lá, manna, þe mínne eft
þurh fyrngeflit folgaþ wyrdeð,
905 íceð caldne nið, fǽhta strúdeð?
Þis is singal sacu. Sáwla ne móton
máufremmende in mínum leng
fǽhtum wunigan, ná cwom eljéodig,
þone ic ǽr on firenum fǽstne talde,
910 hafað mee beréafod rihta gehwylces,
feohgestréona. Nis ðǽt fǽger sið.
Feala mé se hǽlend hearma gefremede,
níða nearoliera, sé ðe in Nazareð
áféded wǽs. Syððan furþum wéox
915 of cildháde, symle cirde tó him
fǽhte mine. Ne mót fǽnige ná
rihte spówan. Is his ríce brád
ofer middangeard, mín is geswiðrod
rǽd under roderum. Ic þá róde ne þearf
920 hleahtre herigean. Hwǽt, se hǽlend mé
in þám engan hám eft getýnde
geómrum tó sorge. Ic þurh Iúdas ǽr
hyhtful gewearð ond ná gehýned éom,
góda geásne, þurh Iúdas eft,
925 fáh ond fréondléas. Gén ic findan can
þurh wróhtstafas wiðereyr siððan
of ðám wearhtreafum. Ic áwecce wið ðé
óðerne cyning, sé ǽhteð þín,

---

ferabatur in aere, dicens : "Quis iterum hic est, qui non permittet me
suscipere animas meorum ? O Jesu Nazarene, omnes traxisti ad te :
ecce et lignum tuum manifestasti adversum me. O Juda ! quid hoc
fecisti ? Nonne prius ego per Judam traditionem perfeci, et populum
concitavi impie agere ? Ecce nunc per Judam ego hinc ejicior.

    ond hê forlǽteð lâre þîne
930 ond mânþêawum mînum folgaþ
    ond þec þonne sendeð in þâ sweartestan
    ond þâ wyrrestan wîtebrôgan,
    þæt ðû sârum forsôht wiðsæcest fæste
    þone âhangnan cyning, þâm ðû hŷrdest ǽr '.
935 Him ðâ glêawhŷdig Iûdas oncwæð,
    hæleð hildedêor (him wæs hâlig gâst
    befolen fæste, fŷrhât lufu,
    weallende gewitt þurh wigan snyttro),
    ond þæt word gecwæð wîsdômes ful :
940 'ne þearft ðû swâ swîðe, synna gemyndig,
    sâr nîwigan ond sæce ræran,
    morðres mânfrêa, þæt þê se mihtiga cyning
    in nêoluesse nyðer bescûfeð,
    synwyrcende, in sûsla grund
945 dômes lêasne, sê ðe dêadra feala
    worde âwehte. Wite ðû þê gearwor,
    þæt ðû unsnyttrum ânforlête
    lêohta beorhtost ond lufan dryhtnes,
    þone fǽgran gefêan, ond on fŷrbæðe
950 sûslum beþrungen syððan wunodest,
    âde onǽled, ond þǽr âwa scealt,
    wiðerhycgende, wergðu drêogan,
    yrmðu, bûtan ende '. Elene gehŷrde,
    hû se fêond ond se frêond geflitu rǽrdon,
955 tîrêadig ond trâg, on twâ halfa,
    synnig ond gesǽlig. Sefa wæs þê glædra,
    þæs þe hêo gehŷrde þone hellesceapan
    oferswîðedne, synna bryttan,

Inveniam et ego quid faciam adversum te : suscitabo alium Regem, qui derelinquet Crucifixum, et mea exequetur consilia, et immittet in te iniqua tormenta : et tunc cruciatus negabis Crucifixum." Judas autem, fremens in spiritu sancto, dixit : "Qui mortuos suscitavit Christus, ipse te damnet in abyssum ignis aeterni." Haec audiens

ond þâ wundrade ymb þæs weres snyttro,
960 hû hê swâ gelêafful on swâ lŷtlum fæce
ond swâ uncŷðig êfre wurde
glêawnesse þurgoten. Gode þancode,
wuldorcyninge, þæs hire se willa gelamp
þurh bearn godes béga gehwæðres,
965 gê æt þêre gesyhðe þæs sigebêames
gê ðæs gelêafan, þe hîo swâ lêohte onenêow
wuldorfæste gife in þæs weres brêostum.

XII.

Ðâ wæs gefrêge in þêre folesceare,
geond þâ werþêode wîde lêded,
970 mêre morgenspel manigum on andan,
þâra þe dryhtnes æ dyrnan weldon,
boden æfter burgum, swâ brimo fæðmað,
in ceastra gehwêre, þæt Crîstes rôd
fyrn foldan begræfen funden wêre,
975 sêlest sigebêacna, þâra þe sîð oððe êr
hâlig under heofenum âhafen wurde,
ond wæs Iûdêum gnornsorga mêst,
werum wansêligum, wyrda lâðost,
þæt hîe hit for worulde wendan ne mealiton,
980 cristenra gefêan. Ðâ sîo cwên bebêad
ofer eorlmægen âras fŷsan
ricene tô râde, sceoldon Rômwarena
ofer hêanne holm hlâford sêcean
ond þâm wîggende wilspella mêst
985 scolfum gesecgan, þe ðæt sigorbêacen
þurh meotodes êst mêted wêre,

funden in foldan, þæt ǽr feala mǽla
behýded wæs hálgum tó téonan,
cristenum folce. Þá ðám cininge wearð
990   þurh þá mǽran wórd mód geblissod,
ferhð gefêonde. Næs þá friegendra
under goldhoman gád in burgum
feorran geférede. Wæs him frófra mǽst
geworden in worlde æt ðám willspelle,
995   blihhende hyge, þe him hererǽswan
ofer êastwegas, áras, bróhton,
hú gesundne síð ofer swonráde
secgas mid sigecwén áseted hæfdon
on Crêca land. Híe se cásere heht
1000 ófstum myclum eft gearwian
sylfe tó síðe. Secgas ne gǽldon,
syððan andsware ếdre gehýrdon,
æðelinges word. Heht hê Elenan hâl
âbêodan beadurófre, gif híe brim † nesen
1005 ond gesundne síð settan mósten,
hæleð hwætmóde, tó þ ếre hálgan byrig.
Heht hire þâ áras ôac gebêodan
Constantínus, þæt hío ciriean þ ếr
on þâm beorhhliðe bêgra rǽdum
1010 getimbrede, tempel dryhtnes,
on Caluarie Crîste tó willan,
hæleðum tó helpe, þ ếr sío hálige ród
gemêted wæs, mǽrost bêama,
þâra þe gefrugnen foldbûende
1015 on corðwege. Hío geefnde swâ,
siððan winemagas westan bróhton
ofer lagufæsten lêofspell manig.
Þâ sêo cwên bebêad cræftum getýde

sundor âsêcean, þâ sêlestan,
1020 þâ þe wrætlicost wyrcan cñðon
stângefôgum, on þâm stedewange
girwan godes tempel. Swâ hire gâsta weard
reord of roderum, hêo þâ rôde heht
golde beweorcean ond gimcynnum,
1025 mid þâm æðelestum corenanstânum,
besetton searocræftum ond þâ in scolfren fæt
locum belûcan. Þær þæt lîfes trêo,
sêlest sigebêama, siððan wunode
æðelum unbræce. Þær bið â gearu
1030 wraðu wannhâlum wîta gehwylces,
sæce ond sorge. Hîe sôna þær
þurh þâ hâlgan gesceaft helpe findaþ,
godcunde gife. Swylce Iûdas onfêng
æfter fyrstmearce fulwihtes bæð
1035 ond geclênsod wearð Crîste getrŷwe,
lîfwearde lêof. His gelêafa wearð
fæst on ferhðe, siððan frôfre gâst
wîc gewunode in þæs weres brêostum,
bylde tô bôte. Hê þæt betere gecêas,
1040 wuldres wynne, ond þâm wyrsan wiðsôc,
dêofulgildum, ond gedwolan fylde,
unrihte æ. Him wearð êce rex,
meotud, milde, god mihta wealdend.

XIII.

Þâ wæs gefulwad, sê ðe ær feala tîda
1045 lêoht gearu . . . . ,
inbryded brêostsefa on þæt betere lîf,

Jerosolymis, et baptizavit eum in Christo. Cum moraretur beata
Helena in Jerosolyma factum est Beatum Episcopum dormitionem

gewended tô wuldre. Hûru, wyrd gescreâf,
þæt hê swâ geléaffull ond swâ léof gode
in worldrîce weorðan sceolde,
1050 Crîste gecwême. Þæt gecýðed wearð,
siððan Elene heht Eusebium
on rǽdgeþeaht, Rôme bisceop,
gefetian on fultum forðsnot/erne
hæleða gerǽdum tô þǽre hâlgan byrig,
1055 þæt hê gesette on sacerdhâd
in Ierusalem Iûdas þâm folce
tô bisceope burgum on innan
þurh gâstes gife tô godes temple
cræftum gecorenne, ond hine Cyriacus
1060 þurh snyttro gepeaht syððan nemde
nîwan stefne. Nama wæs gecyrred
beornes in burgum on þæt betere forð
ǽ hǽlendes. Þâ gên Elenan wæs
môd gemynde ymb þâ mǽran wyrd
1065 geneahhe for þâm næglum, þe ðæs nergendes
fêt þurhwodon ond his folme swâ some,
mid þâm on rôde wæs rodera wealdend
gefæstnod, frêa mihtig. Be ðâm frignan ongan
cristenra ewên, Cyriacus bæd,
1070 þæt hire þâ gîna gâstes mihtum
ymb wundorwyrd willan gefylde,
onwrige wuldorgifum, ond þæt word âcwæð
tô þâm bisceope, bald reordode :

---

accipere in Christo. Beata autem Helena accersivit Episcopum Eusebium urbis Romae, et ordinavit Judam Episcopum in Jerosolyma
Ecclesiae Christi: mutavit autem nomen ejus, et vocatus est Cyriacus.
Beata autem Helena, repleta Dei fide, et intelligens Scripturas per
vetus et novum Testamentum, instructa et repleta Spiritu sancto,
iterum coepit studiose requirere qui in cruce confixi fuerant clavi, in
quibus impii Judaei Salvatorem crucifixerunt: et convocans Judam,

'þû mê, corla hlêo, þone æðelan bêam,
1075 rôde rodera cininge*s*, ryhte getæhtesð,
on þâm âhangen wæs hæðenum folmum
gâsta gêocend, godes âgen bearn,
nerigend fira. Mec þêra nægla gên
on fyrhðsefan fyrwet myngaþ.
1080 Wolde ic, þæt ðû funde, þâ ðe in foldan gên
dêope bedolfen dierne sindon,
heolstre behŷded. Â mîn hige sorgað,
rêonig rêoteð ond geresteð nô,
ærþan mê gefylle fæder ælmihtig,
1085 wereda wealdend, willan mînne,
niða nergend, þurh þâra nægla cyme,
hâlig of hiehða. Nû ðû hrædlice
eallum eaðmêdum, âr sêlesta,
þine bêne onsend in ðâ beorhtan gesceaft
1090 on wuldres *wealdend*, bide wigena þrym,
þæt þê gecŷðe cyning ælmihtig
hord under hrûsan, þæt gehŷded gên,
duguðum dyrne, dêogol, bîdeð'.
Þâ se hâlga ongan hyge staðolian
1095 brêostum onbryrded bisceop þæs folces,
glædmôd êode gumena þrêate
god hergendra ond þâ geornlice
Cyriacus on Caluarie
hlêor onhylde, hygerûne ne mâð,

<hr>

qui cognominatus est Cyriacus, dixit ei: "Quod circa lignum crucis
erat, repletum est desiderium meum: sed de fixoriis qui infixi sunt
imminet tristitia. Sed non requiescam et de hoc, donec Dominus
compleat desiderium meum: sed accede adhuc, et de hoc precare
Dominum." Sanctus vero Episcopus Cyriacus, veniens ad Calvariae
locum una cum multis Fratribus, qui in Domino Jesu Christo
crediderunt per inventionem sanctae Crucis, et quod in mortuo
factum est signum; elevans in coelum oculos suos et manibus simul
percutiens pectus, exclamavit ex toto corde ad Dominum, confitens
priorem ignorantiam, et beatificans omnes qui crediderunt in Christo

1100 gâstes mihtum tô gode cleopode
eallum eaðmêdum, bæd him engla weard
geopenigean uncûðe wyrd
nîwan on nearwe, hwær hê þâra nægla swiðost
on þâm wangstede wênan þorfte.

1105 Leorte ðâ tâcen forð, þær hie tô sægon,
fæder, frôfre gâst, ðurh fŷres blêo
ûp êðigean, þær þâ æðelestan
hæleða gerædum hŷdde wæron
þurh nearusearwe næglas on corðan.

1110 Ðâ cwom semninga sunnan beorhtra
lâcende lîg. Lêode gesâwon
hira willgifan wundor cŷðan,
ðâ ðær of heolstre, swylce heofonsteorran
oððe goldgimmus, grunde getenge

1115 næglas of nearwe neoðan scînende
lêohte lixton. Lêode gefægon,
weorud willhrêðig, sægdon wuldor gode
ealle ânmôde, þeah hie ær wæron
þurh dêofles spild in gedwolan lange,

1120 âcyrred fram Crîste. Hie ewædon þus:
' nû wê scolfe gesêoð sigores tâcen,
sôðwundor godes, þæt wê wiðsôcun ær
mid lêasingum. Nû is in lêoht cymen,
onwrigen, wyrda bigang. Wuldor þæs âge

1125 on hêannesse heofonrîces god '.
Ðâ wæs geblissod, sê ðc tô bôte gehwearf

---

et qui credituri sunt adhuc. Diu autem eo orante, ut manifestaretur
illi signum aliquod, quemadmodum in cruce ita et in fixoriis, in fine
orationis, cum diceret; "Amen," factum est tale signum, quod omnes
qui aderamus vidimus. Magna autem coruscatio de loco illuxit, ubi
inventa est sancta Crux, clarior solis lumine; et statim apparuerunt
clavi illi, qui in Dominico confixi fuerant corpore, tamquam aurum
fulgens in terra; ita ut omnes sine dubio dicerent credentes, "Nunc
cognoscimus in quem credimus." Quos accipiens cum magno timore

þurh bearn godes, bisceop þára léoda,
níwan stefne. Hé þám næglum onféng
egesan geáclod ond þǽre árwyrðan
1130   cwéne bróhte. Hæfde Ciriacus
eall gefylled, swá him séo æðele behéad,
wífes willan. Þá wæs wópes hring,
hát héafodwylm ofer hléor goten,
nalles for torne : téaras féollon
1135   ofer wíra gespon. Wuldres gefylled
cwéne willa. Héo hie on encéow sette
léohte geléafan, láe weorðode
blissum hrémig, þe hire brungen wæs
gnyrna tó géoce. Gode þancode,
1140   sigora dryhtne, þæs þe hío sóð gecnéow
andweardlíce, þæt wæs oft bodod
feor ǽr beforan fram fruman worulde
folcum tó frófre. Héo gefylled wæs
wísdómes gife, ond þá wíc behéold
1145   hálig heofonlic gást, hréðer weardode,
æðelne innoð. Swá hie ælmihtig
sigebearn godes sioððan freoðode.

XIIII.

Ongan þá geornlíce gástgerýnum
on sefan séccan sóðfæstnesse
1150   weg tó wuldre. Húru, weroda god
gefullǽste, fæder on roderum,

---

obtulit Beatae Helenae. Quae figens genua et caput inclinans, ado-
ravit eos.

    Repleta autem sapientia et scientia multa valde, cogitabat quid de
his faceret. Quae cum in semetipsa posuisset omnem exquirere viam
veritatis; Spiritus sancti gratia misit in sensum ejus tale quiddam

ciniug ælmihtig, þæt seo cwên begeat
willan in worulde. Wæs se wîtedôm
þurh fyrnwitan beforan sungen
1155   eall æfter orde, swâ hit eft gelamp
ðinga gehwylces. Þeodewên ongan
þurh gâstes gife georne sêcan
nearwe geneahhe, tô hwan hîo þâ næglas sêlost
ond dêorlîcost gedôn meahte
1160   dugoðum tô hrôðer, hwæt þæs wære dryhtnes willa.
Ileht ðâ gefetigean forðsnotterne
ricene tô rûne. þone þe rædgeþeaht
þurh glêawe miht georne cûðe,
frôdne on ferhðe, ond hine frignan ongan,
1165   hwæt him] æs on sefan sêlost þûhte
tô gelæstenne, ond his lâre gecêas
þurh þeodscipe. Ile hire þrîste onewað :
' þæt is gedafenlic, | æt ðû dryhtnes word
on hyge healde, hâlige rûne,
1170   cwên sêlest. ond þæs ciniuges bebod
georne begange, nû | ê god scalde
sâwle sigespêd ond snyttro cræft,
nerigend fira. Þû ðâs næglas hât
þâm æðelestan corðeyninga
1175   burgâgendra on his brîdels dôn
meare tô mîdlum. Þæt manigum sceall
geond middangeard mære weorðan,
þonne æt sæcce mid þŷ oferswîðan mæge
fêonda gehwylene, þonne fyrdhwate
1180   on twâ healfe tohtan sêcaþ
sweordgenîðlan, þær hîe ymb *sige* winnað,

---

facere, ad commemorationem generationum quae venturae erant, quod
Prophetae pronuntiaverunt ante multas generationes.   Convocans
autem virum fidelem et disciplinatum, cui testimonium perhibebant
multi, dixit ei: Regis mandata custodi et regale sacramentum exerce ;
accipe hos clavos, et fac eos salivares in fraeno equi, qui Regis erit;

wrâð wið wrâðum.   Hê âh æt wîgge spêd,
sigor æt sæcce ond sybbe gehwær,
æt gefeohte frið, sê ƿe foran lædeð
1185   brîdels on blancan, ƿonne beadurôfe
æt gârƿræce guman gecoste
berað bord ond ord.   Þis bið beorna gehwâm
wið æglæce unoferswîðed
wæpen æt wîgge.   Be ðâm se wîtga sang
1190   snottor searuƿancum.   Sefa dêop gewôd,
wîsdômes gewitt.   Hê ƿæt word gecwæð :
" cûƿ ƿæt gewyrðeð, ƿæt ƿæs cyninges sceal
mearh under môdegum mîdlum geweorðod,
brîdelshringum.   Bið ƿæt bêacen gode
1195   hâlig nemned ond sê hwætêadig,
wîgge weorðod, sê ƿæt wicg byrð."
Þâ ƿæt ôfstlîce eall gelæste
Elene for eorlum, æðelinges heht,
beorna bêaggifan, brîdels frætwan,
1200   hire selfre sunu sende tô lâce
ofer geofenes strêam gife unscynde.
Heht ƿâ tôsomne, ƿâ hêo sêleste
mid Iûdêum gumena wiste,
hæleða cynnes, tô ƿære hâlgan byrig,
1205   cuman in ƿâ ceastre.   Þâ sêo cwên ongan
læran lêofra hêap, ƿæt hîe lufan dryhtnes
ond sybbe swâ same sylfra betwêonum,
frêondræddenne, fæste gelæston

---

erunt autem arma inexpugnabilia contra omnes adversarios, victoria
vero erit Regis et pax belli, ut id quod dictum est per Prophetam
impleatur.   " Et erit in illo die quod est in fraeno equi sanctum Domini
vocabitur (Zac. 14, 20)."   Beata autem Helena, qui in Jesu Christo
fide sunt confirmans in Hierosolymis, et omnia perficiens, persecu-
tionem Judaeis immisit, quia increduli facti sunt, et minavit eos a
Judaea.   Tanta autem gratia secuta est Sanctum Cyriacum Episcopum, ut daemones per orationes ejus effugaret, et omnes hominum
sanaret infirmitates.   Beata autem Helena dona multa derelinquens

leahtorléase in hira lifes tîd
1210 ond þæs láttéowes lârum hŷrdon,
cristenum | éawum, | é him Cyriacus
bude bóea gléaw. Wæs se bissceophâd
fægere befæsted. Oft him feorran tô
laman, limséoce, lefe cwómon,
1215 healte, heorudréorige, hréofe ond blinde,
héane, hygegeómre, symle hælo þær
æt þâm bisceope, bóte, fundon
éce tô aldre. Þâ géu him Elene forgeaf
sineweorðunga, þâ hio wæs sîdes fûs
1220 eft tô éðle, ond þâ eallum bebéad
on þâm gumrîce god hergendum,
werum ond wîfum, þæt hie weorðeden
móde ond mægene þone mêran dæg,
heortan gehigdum, in ðâm sîo hâlige ród
1225 gemêted wæs, mærost béama,
þâra þe of eorðan ûp âwéoxe
geloden under léafum. Wæs þâ lencten âgân
bûtan .vi. nihtum ær sumeres cyme
on maias kalendas. Sîc þâra manna gehwâm
1230 behliden helle durn, heofones ontŷned,
éce geopenad engla rîce,
drêam unhwîlen, ond hira dæl scired
mid Mârian, þe on gemynd nime
þære déorestan dægweorðunga
1235 róde under roderum, þâ se rîcesða
calles oferwealdend earme bepeahte. — Finit.

---

sancto Episcopo Cyriaco ad ministerium pauperum, dormivit in pace, septimo decimo Kalendas Maji; demandans omnibus qui Christum diligunt, viris ac mulieribus, celebrare commemorationem diei, in qua inventa est sancta Crux quinto nonarum Majarum. Quicumque vero memoriam faciunt sanctae Crucis, accipiant partem cum Dei genitrice sancta Maria, et cum Domino nostro Jesu Christo, qui cum Patre et Spiritu sancto vivit et regnat, per infinita saecula seculorum.

XV.

Þvs ic frôd ond fûs þurh þæt fæcne hûs
worderæftum wæf ond wundrum læs,
þrágum þreodude ond geþanc reodode
1240   nihtes nearwe. Nysse ic gearwe
be ðære rôde riht, ær mê rûmran geþeaht
þurh ðá mæran miht on môdes þeaht,
wîsdôm, onwráh. Ic wæs weorcum fáh,
synnum ásæled, sorgum gewæled,
1245   bitrum gebunden, bisgum beþrungen,
ær mê láre onlág þurh lêohtne hád
gamelum tô gêoce, gife unscynde
mægencyning ámæt ond on gemynd begêat,
torht ontŷnde, tîdum gerŷmde,
1250   báncofan onband, brêostlocan onwand,
lêoðucræft onlêac, þæs ic lustum brêac,
willum, in worlde. Ic þæs wuldres trêowes
oft, nales æne, hæfde ingemynd,
ær ic þæt wundor onwrigen hæfde
1255   ymb þone beorhtan bêam, swá ic on bôcum fand
wyrda gangum, on gewritum, cŷðan
be ðám sigebêacne. Â wæs secg ôð ðæt
cnyssed cearwelmum, Cên drûseude,
þêah hê in medohealle máðmas þêge,
1260   æplede gold. Ŷr gnornode
Nŷdgefêra, nearusorge drêah,
enge rûne, þær him Eh fore
mîlpaðas mæt, môdig þrægde
wîrum gewlenced. Wên is geswiðrad,
1265   gomen, æfter geárum, geogoð is gecyrred,
ald onmêdla. Ûr wæs geára
geogoðhádes glæm. Nû synt geárdagas
æfter fyrstmearce forð gewitene,

lîfwynne geliden, swâ *Lago* tôglîdeð,

1270　flôdas gefŷsde.　*Feoh* ǽghwâm bið

léne under lyfte, landes frǽtwe

‚gewîtaþ under wolcnum winde geliccost,

þonne hé for hæleðum blûd ástîgeð,

wǽðeð be wolcnum, wédende fereð

1275　ond eft semninga swîge gewyrðeð

in nêdcleofan nearwe geheaðrod,

þréam forþrycced.　Swâ þéos world call gewîteð,

ond ðac swâ some, þê hire on wurdon

âtŷdrede, tîonlêg nimeð,

1280　ðonne dryhten sylf dôm geséceð

engla weorude.　Sceall ǽghwylc ðǽr

reordberendra riht gehŷran

dǽda gehwylcra þurh þæs déman mûð

ond worda swâ same wed gesyllan

1285　eallra unsnyttro ǽr gespreceura,

þristra geþonca.　Þonne on þréo dǽleð

in fŷres feng folc âura gehwylc,

þâra þe gewurdon on widan feore

ofer sîdne grund.　Sôðfæste bîoð

1290　yfemest in þâm âde, êadigra gedryht,

duguð dômgeorne, swâ hie âdréogan magon

ond bûtan carfeðum êaðe geþolian,

môdigra mægen.　Him gemetgaþ eall

eldes lêoma, swâ him éðost bið,

1295　sylfum geséftost.　Synfulle béoð,

mâne gemengde, in ðâm midle þréad,

hæleð higegeômre, in hâtne wylm

þrosme beþehte.　Bið se þridda dǽl,

âwyrgede womsceaðan, in þæs wylmes grund,

1300　léase léodhatan, lîge befæsted

þurh ǽrgewyrht, ârléasra sceolu,

in glêda gripe.　Gode nô syððan

of ðâm morðorhofe in gemynd cumað,

wuldorcyninge, ac hîe worpene bêoð
1305 of ðâm headuwylme in hellegrund,
torngeniðlan. Bið þâm twâm dælum
ungelîce. Môton engla frêan
gesêon, sigora god. Hîe âsodene bêoð,
âsundrod fram synnum, swâ smæte gold,
1310 þæt in wylme bið womma gehwylces
þurh ofnes fŷr eall geclænsod,
âmered ond gemylted. Swâ bið þâra manna æ̂lc
âscyred ond âsceâden scylda gehwylere,
dêopra firena, þurh þæs dômes fŷr.
1315 Môton þonne siðþan sybbe brûcan,
êces êadwelan. Him bið engla weard
milde ond blîðe þæs ðe hîe mâna gehwyle
forsâwon, synna weorc, ond tô suna metudes
wordum cleopodon. Forðan hîe nû on wlite scînaþ
1320 englum gelîce, yrfes brûcaþ
wuldorcyninges tô wîdan feore. Amen.

NOTES.[1]

1. **wæs**, 3d p. s. pret. from **wesan**. Singular, notwithstanding plural subject. Cf. N.E.

geâra, gen. pl., dependent upon **hwyrftum**. The form is also used adverbially (= N.E. *yore*).

2. **geteled rîmes** = *the number told*. Cf. Dickens, "He overmatched me five hundred times told." **geteled** is p.p. from **tellan** (= *to count*), and **rîmes** is gen. sing. (cf. B. 2729). The whole is an adverbial phrase, in which the instrumental is sometimes used instead of the genitive.

3. **þinggemearces**, gen. sg., used adverbially, *according to time*, — as one counts time.

4. **wîntra**. Winter, as a measure of time for year, was frequent in O.E. Cf., also, usage of *winter* and *summer* in N.E.

6. **heo**, *form, shape, hue.* Cf. *hue* in Shakespeare's "Sonnets" (22).

middangeard = the midearth lying between heaven and hell. This word had this signification, no doubt, even before the introduction of Christianity; for the pagans placed their fiends and monsters under the ground, — whether at the bottom of lakes, as Grendel, or under the world, as Loki, — and Wælheal was above the earth, and between them lay the plain upon which mortal man moved. Cf. Grimm's "Mythologie," 754; "Antiq. in A. & E.," 25.

9. **Rômwara.** Cf. **Rômwarena**, 982.

10. **âhæfen**, p.p. from **ahebban.** The word used in reference to the custom of raising a newly elected king upon a shield, in order to exhibit him to the people. Cf. Grimm, "Rechtsalterthümer," 234. Kemble ("Saxons in England," 154, foot-note) remarks that "levatus in regem = **tô cyninge âhafen** continued to be the words in use long after the custom of really chairing the king had, in all probability, ceased to be observed."

---

[1] A number of these notes are transcriptions from the author's "Teutonic Antiquities in Andreas and Eleue" (abbreviated "Antiq. in A. & E.").

68

NOTES.

14. **gumena**, gen. pl. from **guma** (Lat. *homo*, N.H.G. bräutigam, N.E. bridegroom. The N.E. *groom*, save in this compound, has another etymon).

19. **wîges wôma**, *noise of war.* **wîg** is a designation of a heathen god (cf. Grimm's "Andreas und Elene," Preface). The god Tiw seems to have been the god of war, and identical with Mars of classical mythology, which is used in the Epinal Glosses as the rendering of Tiw (cf. Tuesday and Mardi); now **wîg** is rendered in the same glosses by Mars which seems to identify Tiw and Wig (cf. "Antiq. in A. & E.," p. 5; Kemble, in "S. in E.," I. 351). **wôma**, according to Grimm ("A. u. E.") corresponds to *ómi* in Old Norse, which is a name of Oðin, and means *the noise-producing god*; hence **wôma** is in all probability a name of Woden (Oðin), which has lost all of its power except the quality of noise it then attributed. Cf. "Antiq. in A. & E.," pp. 5 ff.

20. **Hreðgotan** = *the renowned Goths* (Zupitza). Cf. Müllenhoff, Haupt's *Zeitschrift*, xii. This union of the Huns and Goths could not have occurred at this time; for the Huns did not appear until A.D. 375. See "Traveller's Song" for another allusion to this union.

21. **Francan.** Some aversion of the author to this people probably gave rise to the addition of their name.

Hugas (?). Grimm reads **Hunas**; Grein translates *Hunen.*

24. **wælhlencan**, pl. of **wælhlenc** (f.) = *coat-of-mail.* **wæl** is found in *Walkyr;* **hlenc** is M.E. *lenke*, N.E. *link.*

wordum ond bordum is a frequently recurring formula, signifying here the noise attending the raising of the battle standard. Cf. Tac., "Hist.," v. 17; "Germ.," XI.

26. **sweotole**, adv., *visibly, clearly,* etc. There exists, however, a substantive, **sweot** (= *crowd*), and this adverb may refer to that substantive. The heroes were assembled there in crowds (*schaarenweise*), and all together.

eal, strongly inflected adj., with loss of *l* in word-end. Cf. Sievers (Cook's edition), § 295, 2.

28. **wulf, earn** 29, and **hrefen** 52. The wolf, eagle, and raven were sacred to the highest god, Wodan, and the attendants of war over which he presided. Cf. Grimm, "A. u. E.," xxvi. f.; Kemble, "S. in E.," i. 343, note; "Antiq. in A. & E.," 7.

29. **ûrigfeðera** (cf. 111), *with moist feathers,* is a not uncommon predicate of the eagle. S., "Judith," 210.

31. **burgenta**, *burg, stadt* (??) (Zupitza). Grimm translates it *Riesenburg,* and makes it refer to some definite locality, but mentions that it may refer to some castle-crowned rock. Grein makes it the land of

the Burgundians. It seems to me to refer to some old castle-crowned rock, some giant's wall; and this view seems supported by analogy in such expressions as enta ærgeweorc (A. 1237), eald enta geweorc (A. 1497, Ruin 2), fyrngeweorc (A. 738). I take it that we have to do with two words here, — burg, the acc. dependent upon ofer, and enta, the gen. pl. of possession. Cf. "Antiq. in A. & E.," 9.

35. fēðan trymedon coredcestum. This is a dark passage. Cf. Zupitza, "Anz: deut. Alt.," v. 43 ff.; "Recension zu Zupitza's erster Ausgabe," in Haupt's *Zeitschrift*. Grimm translates eoredcestum by *electa legio*; Grein, by *turma, legio*; Körner, by *ausgewählte reiterschar*. According to Ten Brink it has the significance of *division, regiment (marschkolonne)* (cf. "Phœnix," 325; "Panther," 52; "Aeðelstan," 24). Wülker translates it by *schaar*. The infantry was strengthened by crowds.

42. cuð, *known*. Cf. uncouth. "Bound on a voyage uncouth." — *Milton*.

ceasterwarum. ceastre from *castra*, the Roman camps, then cities founded on their sites; and later, cities generally.

44. under earhfære, *by means of the circuit of the arrow*. An allusion to the custom, prevalent among Teutonic nations, of sending an arrow around, in any time of danger or sudden attack, to summon the people with despatch (Grimm, "Rechtsalthümer," 162). The word occurs twice in the "Codex Exonicus," and once later. Dietrich translates it *impetus saggitarum*.

49. hilde. *Hild*, goddess of war; = *Bellona*.

52. hrefen. S. 28, 29.

gōl, from galan, *to sing*, with which compare the M.E. *gale*. "In Chaucer's 'Court of Love' the Nightingale is said to cry and *gale*; hence its name nightegale or nightengale." — *Tyrwhitt*. In N.E., *gale* (*to sing*) is obsolete or rare.

54. Napier's collation, used in Zupitza's third edition, shows hlêopon.

56. câfe, as punctuated, an adj. Why not an adv.?

58. sceawedon, 3d p. pl. A change from the expected subject, *he* (the king), to *they* (the army, including the king).

59. þæt þe, which refers to army; he, hie (Ten Brink) would be a more intelligible construction.

64. eaxlgestealna, *shoulder-companions, trusted companions*. The word indicates the serried files of an army, and evidences the comradeship based upon a partnership in dangers and duties. B. 359, 2853.

68. gefær. "Phœnix," 426.

71. swefnes wôma, *vision*, lit. *the noise of a dream*. Cf. 19.

73. hwit. N.E. *white*, by metathesis.

73. nathwyle, *nescio quis*.

74. þonne. Before this word we expect a comparative, which for the translation must be supplied; but we find only a positive form here. Cf. B. 69; Orosius, 2d book, at the end, etc.

76. cofurcumbol means *the sign of the boar*. It has reference to the sign on the helmet, and is used, by synecdoche, for the helmet itself. Grimm ("A. u. E.," xxviii. f.) and Kemble ("S. in E.," i. 357) both connect this with the cult of Freyr, to whom this beast was sacred. It had probably lost its heathen significance.

78. nihthelm tôglâd, *the helmet of night fell apart*, *i.e.* darkness vanished. When night fell, earth was said to have put on her helmet of darkness (cf. A. 1307 ff.). tôglâd expresses, with particular happiness, the breaking or splitting of this helmet (cf. B. 2488). Here the celestial brilliancy of the angel caused the helmet to split (cf. A. 126) and light to prevail.

80. Cf. 1047.

81. þe, ethical dative.

84. findest, with future significance.

90. gimmas. N.E. *gem* comes from Latin *gemma*, through French *gemme*.

91. bôcstafum awrîten. bôcstæf (N.II.G.) *beech stave, beech staff*, *i.e.* little pieces of beech, upon the ends of which characters were cut, hence a name for the characters themselves. awrîtan means *einritzen*, *eingraben*, *i.e.* *cut in*, and refers to the primitive mode of writing; for our word comes from the O.N. *writa*, through this word. Lat. *scribere*, N.H.G. *schreiben*, lives in N.E. *shrive*.

92. mid þys bêacne ðû ... oferswiðesð, *in hoc signo vinces*.

96. þŷ ... þê. Instrumental, and the explanation of N.E. *the, the* before comparatives; as, "the sooner, the better."

II.

97. onlîce, adv., with dat. regimen, rôde.

100. beaggifa, *ring-giver*. Alluding to the custom of the king to distribute rings of gold in the mead halls; hence, a name for a king.

114 ff. This is evidently a kind of formula describing the opening of battle. Note, for instance, the rhyme. It can hardly refer to a hand-to-hand combat, in which the hostile shields clash against each other; for the hurling of spears, in the next line, would have been futile, if not impossible, at such close quarters. Cf. "Antiq. in A. & E.," p. 47.

116. **earhfære**, *Anprall der Geschosse* (Grein), or *Kampf* (Zupitza). Cf., however, 44, and note the aptness of this explanation for this passage.

118. **geolorand** (cf. 50), *yellow border.* The border of the shield served, as we know from the Gnomic verses (" Menology," Grein, " Bibliothek der Agls. Poesie," ii. 346), as a protection or guard for the fingers. It is here used for the shield. Tac. "Germ.," vi.; "Ann.," ii. 14.

131. **sume wîg fornam**, a formula recalling **wyrd**. Cf. **sume drenc fornam** (136), **hine Wyrd fornam** (B. 1206) (" Antiq. in A. & E.," pp. 4 ff.).

141. **gescyrded**, p.p. from **gescyrdan**, *to destroy.* Cf. Sievers, *Anglia*, i. 578; " Wulfstan," 68. ii.; "Andreas," 1315. Grimm has **gescryded** by metathesis.

142. **lŷthwôn**. Cf. Murray, " Dialects of the Several Counties of Scotland."

143. **þanon, þannonne**. M.E. *þanne, þonne, þonnes, þennes;* N.E. *thence.*

151. **prŷðbord** stênan, *bejewel the shield.* Was this a custom after the happy issue of battle? Cf. Grimm, " A. u. E.," 131. **scênan**, *to make shine.*

162 ff. Constantine had just won a most complete victory by virtue of the cross; and now he calls an assembly, to inquire about the unknown God, and asks, —

" þe þis his bêacen wæs
þe mê swâ lêoht ôðŷwde ond mîne lêode generede
tâcna torhtost, ond mê tîr forgeaf
wîgspêd wið wrâðum, þurh þæt wlitige trêo.

There can be no doubt that **tîr, gloria** is closely connected etymologically with Tiw (O.N. *Tyr*), and it was most probably at first another name for the same god. The rune for *t* (*↑*), which means Tir, recalls *♂*, the sign of Mars, with whom Tiw was unmistakably connected. This sign of Mars is of great antiquity (cf. Grimm, " A. u. E.," 156).

It is striking, too, as Grimm further notices, that **tîr** so often occurs with **tacen**, or words from the same root. Thus here, and in E. 754 (**tîre getâcnod, decore insignitum**), B. 1654, and several times in " Juliana." The connection with **torht** is scarcely less noticeable (cf. " Judith," 93, 157). In a word, the Teutonic mind attached great importance to the signs and symbols of the gods; and that of this Tir must have been bright, for that idea seems inseparably connected with this symbol mentioned with Tir.

Now **wîgspêd**, in the next line, is formed of **wîg**, which has been seen to be a name of Mars, and equivalent to Tiw, with which Tir is closely related; and **spêd** is *success;* that is, the word means *the success which Mars grants*, hence success in war. Now this passage denotes the desire of a *heathen* king to find out who an unknown God is, — a God unknown because his sign or emblem (a cross) was unknown; but, as if this showed a lack of confidence in the god of war, upon whom he was in the habit of relying, the heathen king ascribes his success to the heathen God (**wîgspêd**). Indeed, though I am not bold enough to propose a change in the usual rendering of this passage, I mention that a capital *T* and Grein's punctuation — namely, the omission of the 'comma after **forgeaf** — would give us a sentence entirely heathen, — " And Tiw (Mars) granted me Wigspeed (cf. *Godspeed*) against the inimical, through this shining tree "; thus uniting this brightest of signs with the signs of Tiw, in whose martial character this new, unknown God had revealed himself.

179. **on galgan**. Crucifixion was a form of punishment unknown to the Anglo-Saxons; and hence they most frequently described it in the vocabulary of hanging ("Antiq. in A. & E.," 42).

183. **ilcan**, Scotch *Ilk* (Murray, "Dialects," etc.). Not to be confounded with *ilk* (= *each, every*).

190. **fram**, agent. M.E. *of;* N.E. *by*.

191. **æt þâm**, *from this one*. Cf. B. 621, 2229.

192. **þæt** refers to Christianity.

193. **tîd**, *tide;* in Whitsuntide, Shrovetide, "time and tide wait for no man," etc.

III.

194. **sælum**, cf. adj. **gesællig**. M.E. *seliga;* N.E. *silly* (not with its present significance, but equivalent to *happy*).

197. **byhtn**. S. "Guthlac," 116.

198. **ongan** ... **eŷðan = eŷðede**.

dæges ond nihtes, adv., *day and night*. nihtes is adv. gen., from a feminine substantive.

203. **lâr (læran) + smiðas** (N.E. *smith*), *teaching-smiths, i.e.* teachers.

213. **gemyndig**, generally with gen. Cf. 1064; " Harrowing of Hell," 29.

219. **Elene**, *Helena*, hence name of poem. This poem makes no allusion to her English origin.

225. From this point to 272 is independent of original.

226. flote (M.E. *flote*; N.E. *flote*, *float*) = *wave* (Shaks. " Tempest," i. 2).

227. Geofon, which Müller (Haupt's *Zeitschrift*, i. 95) considers as connected with the sea-goddess Gefjon, occurs again, 1201. Merbach ("Das Meer in der Dichtung der Angelsachsen") sees, in the fact that this word occurs only twice in composition, — geofonhus, "Gen." 1321; geofonflod, "Azar." 125, — further proof of the mythological origin of the word.

231. æt wendelsæ seems capable of a twofold interpretation. Either the sea lying between Helen and the cross, *i.e.* separating two lands; or wendel may easily refer, and particularly in connection with on stæðe, to the varying line dividing land and water, *i.e.* the border of the sea; hence, *at shore, near the coast.*

233. ofer mearepaðu. The divisions of land held in common by a tribe or band, or under the control of a lord or king, were called *Marks* (cf. "God save the mark!"). mearepaðu refers to the roads running through these divisions.

235. bordum ond ordum : formula. Cf. wordum ond bordum (24).

236. werum ond wifum : formula.

237. scriðan suggests equine motion. Cf. 238.

238. brimþisan, *rusher over the sea.* Perhaps recalling the horse.

bord, spoken of as receiving the blows of the waves (ýða swengas), is a figurative epithet drawn from the shield in battle, rather than simply the hull of a ship.

239. earhgeblond betrays as much familiarity with the battle as the sea.

241. idese lædan, acc. and inf., objective complement of hýrde.

242. merestræte [from mere, *sea* (cf. N.E. *mermaid*), + stræt (N.E. *street*), *path*], *in the sea-path.*

244. snyrgan under swellingum, *glides along under swelling sails,* —like some bird, perchance a swan. Cf. fugole gelicost glideð on geofone (A. 497).

245. sæmearh plegean recalls the prancing steed.

246. wadan wægflotan suggests the swimmer.

247. cwên, *woman,* — *the* woman, queen. Cf. N E. *quean, queen.*

251. Ms. has saude bewreccene (*sand-whipped*), which is more poetical, and fully as intelligible, as sunde bewreccene.

254. heo refers to ýðhofu.

256. To whom does on corle refer, — Helen ? or is it collective and generic ?

259. **cofurcumbul.** S. 76.

264. I take **sinegim** to be specific, and to refer to the cross which Constantine had had made.

269. **herefeld.** A warrior's conception of fields in general.

273. **Hierusalem.** Cf. **Jerusalem** (1056). The first is the usual form; the second gives the pronunciation, for the word alliterates with *g* and *j*.

IV.

279. **gêmot** recalls the **witena gemot**, or *assembly of counsellors*, whom the king probably appointed, and over whom he presided (Tac. "Germ.," xi.).

291. **wiðwurpon**, regular form; Ms. has **wiðweorpan**.

297. **horn.** According to Sievers (§ 242. 4), instrumental, from **horh**.

300. **spâld.** Cf. **spadl, spatl,** N.E. *spittle*. **Spâld** comes through Northumbrian *spaðl, spalð, spald*.

corðre, from Lat. *cohors*.

309. **webbedan**; for **webbedon** is Mercian or Northumbrian.

320. **eodan**, pret. to **gan** (S. § 430).

330. **cynestôle**, from **cyne [cyning** or **cyn(?)]** + **stol**, which occurs in "Elene" only in composition.

332. **maðelode**, *spoke, made a speech.* There is something formal in this word.

339. Where did Moses prophecy in these words? Cf. Isaiah ix. 6; Joshua v. 14.

345. Psalms xv. 8.

348. **Ic ne wende æfre tô aldre onsion mîne,** *I never turned my face to life,* i.e. to the things of this life.

353. Where does Essaias make this prophecy?

355. Ms. has **þe** instead of **me.**

356. **nâhton = ne âhton.** From **agan** (S. § 420. 2).

358. **man**, indef. pron. Fr. *on*; N.H.G. *man;* N.E. *one.*

þirsceð, from **þirscan**, with metathesis **þrescan.** N.E. *thresh.*

359. **nales = ne + calles, nealles, nales.** Cf. **nalas, nalæs.**

V.

366. **meotod.** This word, which Vilmar ("Alterthümer in Heliand") conceives as *measurer* (cf. Grein, "Sprachschatz," 2. 240), refers, according to him, in the first instance to the measuring god or god who sets boundaries, — i.e. perhaps Thunar, who measured with the hammer, from which were derived those peculiar and prevalent

measures by means of a throw (Grimm, "Deutsche Rechtsalthümer, 54 ff.). The indications are, however, that the god of land-measures, of boundaries, etc., among the Saxons, was Woden. Wanborough (formerly Wodensburh), Wonston (formerly Wodenstan), and numerous others (see Kemble, "S. in E.," i. 344), show his connection with land, while, according to the same author, there are numerous instances in charters of the use of Woden's name in connection with boundary trees, stones, or posts. Hence this mcotod, which had, no doubt, lost -all of its heathen significance, probably referred originally to Woden, as the god of boundaries.

373. gên. Cf. *again*.

414. Indirect question is usually expressed by optative.

439. þe hit siðð̄an cyð̄de sylfa his eaferan, *which he himself afterwards told his descendant.*

447. mîn swæs sunu. Usual form, mîn sunu se swæs.

452. in woruld weorulda, *in seculum seculi* (Lat. orig.). Cf. *in secula seculorum.*

VI.

461. nergend, from nerian (B. 573). Goth. *nasjan* (cf. *nasjands*).

466. unaseegendlic, *inenarrabile.*

479. sume hwile, temp. acc., *somewhile.*

483. þrêo niht, pl. fem. with omission of final *e*, or perhaps to be explained as neut. pl.

487. hine is supplied on account of verse.

489. The tangle by which Judas is made the brother of the first martyr, Stephen, the son of Simon and grandson of Sachias, is unintelligible; but the confusion did not originate with Cynewulf. Cf., for instance, "Die Kreuzeslegenden in Leabhar Breac."; Gustav Schirmer, "St. Gallen" (86) (" Leipziger Dissertation," pp. 12–13, 35–36).

501. miltse. Cf. milde (*d* before *s* became *t*).

522. lêoð̄rûne, *secret song, secret instruction, admonitio per carmen.*

533. tô gecyð̄anne, inflected infinitive. S. § 363. 1.

539. nûð̄â, emphatic form of nû.

540. þyslîc (from þýs), instrumental of sê + lîc (*thusly*), *thus.*

VII.

547. In the Ms. stands weoxon word ewidum (where word must be construed as plural), *the words increased in* (much) *speaking.* This is intelligible; and hence the change to wrixledan is to be rejected.

548. on healfa gehwǽne (gehwǽne, for gehwone, *each*), acc. sg. masc. Cf. S. § 347.

583. under womma scéatum (séeat, according to Grein, *latebra*, *latibulum*), *in the womb of sins*.

585. betǽhton, from betǽcan. takan means both *give* and *take*.

600. tô gîsle, *zum Geisel* (that is, for torture, in order to evoke from him the desired information).

610. rex (Lat.) = *king*, but here equal to *queen*.

618. beneah, s. S. 424. 11.

VIII.

622. eard has nothing to do with eorðe.

629. *Whether he renounced the hope of heaven, as was in his mind, and this kingdom under the heavens, for the present, or revealed the cross.* The two members of this disjunctive sentence are not complete, nor clear, unless we can interpret rîce under roderum as parallel with heofonrîces, whereas it seems to be in antithesis. It would then mean *whether he should refuse to reveal the cross, and hence renounce heaven, or reveal it and in consequence claim heaven.*

633. Cf. 304.

635. *I cannot report* (supply *more exactly*).

636. forðgewitenra, part. from forðgewitan, and best translated by relative clause.

640. cnihtgeong hæleð, *a young man* (still) *in the period of youth.*

645 ff. See original. This allusion to the Trojan War would hardly have been retained had it not been well known to the poet's public.

647. þonne. After an implied comparison. open ealdgewin þonne, *a known battle in olden times* (more remote) *than*, etc.

649. hwæt = *how many.*

661. Helen seems to have had the power of divination; else how did she know what Judas had told his companions?

668. wénde him trâge hnâgre, *he feared the deplorable evil.* him is reflexive pronoun.

685. þurh corne hyge, *in her angry soul* (*i.e.* not aloud).

691. See original.

IX.

709. Ten Brink proposes seráf (from serîfan); but this is used only of God. See Lat. original.

720. Here begins the prayer. Compare such occurrences in "Crist" and "Juliana."

749. wlitegaste. *a*, as connecting vowel, is frequent in Kentish in superlative. wlitegaste refers to wôða.

750. The hierarchies of angels are several times mentioned in O.E. First are mentioned six angels with six wings each, of whom four are continually doing service before the eternal Judge. These seem to correspond to the four beasts (Rev. iv. 7); they form a heavenly chorus, and are called "cherubim." The other two are "seraphim"; and their duty is to guard paradise, and the tree of life, with fiery swords. The fall of the evil angel and his cohorts is mentioned in the same prayer. The archangels (hêahengla, 751) may or may not have represented another class. The passage concerning the seraphim, who guarded the garden of Eden (756), is taken from Gen. iii. 24, where, however, these guardians are called "cherubim." Should the order in which they are named here (and in "Andreas," 719) be intended to indicate relative rank, then it is singular that this order should be just the reverse of that usually assigned them. Cf. Skeat, "Piers the Plowman," p. 109; "Antiq. in A. & E.," 19, 20.

756. neorxnawang, *paradise*. The first part of this word is dark; but the constituent wang recalls the "fields of the blessed," etc.

766. in dracan fæðme, *in the embrace of the dragon*. A part of the Saxon conception of hell was that it was a huge monster, whose mouth was the entrance. Cf. Grein ("Dichtungen der Angelsachsen"), "Die Hölle selbst ward als Drache gedacht"; Plates IV. and XI. of the Cædmon Ms., Ellis's "Archælogia," vol. xxiv.

773. Notice Lat. original.

783. Notice unusual position of þurh ðâ.

788. *Bones of Joseph* — where?

790. þurg þæt beorhte gesceap, of the image of the cross.

791. goldhord. Reference, probably, to cross, without any figurative meaning.

802. *in secula seculorum* = â bûtan ende.

X.

818. fêam [feawum, feaum, fêam]. Cf. A. 615.

825. wigges lêan, *reward of the warrior*. Reference to the reward of Walhalla (S. "Antiq. in A. & E.," 17 f.).

831. feor seems to signify *deep*.

832. niðer, adv., qualifying nêolum.

835. begraucne. *u* is an unusual form for O.E.

872. gefærenne man, *departed man*. Death, as an entrance upon a

journey, partakes at the same time of Christianity and heathenism: for the former uses such language; the latter held such a doctrine in various forms.

XI.

900. **fcond.** The devil — not his son (cf. "Andreas," "Juliana," etc.) — is represented as endowed with the power to fly, and as visiting the earth.

909. Allusion to Christ's death as a malefactor, and his burial.

922. Judas Iscariot.

924. Judas, later Cyriacus the bishop.

928. Julian the Apostate.

XII.

983. **holm.** Grein compares this word denoting the appearance of the sea as rising, and not as a flat surface, with Russian *cholm* and Lat. *culmen*, both denoting elevation. Cf. **ofer hêanne holm**, *over the high sea.*

1001. **Is sylfe** used reflexively?

XIII.

1047. **wyrd.** Among the appellations of the Deity occurs **wyrda wealdend.** It is easy to translate this *Controller of Events*, and to contend, as Köhler ("Germanische Alterthümer in Beowulf," S. 5) does, that the word had lost all its associations with the Norse *Wyrd* or, as the name is in N.E., *Weird.* In this place, **wyrd** is personified. Cynewulf, recalling the checkered and singular career of Judas, — who, from the most ardent of all opponents to surrender to Helen, becomes a most faithful and steadfast defender of Christianity, — exclaims. "Verily, Weird decreed that he should become so faithful," etc.; recording, thus, his belief in fatalism, and attributing this to one of the sisters who presided over the destinies of men. If we recall, now, the expression in 80, it may be added, that, had the poet used this expression deliberately and in its full sense, he would not have been heathenizing God, but rather elevating him above the highest powers of heathen belief, — for even the gods were controlled by the decrees of the Norns, — and giving him a controlling power over the controlling powers of heathen belief.

1059. **Cyriacus** is henceforth the name of *Judas.*

1078. **mec** is old form; in younger poetry, **me** is frequent.

1114. **grunde geteuge,** *near the surface, on the ground* (Zupitza).

XIV.

1156. ðinga gehwylees. genitive with gelimpau. Cf. "Dan." 114. Generally with dative.

1158. hwan is instrumental case. Cf. "Sat." 527 ; "Crist," 32 ; "Guðlac," 521.

1185. on blancan. Cf. Riddle, 23. 18.

1196. byreð, for biereð.

1227. leneten. The year was divided into seasons, — *spring* (leneten), *summer* (1228), *fall* is not mentioned, and *winter* (4). Summer began on the 7th of May ; making the seasons, granting their equal duration of three months each, begin on the 7th of May, 7th of August, 7th of November, and 7th of February : which would make midsummer fall about the 21st of June, the time of the summer solstice : midwinter, about the time of the winter solstice, December 21st ; while the middle of fall and of spring coincide very nearly with the autumnal and vernal equinoxes (Grein, "A. u. E.," xxiv., and "Nachträge," 171).

1232. dröam has the primary meaning of *noisy joriality;* and the derived meaning of *blessedness* is removed by several links in the chain that unites them.

XV.

1237. frôd, *prudent, wise, the age of wisdom; i.e. old.* Grimm translates frôd ond fûs, *prudens ac promptus.* fûs means *ready,* — then *ready* for something, which the context seems to indicate to be death.

hûs, *house, habitation.* Refers, in my opinion, to the body; others think, to the world.

1238. wæf, his own work ; læs, his compilation from other sources.

1239. reodode is not found elsewhere.

1240. nihtes nearwe (*oppression of night*) seems to suggest sleeplessness, caused by engrossing interest in his work.

1240 ff. That is, that the extended knowledge derived from his reading and aided by his reflection, had given him a clearer insight into the real significance of the cross.

1245. Is biter (= *bitter necessity*) neuter or feminine ?

1246. þurh lëohtne hâd, *in a remarkable manner.* Formerly thought to be indicative of clerical station.

1249. torht. Cf. "Gen." 2890 ; B. 313.

tîdum gerŷmde, *prolonged my days.* Why dative ?

1257. Instead of seeg, read sæc (*strife*).

1258. cên (ħ), rune for *c*.

1260. æplede. Cf. "Phœnix," 500; "Juliana," 688; Haupt's *Zeit-schrift*, xi. 420.

yr (ᛣ) rune for *y*, *bow*. Cf. Wülker's "Grundriss," 158–165.

1261. nyd (ᚾ), rune for *n*, *need*.

1262. eh (ᛖ), rune for *e*, *horse*.

1264. wên (ᚹ) rune for *w*, *hope*.

1266. ur (ᚢ) rune for *u*, *aurochs*.

1269. lago (ᛚ) rune for *l*, *sea*, *lake*.

1270. feoh (ᚠ), rune for *f*, *cattle*.

The runes, taken together, give ᚻᛣᚾᚹᚢᛚᚠ (*Cynewulf*). This was discovered by Kemble. Cf. "Grundriss," p. 148.

1276. *Cave of the winds.*

1277. þrêam. Cf. "Daniel," 294; "Creation," 41. Here begins a description of purgatory.

1294. eldes. Cf. "Crist," 1060; B. 3125.

GLOSSARY.

â, always, aye, 744, 802, 804, 896, 1029, 1082, 1257.

æ, f., law. dryhtnes æ, 198, 971; þurh rihte æ, 281; Moyses æ, 283. ćowre æ æðelum + cræftige, = versed in the origin of our law, 315; scriptures (written law), revelation, 393, 397; faith, religion, gospel (unrihte æ = false religion), 1042. æ hælendes, 1063.

âbannan, red. vb., to proclaim, to order, 84.

âbêodan, sv. II., to bid, 1004; pret. âbead; swa him se âr âbead, as the messenger commanded him, 87.

âbrêotan, sv. II., to break to pieces, to destroy, to kill, 510.

æbylgð, n., offence, sin, transgression, 401, 513.

ac, but, (however) 355, (on the contrary) 222, 450, 469, 493, 569, 863(?), 1304.

âcennan, wv. I., to bring forth, bear (child); p.p. âcenned, 5, 178, 330, 639, 776, 816.

âcîgan, wv. I., to call, summon (pret. âcîgde), 603.

æclæca (= ægl-) m., monster; eatol æclæca, dire monster (i.e. devil), 902.

æclêaw, s. æglêaw.

æcræft, knowledge of the law, religion; æcræft eorla (= Jews) 435.

âcweðan, sv. V., to utter, pronounce, express (pret. âcwæð), 1072.

âcyrran, wv. I., to turn away from, to avert, 1120.

âd, m., fire; âde onæled, burnt with fire, 951; funeral pile, 585; pyre, yfemest in þâm âde, uppermost on this pyre, 1290.

æðelcyning, m., noble king (of Christ), 219; æðelcyninges rôd.

æðele, noble, 275, 300, 476, 545, 591, 647, 662, 733, [1029], 1074, 1107, 1131, 1146, 1174; glorious, 787; costly, valuable, 1025.

æðeling, m., nobleman, prince, (of Constantine) 12, 66, 202, 1003, (of Constantine's followers) 99, (generically) 393, (of Helen's followers) 846, 1198, (of Christ) 886.

æðelu, n. pl., origin, source (dat., ćowre æ æðelum + crætige, 315, s. æ), race, sect. Israhéla æðelu = the race of the Israelites, 433, [properties, 1029].

âdrêogan, sv. II., endure, bear, suffer; inf., 705, 1291.

âfêdan, wv. I., bring up, rear; p.p. âféded, 914.

æfen, n., evening, 139.

[æflian, 'comparare,' Gm. 1260.]

æfre, ever, (rendered with nega-

82 GLOSSARY.

tive, hence = never) 349, 361, 524, 572, (rendered without negative, = ever, at any time) 463, 448, 507, (without negative) 961 ; [always, 451].

æfst, n., hate ; æfstum, dat. sg., 207 ; æfst (acc. sg.) wið âre, hatred with favor, 308 ; for æfstum, = out of hatred, 496 ; æfst, acc. sg., 524.

æfter (with dat.), after (temporal or local), 233, 430, 490, 1034, 1155, 1265, 1268 ; about, 828 ; throughout, 972 ; during (æfter woruldstundum = during my sojourn in the world, 363); behind, upon, 135, 675.

âfyrhtan, wv. I., to make afraid, terrify ; p.p. âfyrhted, = frightened, 56.

âgalan, sv. VI., to sing, to strike up (a song, etc.); pret. âgól, fyrdlêoð âgól wulf, the wolf struck up his song of battle, 27 ; Dauid ... dryhtlêoð âgól, David sang a song for the people, 342.

âgan, p.p., to have, possess ; 2d p. sg. âhst, 726 ; 3d p. sg. âh, 1182 ; 3d p. sg. opt. âge, 1124. (S. § 420. 2.)

âgân, âgangan, red. vb., pass, go ; p.p. âgangen, 1 ; p.p. âgân, 1227.

âgen, own, 179, 422, 590, 1077.

æghwâ, prn., each one, every one ; dat. sg., æghwâm, 1270.

æghwylc, prn., each, 1281.

âgifan, sv. V., render, give ; andsware âgifan, 167, 545; 3d pret. sg. andsware âgeaf, 455, 462, 619, 662 ; pret. pl. (not w.s. form), âgêfon, delivered, surrendered, 587.

æglâec, n., terror, distress, oppression, 1188.

æglêaw, wise in the law, 806 ; æclêaw, 321.

âhangen, s. âhôn.

âhebban, sv. VI., raise, lift up, 10, 17, 29, 112, 724, 844, 862, 868, 879, 885, 976; ic ûp âhôf eaforan ginge, etc., I brought up (reared) a young heir, 353.

âhôn, red. vb., hang, crucify ; pret. pl. âhêngon, 210, 475 ; pp. âhangen, 180, 245, 445, 671, 718, 1076; acc. p.p. âhangnan, 453, 687, 798, 934.

æht, f., council, assembly, deliberation, 473.

æht, f., possession, property, 905, 916 ; power, 908.

âhýðan, wv. I., plunder, loot, 41.

al, s. eal.

ælârend, instructor in faith, expounder of law, 506.

æle, prn., every one, each, 1312.

ald, s. eald.

aldor, m., prince (of Constantine), 97, 157.

aldor, n., life, 132, 349, 571, 1218.

aldordôm, authority, dominion, 768.

âlesan, sv. V., select, choose ; p.p. âlesen, 286, 380.

ælfylce, n., strange land, foreign land, 36.

all, [1266,] = eall.

ælmihtig, almighty, (of God) 145, 866, 1084, 1091, 1152, (of Christ) 800, 1146.

âlŷsan, wv. I., loose, release (redeem, ransom) ; âlŷsde lêoda bearn of locan dêofla, released the children of men from the snares of the devil, 181.

âmerian, wv. I., free from dross, purify, refine, 1312.

âmetan, sv. V., measure out, (2d p. sg. pret. âmæte, thou measurest out, etc.), measure out to, allot, grant; 3d p. sg. pret. âmǽt, the mighty king granted, etc., 1248.

ân, one, 417; acc. sg. m. ǽnne, 585, 599; gen. pl. ânra, in the formula ânra gehwylc, every one, every, 1287.

anbîd, n., expectation; on anbide, in expectation, 885.

ânboren, only-begotten; cyning ânboren, the only-begotten king, 392.

[anbrôce, f., building material, wood? (Gm. 1029)], and

anda, m., vexation, cause of indignation, 970.

andsæc, n.(?), opposition, resistance; andsæc fremede, I offered opposition, resisted, 472.

andswaru, f., answer, 166, 318, 375, 455, 462, 567, 642, 662, 1002.

andswerian, wv. II., answer; 3d p. pret. pl. answeredon, 396.

andweard, present, 630.

andweardlîce, adv., at present, now, 1141.

andwlita, m., countenance, face, 298.

andwyrde, answer, 545, 619.

ǽne, once, a single time, 1253.

ânforlǽtan, red. vb., give up, surrender, desert; 3d p. sg. pret. opt. ânforlête, 630; 2d p. sing. pret. ind. ânforlête, = relinquishedst, 947.

ânhaga, m., solitary (man), recluse, 604.

ânhȳdig, of one mind, fixed in mind, determined, 848; elnes ânhȳdig, determined in zeal, zealous, 829.

ǽnig, prn., any: (1) subst. w. gen., 159; (2) adj., 166, 538, 567, 660, 916.

ǽnlic, unique, excellent, glorious, 74, 259.

ânmôd, unanimous, with one mind, 396, 1118.

æplede, apple-shaped, 1260.

âr, m., ambassador, messenger, (of the angel) 76, 87, 95, (of Helen's messengers) 981, 996, 1007; âr selesta, O best ambassador, — i.e. one who bears the message of one king to another, hence mediator, — (spoken of Cyriacus), 1088.

âr, f., honor, 714; favor, 308.

ǽr, adv., formerly, before, 74, 101, 240, 459, 478, 572, 602, 604, 707, 717, 882, 909, 922, 934, 975, 987, 1044, 1118, 1122, 1144, 1285.

ǽr, prep. with dat. before; ǽr sumeres cyme, before summer's advent, 1228.

ǽr, conj., before, with opt., 447, 676; with ind., before, until, 863, 1241, 1246, 1254; ǽrþan, 1084.

ârǽran, wv. I., raise, build, erect, 129, 887. ârǽred, elated, 804.

ǽrdæg, m., dawn, 105.

areccan, wv. I., expound, report, 635.

ǽrest, first, at first; cf. ǽr, ǽrra, ǽrost, 116.

ârfæst, gracious, merciful, 12, 512.

ǽrgewyrht, n., prior action, former deed, 1301.

ǽriht, n., faith (a system of doctrines), law of the covenant (Gn.), 375; code of law, faith, 590.

ârîsan, sv. I., arise, 803; rise (of resurrection); pret. sg. ârâs, 187, 486; pret. sg. ârâs, 885 (of the young man raised from the dead)

ârlêas, dishonored, wicked, godless, 836, 1301.

ǽrra, adj. comp., former, 305.

ârwyrðe, worthy of honor, venerable, 1129.

ǣrþan, s. ǣr.

âsǣlan, wv. I., to fasten with ropes, illaqueate, ensnare, fetter; synnum âsǣled, fettered by sins, 1241.

æse, m., ash, a lance made of ash, a lance. [140].

âsceâdan, red. vb., hold aloof; ic symle mec âsceâd þâra scylda, I held myself aloof from their guilt always, 470; separate, to separate from impurities, to purify, 1313.

æscrôf. renowned for skill with the spear, spear-strong, warlike, 202, 275.

æsewíga, m., lancer, 259.

âscyrian, wv. I., separate, free, 1313.

âsêcan, âsêcean, wv. I., to seek out, select; imperative pl. sundor âsêcaþ,407; inf. sundorâsêcean,1019.

âsêoðan, sv. II., free from dross, refine, purify, 1308.

âsettan. wv. I., place, lay, set, 847,863,877; perform, accomplish; sið . . . âseted hæfdon, = had made a voyage, etc., 998.

âspyrigean, wv. I., search out, spy, find out; discover, 407.

âstîgan, sv. I., ascend, 795; 3d p. sg. pret. âstâh, 188, 900; starts up (of the wind), 1273.

âsundrian, wv. II., separate, free, 1309.

æt, prep. w. dat., at, in : (1) locative, 137, 231, 251,390, 628, 1178, 1182, 1183, 1184, 1186, 1189; (2) specification (æt þâm dægweorce, = upon this day's work, 146; æt þære gesylhðe, = in regards to this view, etc.,965); (3) source(æt þâm,=from him, 191; æt þâm bisceope, 1217); (4) means (æt þâm willspelle, = through this good news, 904).

ætsomne, together, 834.

âtýdran, wv. I., beget, 1279.

ætŷwan, wv. I., show, reveal; p.p. ætŷwed, 69.

âþrêotan, sv. II., to be oppressive, burdensome; 3d p. sg. pret. âþrêat, 368.

âwa, always, everlasting, 951.

âweaxan, sv. VI., grow up; 3d p. sg. pret. opt. âwêoxe, 1226.

âwêcean, wv. I., awake, arouse (3d p. sg. pret. âwehte, 304, 946; âweahte, 782); incite (ic âwecce wið ðe ôðerne cyning, 927).

âwendan, wv. I., turn; þæt êow þæt lêas secal awended weorðan to woruldgedâle, that for you this falsehood should be turned to separation from the world (i.e. death), 581.

âweorpan. sv. III., throw, hurl, 763; scorn, reject, contradict, oppose, 771.

âwer = âhwǣr, somewhere, 33.

æwita, m., a man versed in the law, 455.

âwrîtan, sv. I., write upon, inscribe, 91.

âwyrged, accursed, despised; âwyrgede womsceaðan, the accursed sin-besmirched enemies, 1299.

B.

bæð, n., bath; fulwihtes bæð, 490, 1034.

bæðweg, m., bath-way, sea-way, sea, 244.

bǣl, n., fire, funeral pile, pyre, [578].

bǣlfŷr, funeral pile fire, [578].

bald, bold, 412, 593; boldly (adv.), 1073.

baldor, m., prince, (of David) wigona baldor, 344.

bân, n., bone; bân Josephes, 788.

bâncofa, m., bone-chamber, body, 1250.

bannan, red. vb., call, summon, bid, order, 45.

bǣr, f., bier, 873. [beran.]

be, prep. with dat., by, with [(specification) be naman, by name, 78, 505, 756]; by [(over, — nearness, motion alongside), be wolcnum, by the clouds, 1274]; about, concerning, in reference to (be þâm sigebéame (-beacne), 168, 420, 444, 665, 861, 1257; be þâm lifes (wuldres), tréo, 706, 867; be Nǣre róde, 601, 1241; be godes bearne, 562; be þâm (demonstrative), 337, 342, 1068, 1189; be cow (personal), 350).

bêacen, beacon, sign (of the cross), 92, 100, 109, 162, 842; gedó mi, fæder engla, forð bêacen þin, show forth now, father of angels, thy sign, 784; þæt bêacen (of the nails), 1194.

[bêacenige, m., sign, K. 842.]

[bêaceninga, ' wäre ominose, fausto omine, feliciter,' Gm. 842.]

beadu, f., battle, war, 34, 45.

beadurôf, renowned in war, distinguished in battle, 152, 1004, 1185.

beaduþrêat, m., battle-throng, troops, army, 31.

bêaggifa, m., ring-giver, king; beorna bêaggifa (of Constantine), 100, 1199.

bealu, n., evil, wrong, injury, 403.

bealudǣd, f., evil deed, sin, 515.

bêam, m., tree, tree of the cross, cross, 91, 217, 424, 851, 865, 887, 1013, 1074, 1225, 1255.

bearhtm (865), breahtm (39), beorhtm (205), m., noise, clang, sound.

bearn, n., child, son (of Christ), bearn, 354, 446, 783; æðelust bearna, 476; bearn wealdendes, 391, 851; godes bearn, 179, 525, 562, 814, 837, 964, 1077, 1127; léoda bearn, = children of men, 181.

bebêodan, sv. II., bid, command; 3d p. sg. pret. bebéad, [378], 710, 715, 980, 1018, 1131, 1220; p.p. beboden, 224, 412.

bebod, n., command, 1170.

bebûgan, sv. II., avoid, 609.

bêe, s. bôe.

beclingan, sv. III., surround, enclose, shackle, 696.

becuman, sv. IV., come, reach, 142.

bedǣlan, wv. I., deprive of, rob, [1244].

bedelfan, sv. III., hide by digging, bury; p.p. bedolfen, 1081.

bedyrnan, wv. I., hide, conceal, secrete, 584, 602.

befæstan, make fast; p.p. befæsted, 1300; make safe, entrust to, commit; p.p. befæsted, 1213.

befeolan, sv. IV., grant, bestow upon; p.p. befólen, 196, 937.

befôn, red. vb., embrace, encompass, seize; 3d p. sg. pret. befeng, 843.

beforan, prep. with dat., before, 108; adv., before, beforehand, 1142, 1154.

begangan, red. vb., execute, fulfil, 1171.

bêgen, prn., both, nom. neut. bû, 614, 889; gen. bêga, 618, 964; bêgra, 1009; dat. bǣm, 805.

begêotan, sv. II., pour into; 3d p. sg. pret. begêat, 1248.

begitan, sv. V., obtain, achieve, procure; 3d p. sg. pret. begeat, 1152, [1248].

begrafan, sv. VI., bury, cover, hide ; gréote begrauene, buried in the sand, 835; foldan begræfen, hid in the earth, 971.

behealdan, red. vb., hold, keep, inhabit; 3d p. sg. pret. wie behéold hálig ... gäst, the Holy Ghost inhabited the dwelling, 1144 ; behold, gaze on, observe; 3d p. sg. pret. behéold, 111, 243.

behelian, wv. I., hele (Gower), conceal, hide, 429, 831.

behlidan, sv. I., shut, close; sie ... behliden helle duru, may the door of hell be closed, 1230.

behȳdan, wv. I., hide, conceal, 793, 988, 1082.

belíðan, sv. I., rob, deprive of ; life belidenes lic, body robbed of life, 878.

belûcan, sv. II., enclose, lock up, 1027.

bemíðan, to hide, keep secret, 583.

bên, f., prayer, request, 1089.

*benugan, s. note 618; beneah with gen, to have at one's disposal ; þonne hé bega beneah, when he has both at his disposal, 618.

béodan, sv. II., offer (him wæs hild borden), 18; present, declare, (wære béodan), to declare protection, 80 ; bid, order, command (swá him sio cwén béad), 378; announce, proclaim, 972; 3d p. sg. pret. opt. þe him Cyriacus bude, 1212.

beofian, wv. II., tremble, shake, 759. s. bifian.

béon (often with future significance); bið, 339, 340, 432, 435,

[451], 526, 606, 1029, 1187, 1194, 1270, 1294, 1298, 1306, 1310, 1312, 1316; bioð, 1289; beoð, 1295, 1304, 1308.

beorg, m., mountain, mount, hill, 510, 578.

beorgan, sv. III., with dat., save ; sume ... féore burgon, some saved life, etc., 134.

beorghlið, n., 788; beorhhlið, mountain slope.

beorht, bright, lucid, shining, glittering, gleaming, brilliant, glorious, sublime, 88, 489, 783, 790, 822, 948, 1080, 1110, 1255.

beorhte, adv., brightly, brilliantly, 92.

beorhtm, s. bearhtm.

beorn, m., man (usual in poetry), hero, 100, 114, 186, 253, [614], 710, 805, 873, 1062, 1187, 1199.

berǽdan, wv. I., rob, deprive, 498.

beran, sv. IV., bear, carry, lead ; beran ût þræce, to lead out to battle, 45; beran béacen godes, to bear the standard of God, 109; berað bord ond ord, they bear shield and spear, 1187; sé þæt wieg byrð, who guides (directs) this horse, 1196.

beréafian, wv. II., rob ; p.p. beréafod, 910.

bescûfan, sv. II., shove, push, hurl, 943.

besencan, wv. I., to sink, [721].

beséon, sv. V., intr., see, look, 83.

besetton, wv. I., set about, adorn (with jewels), bejewel, 1026.

besylean, wv. I., weaken ; sârum besyleed, 697.

betǽcan, wv. I., to commit, deliver, surrender ; 3d p. pl. pret. betæhton, 585.

betera (s. gōd), comp. better, 506; acc. m. beteran, 618; acc. ntr. betere, 1039, 1016, 1062.

Bethlem, Bethlehem, 391.

betwêonum, prep. with dat., between; here with gen., among (sylfra betwêonum, 1207).

beþecean, wv. I., cover; 3d p. sg. pret. ind. beþeahte, 1236; beþeaht, 76, 884; 3d p. pl. pret. ind. beþeahton, 836; p.p. beþehte, 1298; regularly beþeaht, (s. Sievers, 407, a).

beþringan, sv. III., oppress, burden; sûslum (bisgum) beþrungen, 950, 1245.

beþurfan, pret. pres., impersonal; wisdômes beþearf, there is need of wisdom, 543.

beweorcean, wv. I., work, adorn, ornament, 1024.

beweotigan, wv. II., attend to, perform, 745.

bewindan, sv. III., wrap, envelop, encase; lēohte bewundene, wrapped in light, 734; present, deliver, [213].

bewrecan, sv. V., whip, lash; sunde bewrecene, sea-lashed, 251 (s. note 251).

biở, s. bêon.

bîdan, sv. I., with gen., wait for, await (bîdan beorna geþinges, to await the fate of the men, 253); intr. wait, tarry; 3d p. sg. pret. bâd, 329; pres. ptc. bidende, 484; 3d p. sg. pres. bideở, 1093.

biddan, sv. V., ask, beg; with acc. of pers. + þæt, pret. bæd, 494, 1069; beg earnestly, pray (with þæt), 3d p. sg. pret., 600, 1101; biddan, 790, 814; imperative bide, 1090.

bifian, s. S. 416, note 5.

bigang, m., course; wyrda bigang, course of events, 1124.

bil, bill, n., sword, 122, 257. Cf. policeman's billy (?).

bîoở, s. bêon.

bisceop, m., bishop, 1052, 1057, 1073, 1095, 1127, 1217, [biscop, biscep] [episcopus].

bisgu, f., trouble; dat. pl. bisgum beþrungen, by troubles oppressed, 1245.

bisittan, sv. V., to sit in; with acc. æht bisæton, they sat in council, 473.

bisseophâd, m., bishopric, bishop's dignity, 1212.

biter, adj., bitter, fierce (bitter necessity, 1245).

bitre, adv., bitterly, painfully, [1245].

blâc, white, bright, brilliant, 91.

blǣd, m., good fortune, 162; prosperity, glory, 354, 489; happiness, 826.

blanca, m.; on blancan, = on the white horse, 1185.

blêo, n., color, appearance, hue, form, 759, 1106.

blîde, blithe, glad, happy, 96, 246; friendly, gracious, 1317.

blind, blind, 1215.

blindnes, f., blindness, 299, 389.

blinn, n. (?), end, ceasing; bûtan blinne, without end, 826.

bliss, f., bliss, joy; dat. pl. blissum hrêmig, = rejoiced with bliss, 1138.

bôc, f., book; (on godes) bôcum, 204, 290, 826; þurh hâlige bêc, 304, 670, 853; bôca gleaw, 1212; on bôcum, 1255.

bôcstæf, m., letter, character; bôcstafum âwriten, 91.

boda, m., messenger, ambassador, 77, 262, 551.

bodian, wv. II., announce, 1141.

bold, n., house, [162].

bord, n., (board), shield; bord ond ord, 1187; borda gebrec, 114; wordum ond bordum, 24; bordum ond ordum, 235; board, hull, 238.

bordhaga, m., protection of the shield; under bordhagan, 662.

bordhreða, m., cover of the shield (Heyne, "Beowulf," 2204); ornament of the shield (Zupitza), shield, 122.

bôt, f., reparation, reform, remedy, healing, atonement, 280, 389, 1217; repentance, 515, 1039, 1126.

brâd, broad, extended, 917.

breahtm, s. bearhtm.

brecan, sv. IV., break, 122, 244; 3d p. pl. pret. brǽcon.

bregdan, sv. III., weave, plait; brogden byrne, plaited corselet, 257.

brêost, n., breast, bosom; dat. pl. brêostum, 595, 967, 1038, 1095.

brêostloca, m., breast-lock, bosom's recess, soul, 1250.

brêostsefa, mind (heart), in the breast, 805, 842, 1040.

brîdels, m., bridle, reins, 1175, 1185, 1199.

brîdelshring, m., bridle-ring, 1194.

brim, n., surging flood, breakers (of the sea), sea (ocean), 253, 972, 1004.

brimnesen, 'iter marinum' (Gm.), das glückliche überstehen der seefahrt, (Gn.), [1004].

brimþisa, m., rusher over breakers (brandungsrauscher, Gn.), ship, 238.

brimwudu, sea-wood, ship, 244.

bringan, wv. I., irreg. (cf. S., § 407, a), bring; 3d p. sg. pret. brôhte 1130; 3d p. pl. pret. brôhton, 873,

996, 1016; p.p. gebrôht, seldom (cf. S., § 407, a, 7); bremgen, 1138.

brôðor, m., brother, 489, 510, 822.

brogdenmǽl, drawn sword (cf. Sweet) (das geschwungene schwert, Gn.), sword with spiral sign, 759.

brôhte, s. bringan.

bront, steep, high, 238.

brûcan, sv. II., with gen., use, enjoy, [151], 1251, 1315, 1320.

brytta, m., dispenser, distributor, 162, 194; originator, author, 958.

bryttian, wv. II., divide, rend asunder, destroy, 579.

bû, s. bêgen.

burg, f., stronghold, fortress, [31]; gen. sg. byrig, castle (city), 864; dat. sg. byrig, castle (city), 822; city, 1000, 1054, 1204; gen. pl. burga, cities, 152; dat. pl. burgum, cities, 412, 972, 992, 1057, 1062.

burgâgend, possessing castles (citadels), 1175.

bûrgeat, n., tor (nach Ettmüller), 31.

Burgendas, -dan, pl. m., Burgundians, [31].

[burgent (?), f. (?), burg, stadt (??), 31 Zupitza]; s. burg and ent.

burggeat, n., city gate, [31].

burgsittend, city-dweller, citizen, 276.

burgwîgend, warrior of the city or castle, defender of the city or castle, 34.

bûtan, prep. with dat., without; (à) bûtan ende, 802, 811, 894, 953; bûtan blinne, 826; bûtan earfeðum, 1292; save, except, bûtan VI. nihtum, save six nights, 1228; with acc. (?), except; bûtan þec, except thee, 589.

bûtan, conj., unless; bûtan þû

forlǽte þa lëasunga, unless thou desist from these lies, 689.

byldan, wv. I., incite, impel, encourage, 1039.

bŷme, f., trumpet, 109.

byrgen, f., grave, tomb, 186, 484, 652.

byrig, s. burg.

byrne, f., corselet; brogden byrne, linked corselet, 257.

byrnwî(g)gend, corselet-warrior, mailed-warrior, [34], 224, 255.

C.

câf, quick, vigorous, bold, 56.

Caluarie, Calvary, 676; on Caluarie, 672, 1011, 1098.

campwudu, m., battle-wood, 51.

can(n), s. cunnan.

carcern, n. (Lat. carcer), prison; of carcerne, 715.

câserdôm, m., empire, 8.

câsere, m., emperor, (of Constantine) 42, 70, 175, 212, 262, 330, 416, 551, 669, 999.

cearwelm, m., agitation of grief, wave of trouble; cnyssed cearwelmum, beaten by the waves of trouble, 1258.

cêas, f., strife, battle, 56.

ceaster, f., city, (of Jerusalem); gen. ceastre, 384; acc. ceastre, 274, 846, 1205; gen. pl. ceastra, 973 [castra].

ceasterware, pl., dwellers in the city, citizens, 42.

cempa, m., fighter, warrior, champion, [1258].

cêu, m., resin (rosin); name of the rune for c(k), (h), 1258 (s. note 1258).

cennan, wv. I., engender, beget (cende, 354), bring forth, bear, be born (cenned, 346, 392), procreate, give life to (3d p. pl. pret. cendan (cendon), 508), create, give, apply (þám wæs Júdas nama cenned, to him was the name Judas given, 587).

cêol, m., keel, ship, 250.

ceruphîn, cherubim, 750.

cild, n., child; in cildes hâd, 336, 776.

cildhâd, m., childhood, 915.

cining, s. cyning.

Ciriacus, s. Cyriacus.

cirice, f., church (Scottish kirk), 1008.

cirran, wv. I., turn; 3d p. sg. pret. cirde; from cyrran, 2d p. sg. pres. cyrrest, thou turnest thyself, betakest thyself, etc., 666.

clǽne, clean, pure; on clǣnra gemang, into the hosts of the pure, 96; clǣnum stefnum, with pure voices, 750.

cleopigan, wv. II., cry, exclaim, 696; 3d p. sg. pret. cleopode, 1100; 3d p. pl. pret. cleopodon, 1319.

clom, m., fetter, 696.

clynnan, wv. I., resound; campwudu clynede, 51.

cnêo, n., knee, 848; cnêow, 1136.

cnêomâgas, pl., compatriot, companions of race, blood relations, 587, 688.

cniht, m., boy, 339.

cnihtgeong, in the period of boyhood (of youth); cnihtgeong hæleð, a young man in the days of youth, 640.

cnyssan, wv. I., strike, beat; cnyssed cearwelmum, 1258.

côlian, wv. II., cool, grow cold, be cold; leomu côlodon, limbs were cold, 883.

collenferhð, of elated mind, proud, courageous, 247, 378, 849.

Constantīnus, Constantine, 79, 103, 1008; gen. Constantines, 8; dat. Constantino, 145.

corðor, n., crowd, multitude, following, retinue; dat. sg. on corðre, 70; on wera corðre, 304, 543; acc. sg. corðre, 691; gen. pl. corðra, 374.

cræft, m., craft, power, ability, skill, art, knowledge, 154, 374, 558, 595, 1018, 1059, 1172.

cræftig (crafty), skilled, powerful, 314, [315(?)], 419.

Crēcas, pl., Greeks; on Crēca land, 250, 262, 999.

Crîst, Christ, 460; gen. Cristes, 103, 212, 499, 973; dat. Criste, 678, 1011, 1035, 1050, 1120; acc. Crist, 798.

cristen, Christian (used substantively); cristenra gefēan, joy of the Christians, 980; cristenra cwēn, queen of the Christians, 1069: (adjectively), cristenum folce, to the Christian people, 989; cristenum þeawum, to Christian usages, 1211.

cûð, known, familiar, 42, 1192.

cûðe, s. cunnan.

cuman, sv. IV., come, 279, 1205; 3d p. pl. pres. cumað, 1303; 3d p. sg. pret. côm, 150; cwôm, 549, 871, 908, 1110; 3d p. pl. pret. cwômon, 274, 1214; p.p. cymen, 1123.

cunnan, pret. pres. (1) know; 1st p. sg. pres. can, 635, 683; cann, 684; pl. pres. cunnon, 399, 531, 535; pret. sg. cûðe, 1163; pret. pl. cûðon, 328, 393, 398; opt. pl. cunnen, 374. (2) know how (understand), be able, can; 1st p. sg. pres. can, 610, 925; pl. pres. cunnon, 317, 648; pret. pl. cûðon, 167, 281, 284, 1020:

opt. 2d p. sg. cunne, 857; opt. pl. cunnen, 376.

cwacian, wv. II., quake, 758.

cwalu, f., torture, violent death, murder, 499.

cwealm, m., destruction, death, 676.

cweðan, sv. V., say, speak; cweðaþ, 749; cwæð, quoth, 667; cwædon, 169, 871, 1120.

cwên, f., woman, the woman, queen (of the emperor's mother), 247, 275, 324, 378, 384, 411, 416, 533, 551, 558, 605, 662, 715, 849, 980, 1018, 1069, 1152, 1170, 1205; dat. cwêne, 587, 610, 1130; gen. sg. cwêne, 1136.

cwic, quick, living, alive, 691.

cwide, m., speech, address [547].

cwôm, s. cuman.

cwylman, wv. I., afflict, torture-to-death, kill, 688.

cÿðan, wv. I., make known, show, tell, 161, 175, 199, 318, 540, 558, 566, 661, 671, 854; pres. (with future significance), cÿðe, I will reveal, 702; pret. cÿðde, [439]; p.p. cÿðed, 827; imperative cÿð, 607; wundor cÿðan, to work a miracle, 1112.

cyme, m., arrival, 41; advent, 1228; appearance (act of appearing), 1086.

cyman, s. cuman.

cyn, cynn, n., family, race, people, 188, 209, 305, 521, 591, [837], 898, 1204.

cynestôl, m., royal seat, throne, 330.

cyning, king (of earthly kings frequently), e.g. 13, 32, 51, 56, etc., 342; (of God), 79, 145, 291, 404, 1248; (of Christ), 392, 800.

[cyninge, f., queen, (610)].

Cyriacus, proper name, 1059, 1069, 1098, 1211; Ciriacus, 1130. The changed name of the second Judas.

cyrran, s. cirran.

D.

dǽd, f., deed, action, 386, 1283.

dǽdhwæt, powerful in deed, 292.

dæg, m., day; gen. sg. dæges, 140; adv. dæges, by day, 198; dat. sg. dæge, 185; acc. dæg, 312, 697, 1223; instrumental, by þriddan dæg, on the third day, 485; gen. pl. dagena, 193, and daga, 358.

dægweorc, n., day's work, 146.

dægweorðung, f., celebration of a day, festival, 1234.

dǽl, m., deal, part, division, 1298, 1306; share, lot, 1232.

dǽlan, wv. I., divide, be divided, 1286.

Danûbie, f., dat. 37, acc. 136, Danube.

dareðlácende, spear-contenders, lancers; dareðlácende, 37; dareð-lácendra, 651.

daroð, m., spear, javelin, lance (140).

daroðæsc (?), m., n. (?), spear of ash, [140].

Dâuid, David; Dâuid cyning, 342.

dêad, dead, 882; dêadra, 651, 945.

dêað, m., death, 187, 302, 303, 477, 500, 584, 606, 780.

dêaðcwalu, f., death-throe; drêogað dêaðcwale, they suffer death-throes, 766.

deareð, s. dareð.

dêgol, n., concealment, obscurity, 336.

delfan, sv. III., delve, dig, 829.

dêma, m., judge, 746, 1283.

dêman, wv. I., deem, judge, condemn; dêman tó dêaþe, 303, 500; damn, 311.

dêoful, m., devil; gen. sg. dêofles, 1119; gen. pl. dêofla, 181, 302.

dêofulgild, n., sacrifices to the devil, idolatry, idol, 1041.

dêogol, secret, hidden, concealed, 1093; dýgol, 541.

dêop, deep (deep buried), secret, hidden, 584; deep. heavy; dêopra firena, of deep sins, heavy transgressions, 1314.

dêop, adv., deeply, to a great depth, 1190.

dêope, adv., deeply, to a great depth, 1081.

dêophycgende, engaged in deep thought, pensive, 352, 882.

dêoplîce, adv., thoroughly; sup. dêoplicost, most thoroughly, 280.

dêore, s. dŷre.

dêorlîce, dearly, preciously, gloriously; sup. dêorlicost, in most glorious wise, 280.

dierne, s. dyrne.

disig (cf. dysig), foolish, 477.

dôgorgerîm, number of days; dat. adverbially, dôgorrimum, 705; dogorgerimum, 780.

dôm, m., doom, judgment, 1280; ordeal (þurh þæs dômes fŷr), through the fire of this ordeal, 1314; choice, will (dôma geweald), power over wills, 726; glory (dôm unscyndne), blameless glory, 365; dôm, 450; happiness (dômes lêasne), deprived of happiness, 945.

dômgeorn, eager for glory, 1291.

dômweorðung, f., honor through glory, glorious honor, 146.

dôn, irr. vb. (S. 129), do; imperative dô, do, 541; put, place, affix, attach, 1175.

draca, m., dragon, 766 (s. note 766) [draco].

drêam, m., joy, blessedness, [451]; dream unhwilen, eternal joy, 1261.

drene, m., drowning; sume drene fornam, drowning snatched away some, 136.

drêogan, sv. II., endure, suffer, tolerate, bear; wergðu drêogan, 211, 952; drêogað dêaðewale, 766; pret. nearnsorge drêah, 1261.

drifan, sv. I., drive, 358. [drûsan, sv. II., full, 1258.]

drûslan, wv. II. (?), become turbid, be lazy, burn badly; cen drûsende, rosin burning badly, 1258.

drŷge, dry; in drŷgne sêað, into the dry well, 693.

dryhten, Lord (of God), 81, 193, 198, 280, 292, 352, 365, 371, 726, 760, 948, 971, 1010, 1140, 1160, 1168, 1206, 1280; (of Christ) 187, 346, 491, 500, 717, 897.

dryhtlêoð, n., song for the people (national song), 342.

dryhtseipe, m., valor, heroism, 451.

dûfan, sv. II., plunge, thrust; pret. bil in dufan, they thrust in the swords, 122.

dugan, avail, be worth, [451].

dugoð, uð, f., worth, excellence, joy; duguða lêas, deprived of joys, 683; throng, multitude, 1201; heavenly hosts, duguða dryhten, 81; mankind, men, 450, 1093, 1160.

dûn, f., dune, hill, 717.

duru, f., door; helle duru, 1230.

dŷgol, s. dêogol.

dynman, wv. I., make a noise (cf. v. a. din), 50.

dŷre, dear, beloved, 292; precious, glorious; sup. dêorestan, 1234.

dyrnan, wv. I., hide, secrete, keep secret, 971; pret. pl. dyrndun, 626.

dyrne, secret, hidden, concealed, 723, 1093; dierne, 1081.

dysig, n., folly; mid dysige þurhdrifen, pervaded with folly, 707.

dyslie, foolish; acc. dyslice dæd, foolish deed, 386.

E.

êac, adv., also, 742, 1007; swylce êac, also, likewise, 3; with ond (frequent elsewhere), 1278.

êaðe, adv., easily, 1202.

êadhrêðig, rejoicing in prosperity, triumphant, blessed; sêo êadhrêðige Elene, 266.

êadig, rich, happy, blessed, 806; sêo êadige, 619; êadigra gedryht, 1290.

êaðmêdu, f., reverence; pl. eallum êaðmêdum, 1088, 1101.

êadwela, m., riches, prosperity, 1316.

eafera, m., child, descendant, heir, 439; eafora, 353.

êage, n., eye; gen. pl. êagena, 298.

eal, eall, (1) all (without substantive); gen. sg. ealles, 512, 1236; nom. pl. ealle, 1118; gen. pl. ealra, 187; eallra, 370, 475; dat. pl. eallum, 1220; acc. pl. ealle, 385: (with substantive), nom. sg. eal, 20 (?), 753; gen. sg. neut. ealles, 486; gen.

sg. f. eallre, 446; dat. sg. ealre, [293]; acc. sg. m. ealne, 731; neut. eall, 1197; gen. pl. eallra, 422, 483, 519, 894, 1285; ealra, 769; alra, 645; allra, 816; dat. pl. eallum, 1088, 1101. (2) entire, whole; ealle gesceaft, whole creation, 729; þeos world call, this whole world, 1277. (3) every; ealre synne, 772; adv. entirely, wholly; eal, 856; eall, 1131, 1155, 1293, 1311; eallra, in all, 649.

eald, old, 207, 455, 905; ald, 252, 1266; comp. yldra, elder, older, 159; min yldra, my father, 462; yldra fæder, grandfather, 436.

ealdfeond, m., old foe, hereditary foe, embittered adversary, 493.

ealdgewin, n., battle in olden days (of the Trojan war), 647.

earc, f., ark, ark of the covenant; æt godes earce, 399.

eard, m., country, home, dwelling-place, 509, 622.

earfeðe, n., hardship, distress, torture, 700, 1292.

earhfaru, f., the circuit of the arrow (s. note 44 and 116); (pfeil-flug, kampf, Zupitza) (Umlauf des Heerpfeils, 44; Anprall der Geschosse, 116 (Grim.)). Impetus sagittarum (Dietrich).

earhgeblond, n., sea, 239.
earm, m., arm, 1236.
earn, m., eagle, 29, 111.
eart (2d pers. sg. ind. of béon). art, 809, 815.

éastweg, m., eastern road, path from the east, 255, 996.

eatol, dreadful, dire, terrible; eatol æclæca, dire monster, 902.

eaxlgestealla, m., shoulder-companion, trusted friend, 64 (s. note 64).

Ebréas, pl., Hebrews, 287, 448.
ebréisc, Hebrew; ebréisce æ, 397; weras ebresce = Ebréas, 559; on ebrise, in Hebrew, 725.

éce, eternal, everlasting; éce lif, 526; écra gestealda, everlasting mansions, 802; éces éadwelan, 1316; éces déman, 746; éce cining, 800; éce rex, 1042.

éce, adv., eternally, continually, forever, 1218, 1231.

éðe, easy, agreeable, pleasant; superl. éðost, 1294.

éðel, country, native land, home, 1220, [1294].

éðgesýne, readily seen, visible, 256.

éðigean, wv. II., breathe, ascend, 1107.

ednīowunga, anew (cf. geednīwian, to renew), 300.

édre, adv., immediately, forthwith, at once, 649; syððan ... édre, as soon as; syððan andsware édre gehýrdon, 1002.

efnan, wv. I., do, perform, execute, 713.

eft, adv., again, 143, 148, 382, 514, 516, 903, (921), 924, 1000, 1155, 1220, 1275; afterwards, later, 255, 350, 500.

egesa, m., fear, terror (consternation, dismay); egsan geáclad, with fear disquieted, 57, 1129; egesan hwópan, to threaten with terror, 82; egesan geþréade, by fear oppressed, 321.

égstréam, m., sea-stream, current, river (of the Danube); égstréame néah, 66; sea, (on égstréame, 241).

eh, m., n. (?), horse, name of the rune for e, (ᛖ), 1262.

éhtan, wv. I., with gen. pursue;

pret. éhton elþéoda, 139; persecute (sé éhteð þin, who will persecute thee, 928).

elde, pl., 476; ilde, 521; ylde, [451], 792; men.

éled, m., fire, (1294).

Elene, Helen, 219, 266, 332, 404, 573, 604, 620, 642, 685, 953, 1051, 1198, 1218; gen. Elenan, 848; dat. Elenan, 1003, 1063.

ellen, n., courage, strength, zeal; elnes oncýðig, unacquainted with strength, powerless, 725; elnes ânhýdig, determined in zeal, 829.

elþéod, f., strange nation, hostile nation, enemy, 139.

elþéodig, strange, hostile (without substantive); elþéodig, 908; elþeodige, 57, 82.

ende, m., end, 590, 802, 811, 894, 953; limit, boundary, lifes æt ende, at the limit of life, 137; on Rôwwara rices ende, on the boundary of the empire of the Romans, 59.

endelif, n., end of life, 585.

enge, narrow; fram þâm engan hofe, out of this narrow (contracted) court, 712; in þâm engan hâm, in that contracted home (i.e. hell); enge rûne, close secret, 1262.

engel, m., angel; gen. pl. 79, 476, 487, 773, 777, 784, 858, 1101, 1231, 1281, 1307, 1316; dat. pl. englum, 622, 1320.

engeleyn, n., race of angels, 733.

ent, m., giant (31).

éode: pret. to gân (s. S. § 430), went, went away; eode, 1096; eodon, 411, 557, 846; eodan, 320, 377.

coforcumbul, n., sign of the bear (an image on the helmet), helmet, 259; eofur-, 76.

cofot, n., sin, guilt, crime; un-

scyldigne cofota gehwylces, innocent of every sin, 423.

eofulsæc, n., blasphemy, 524.

éom; 1st p. sg. pres. ind. of béon, am; ic (the devil) . . . éom, etc., 923.

eorcnanstân, m., precious stone (cf. eorclanstân, B. 1209); mid þâm æðelestum eorcnanstánum, with the most costly precious stones, 1025.

eorðcyning, m., earthly king; þâm æðelestan eorðcyninga, to the noblest of the kings of earth, 1174.

corðe, f., earth, 753; dat. for eorðan, 591; on eorðan, 622, 878, 1109; of eorðan, 1226; acc. eorðan, 728, 829; instr. eorðan, 836.

corðweg, m., path of earth, earth; of eorðwegum, from the paths of earth, 736; on eorðwege, on earth, 1015.

éoredcest, f., crowd (?); féðan trymedon éoredcestum, the infantry was strengthened by crowds, 36 (s. note 36).

eorl, m., earl, warriors, (of Constantine's retinue) 12, 66; (of Helen's retinue) 225, 256, 275, 620, 848, 1198; (of the Jews) 321, 332, 404, 417, 435; (of Moses) 787; (Judas is) eorla hléo, 1047. Selection on account of excellence is the dominant factor in this word.

eorlmaegen, n., multitude of noble men, 981.

corre, s. yrre.

éow, pers. prn., you; dat. pl. from ðû, thou, 298, 309, 339, and frequently.

éow, pers. prn. you; acc. pl. from ðu, thou, 295, 318, 368, and frequently.

éower, poss. prn., your, 305, 315, 375, etc.

ermðu, f., misery; yrmðu, 953; | pl. in ermðum, 768.

Essáias, Essáias, 350.

êst, favor, love grace; þurh meotodes êst, 986.

Eusebius, Eusebius; acc. Eusebium, 1051.

êwigean, wv. I., to show one's self, [1107].

F.

fæc, n., period of time, interval, while; ymb lytel fæc, after a little while, 272, 383; on swá lytlum fæce, in such a little while, 960.

fæcne, deceitful, delusive, 577; uncertain, unreliable, 1237.

fæder, m., father, (of God) 784, 891, 1084, 1106, 1151; (of earthly relationship) 343, 463, 517, 528; min yldra fæder, my grandfather, 436; dat. fæder, 438, 454; pl. fæderas, forefathers, ancestors, fathers, 388, 398, 425, 458.

fæderlic, paternal, ancestral; þá fæderlican láre, ancestral teaching, 431.

fæðm, m., fathom, expanse; sæs sidne fæðm, the wide expanse of waters, 729; outstretched arms, encircling arms (on fæðme, 881); embrace (in dracan fæðme, in the embrace of the dragon, 766).

fæðman, wv. I., embrace, encircle, surround, 972.

fæge, doomed to death (nothing to do with N.II.G. feige, cowardly), 117; dead ofer þæt fæge hús, over that dead frame, 881.

fæger, fair, beautiful, joyful, 98, 242, 891, 911, 949.

fægere, adv., beautifully, admirably, 743, 1213.

fáh, colored, stained, variegated, spotted; weorcum fáh, spotted by works, 1243.

fáh, hostile, guilty, abhorred (of the devil), 769, 925, (1243?).

fæle, faithful, good, lovely; fæle friðowebba, lovely weaver of peace, 88.

fámig, foamy, foaming, 237.

fær, n., journey, warlike journey, war, [93].

fær, m., danger, 93, 646.

faran, sv. VI., go, travel, march, march thither, advance; pret. sg. fór, 27, 35, 51; pret. pl. fóron, 21, 261; þe geond lyft farað, who fly through the air, 734; færeð (of the wind), 1274.

fæst, fast, firm, secure, 252, 723, 771, 883, 909; fæste on fyrðe, 570; fæst on ferhðe, 1037, steadfast in heart.

fæste, adv., fast, firmly, steadfastly, [213], 933, 937, 1208.

fæsten, n., fastness, 134.

fæstlice, adv., firmly, securely, 427, 797.

fæt, vessel, casket, 1026.

fêa, few; þeah hira fêa wæron, although there were few of them, 174; fêam siðum, few times, seldom, 818.

feala, with gen., many; obj. acc. feala wundra, 362, 778; feala hearma, 912; dêadra feala, 945; adv. acc. feala mæla, 987; feala tida, 1044; nom. feale, is nú feale siðþan forðgewitenra, etc., 636 (s. S. 275). [Ger. viel.]

feallan, red. vb., fall; pret. pl. fêollon, 127, 1134.

fearoðhengest, m., seahorse, ship, 226.

fêða, m., infantry-man, foot-soldier, infantry, army; fêðan, 35.

fēðegest, m., guest coming on foot, newcomer, stranger; pl. fē-ðegestas, 845.

feng, m., grip, embrace; in fȳres feng, in the fire's embrace, 1287.

fēogan, fēon, wv. III., hate, 360; pret. pl. fēodon, 356.

feoh, n. (Ger. vieh), cattle, possessions, money. Name of the rune for f. (ᚠ), 1270.

feohgestrēon, n., possessions, riches; gen. pl. feohgestrēona, 911.

fēond, enemy; gen. pl. fēonda, 68, 108, 1170; acc. pl. fēond, 93 (S. 286). (Of the devil), 207, 900, 954; gen. sg. fēondes (721?).

fēondscipe, m., enmity, hatred; þurh fēondscipe, 356, 498.

feor, far, distant (from the surface), deep; on .xx. fōtmǣlum feor, twenty feet deep, 831; distant (from present), remote past, far back in the past, 1142.

feorh, m. n., life; gen. sg. feores, 680; dat. sg. feore (!), 498; acc. pl. feore, 134; period of time, time; tō widan feore, for extended time, for eternity, forever, 211, 1321; on widan feore, throughout (in) extended time, 1288 (S. 273).

feorhlegu, f., life's end, death, murder; tō feorhlege, 458.

feorhneru, f., preservation of life, rescue, deliverance, salvation, 898.

feorran, adv., from afar, 993, 1213.

fēower, four, (744).

fēran, wv. I., go, march, journey, 215.

ferhð, m. n., soul, mind, heart; ferhð, 174, 901; dat. sg. on ferhðe, 1037, 1164; on fyrðe, 463, 570, 641; in fyrhðe, 196; acc. sg. ferhð, 797;

acc. pl. ferhð, 427: (adverbially) life time (widan fyrhð, 761; widan ferhð, 891), throughout eternity, eternally.

ferhðglēaw, wise in heart, wise; 327; fyrhð-, 881.

ferhðsefa, life-spirit, mind, heart; on ferhðsefan, 316, 850, 895; on firhðsefan, 213); on fyrhðsefan, 98, 1079; acc. fryhðsefan, 534.

ferian, wv. I., carry, bear, 108. Cf. N.E. ferry.

fēt, s. fōt.

fiðru, n. pl., feathers, wings; mid syxum fiðrum, with six wings, 743.

fifelwǣg, m., sea-monster's waves, sea, 237.

fifhund, five hundred, .d., (379).

findan, sv. III., (1) find, 924; 2d p. sg. pres. findest, 84; 3d p. pl. pres. findaþ, 373, 1032; pret. sg. fand, 202, 1255; also funde, 831 (s. 386, n. 2); pret. pl. fundon, 327, 379, 1217; pret. opt. funde, 1080; p.p. funden, 974, 987. (2) find out, discover, 632, 641.

finger, m., finger; þurh fingra geweald, 120.

firas, m. pl., men; nerigend fira, 1078, 1173; fira cynne, 898.

firen, f., transgression, sin; on firenum, 909; dēopra firena, 1314.

firhð-, s. ferhð-.

flān, m. f., arrow; flāna scūras, showers of arrows, 117.

flēogan, sv. II., fly; pret. pl. daroðas flugon, spears flew, 140.

flēon, sv. II., flee; pret. pl. flugon, 127, 134.

fliht, m., flight; on flihte, a flight, on the wing, in motion, 744.

flōd, m., flood, flow of the tide,

current; flódas gefýsde, currents set in motion, 1270.

flōdweg, m., current's road, water-way, sea, [215].

flot, n. [from fléotan, to float], [water deep enough to float a ship (B.)]; sea (Grein), swimming, sea-voyage (Z.); tó flote fysan, to prepare for the sea-voyage, 226.

fōdder, n., fodder (Ger. futter), 360.

folc, n., folk, people, nation, 872, 1287; gen. sg. 157, [213], 499, 1095; dat. sg. folce, 415, 895, 989, 1056; acc. sg. folc, 117; instr. sg. folce, 891 : pl. men, people, 362 ; gen. folca, 27, 215, 502; dat. folcum, 1143.

folcscearu, f., folkshare, part of a people, nation, people ; on þyne folcscere, 402 ; in þǽre folcsceare, 908.

foldbūende, pl., earth-dweller, inhabitant of earth, 1014.

folde, f., earth ; foldan getyned, 702 ; foldan begrǽfen, 974 ; in foldan, 987, 1080.

foldgrǽf, n., earth-grave ; of foldgrǽfe, out of its earth-grave, 845.

foldweg, m., earth-way, road over the earth ; feran foldwege, 215.

folgađ, m., following, retainers, retainers' service, 904.

folgian, wv. II., follow, obey, be subject to ; manþéawnm minum folgaþ, he is subject to my sinful usages, 930.

folm, f., hand ; his folme, 1066 ; hǽ đenum folmum, 1076.

for, prep., for. I. with dat. (1) local, before, in the sight of, in the presence of, 4, 110, 124, 170, 175, 180, 332, 351, 362, 404, 406, 417, 587, 591, 596, 620, 688, 782, 979, 1198, 1273; (2) causal (objective), because of. on account of, 63, 491, 521, 677, 703; (subjective), out of, from, for. on account of, 496, 561, 687, 1134; (3) in regard to (for þám næglum, in regard to the nails, 1065). II. with acc., for, in the place of, instead of, 318, 546.

fōr, f., journey, [1262].

foran, adv., before, in front, 1184.

forđ, adv., forth. I. (with verbs of motion giving direction); forđ onsendan, send forth, 120 ; gedo-forđ, show forth, disclose, 784 ; forđ gewitan, go forth, depart, die, 636, 1268; forđ . . . up eđigean, ascend, 1105. II. (temporal), (1) forth, from now on, from this time on, 318, 1062; fram orde ođ ende forđ, from the beginning (even) until the end, 590; ođ þæt æfen forđ fram dæges orde, from the beginning of day (even) until evening, 139 (in these two phrases it gives direction in time) ; (2) continually, 192, 213.

forđgewitan, sv. I., go, vanish ; forđgewitenra, 636.

forđsnoter, forđsnotter, very wise ; acc. m. forđsnoterne, 1053 ; forđsnotterne, 1161 ; gen. pl. forđ-snotterra, 379.

fore, prep., before, with dat. or acc. (1) (local), mé fore, before me, 577; fore onsýne, before the sight, 746; fore Elenan cnéo, before Helen's knee, 848; (2) (temporal), ūs fore, before us, 637.

fore, adv., before, beforehand, aforetimes, once upon a time, once, 345, 1262.

foresnotter, very wise, [379].

forepanc, m., forethought; pl. nähton forepancas, they had no forethought, 356.

forgifan, sv. V., give, grant, bestow; pret. sg. forgeaf, 144, 164, 354, 1218.

forlæran, wv. I., mis-teach, lead astray by false teaching, seduce, 208.

forlætan, red. vb., (1) let (with inf.); pret. sg. forlet . . . sécan, 598; imperative, forlæt . . . ástigan, 793. (2) with adverb of direction; pres. opt. mé of . . . úp forlæten, let me up out of, 700; pret. opt. hine of . . . úp forléte, 712. (3) let go, relinquish, abandon, renounce; pres. opt. þa fæderlican lâre forléten, 432; bûtan þú forlæte þa léasunga, unless thou desist from this lying, 689; pres. ind. (with future significance); hé forlæteþ lâre þine, he will renounce thy teaching, 929.

forniman, sv. IV., take away, snatch away, 578; pret. sg. fornam sume wig fornam, 131; sume drenc fornam, 136.

forsécan, wv. I., to follow closely, to punish, persecute; sârum forsôht, 933.

forséon, sv. V., scorn, abhor; pret. pl. forsâwon, 1318; forsegon, 389 (S. 391. 5).

fortyhtan, wv. I., mislead, lead astray; pret. sg. fortyhte, 208.

forþan, forðan, for that, therefore, on that account, 309, 517, 522, 1319.

forþryccan, wv. I., crush, oppress; þréam forþrycced, 1277.

forþylman, wv. I., surround, envelop; þéostrum forþylmed, enveloped in darkness, 767.

forwyrd, f., destruction; in wita

forwyrd, in the destruction of hell, 765.

fôt, m., foot; pl. fét, 1066.

fôtmæl, n., foot-measure, foot, 831.

fram, prep. with dat. (instr.). (1) from (motion away); fram rûne, 411. (2) from (measure of distance — in time), 140; (from), 590. (3) from (with idea of separation), 296, 299, 301, 1120, 1309. (4) from, by (agent with passive), 190, 701, 1142. (5) from, out of (source), 712.

Francan, pl., Franks, 21.

frætwan, wv. irr. (S. 408. 6), adorn, 1190.

frætwe, f. pl., ornament; frætwum beorht, bright with ornaments, 88; landes frætwe, the ornaments of the land, 1271.

fréa, m., lord, king (of God), 680, 1307; (of Christ), 488, 1067.

frécne, terrible; on þâm frécnan fære, in the terrible danger, 93.

fremman, wv. I., do, accomplish, 646; exercise, offer (andsæc fremede, I offered opposition, 472; wiðersæc fremedon, they offered contradiction, 569); commit, (þæt þú hospcwide, æfst né cofulsæc æfre ne fremme, that thou mayest never commit scornful speech, hate or blasphemy, 524).

fréobearn, n., noble child; cyninges fréobearn, the King's noble child, 672.

freoðian, wv. II., have a care for, protect, guard; freoðode, 1147.

fréond, m., friend, 954; pl. frŷnd, 360 (S. 286).

fréondléas, friendless, 925.

fréondræddon, f., friendship; fréondræddenne, 1208.

fricca, m., herald; hreopan

(hreopon) friccan, the heralds made proclamation, 54, 550.

frieggan, sv. V., inquire, ask, 157, 560; friegendra, 991.

friŏ, m. n., peace, protection, safety, 1154. [Ger. friede].

friŏcléas, peaceless, deserted of peace, 127.

friŏian, s. freoŏian.

friŏowebba, m., weaver of peace; fæle friŏowebba (of the angel), 88.

frignan, sv. III., ask; frignan ongan, 443, 570, 850, 1008, 1104; 2d p. sg. frignest, 589; 3d p. sg. frigneŏ, 534; p.p. frugnen, 542.

frigu, f., love; þurh weres frige, 341.

frôd, prudent, wise, 343, 431, 438, 463, 531, 542; frôdne, 1104; frôdra, 637; experienced, old, frôd, 1237. Adverb, wisely; frode, 443.

frôfor, f., consolation, joy; gen. sg. frôfre gast, 1037, 1106; dat. sg. tô frôfre, 502, 1143; gen. pl. frôfra mæst, 196, 993.

from, s. fram.

from, active, bold, brave; fyrdrincas frome, warriors bold, 261.

fromlîce, adv., boldly, quickly, 454.

fruma, m., beginning, origin (fram fruman worulde, from the beginning of the world, 1142); originator, author, 772, 793, 839; the first, the chief, prince (herga fruman, 210, [213. 518]).

frymŏ, m. f., beginning, 345, 502.

frŷnd, s. frêond.

ful, full, 752, 939. Adv., fully, full; ful geare, 167; ful gere, 860.

fûl, n., foulness, uncleanliness, impurity, 769.

fultum, m., help; on fultum, in help, 1053.

fulwiht, f. n. m. (?), baptism; þurh fulwihte, 172; fulwihte onfêng, receive baptism, 192; onfêng . . . fulwihtes hæŏ, 490, 1034.

furŏum, even, just; syŏŏan furŏum, just as soon as, 914.

furŏur, further, more, 388.

fûs, ready, ready for (with gen.); siŏes fûs, ready for the journey, 1219; ready to die, 1237.

fylgan, wv. I., follow; gedwolan fylgdon, followed error, 371.

fyllan, wv. I., fell, cause to fall, discard; gedwolan fylde, he discarded error, 1041.

fyr, comp. to feor, [646].

fŷr, n., fire; ŏurh fŷres bléo, through the form of fire, 1106; in fŷres feng, in the embrace of fire, 1287; þurh ofnes fŷr, 1311; þurh þæs dômes fŷr, through the fire of this ordeal (purgatorial), 1314.

fŷrbæŏ, n., fire-bath, hell-fire; on fyrbæŏe, 949.

fyrd, m., army; fyrda mæst, 35.

fyrdhwæt, brave in war, warlike, 21, 1179.

fyrdlêoŏ, n., war-song; fyrdlêoŏ ágól wulf, the wolf sang his battle-song, 27.

fyrdrinc, m., warrior; fyrdrincas frome, 261.

fŷrhât, hot as fire, ardent; fŷrhât lufu, 937.

fyrhŏ, s. ferhŏ.

fyrhŏwêrig, sad at heart, sorrowful; fyrhŏwêrige, 560.

fyrmest, adv., first, at first, 68; first of all, especially, 316.

fyrn, adv., formerly, in olden days, of yore, long ago, 632,641,974.

fyrndagas, m. pl., days of yore; (on) fyrndagum, 398, 425, 528, [722].

fyrngellit, n., old strife; þurh fyrngellit, 904.

fyrngemynd, n., recollection of former deeds, history, 827.

fyrngewrit, n., old writing, ancient scripture; þurh fyrngewrito, 155; fyrngewritu, 373, 431, 560.

fyrngid, n., ancient word, ancient prophecy; fyrngidda fród, 542.

fyrnweota, m., wise old man, prophet; fród fyrnweota (of David), 343; fród fyrnwiota (of Sachius), 438; þurh fyrnwitan, 1154.

fyrst, m., space of time, time (Ger. frist); nihtlangne fyrst, 67; æfter fyrste, 490; vii. nihta fyrst, 694.

fyrstmearc, f., definite time, appointed time; æfter fyrstmearce, 1034, 1268.

fyrwet, n., curiosity, desire of knowledge; mec . . . fyrwet myngaþ, desire of knowledge reminds me, etc., 1079.

fysan, wv. I., hasten, make haste, prepare one's self; tó flote fysan, to get ready for the sea-voyage, 226; fysan . . . tó ráde, get ready for the journey, 981.

G.

gád, n., lack, 992.

galan, sv. VI., sing, scream; hréfen úppe gól, the raven screamed on high, 52; þá wæs . . . sigeleoð galen, 124.

gælan, wv. I., hesitate, delay; scealcas ne gældon, the servants did not delay, 692, 1001.

galdor, m., sound, tone, song, speech; galdrum cýðan, 161.

galga, m., gallows, cross; on galgan, 179, 489, 719.

gamel, old, aged; me . . . gamelum tó géoce, to me an old man for my assistance, 1247.

gang, m. [Ger. gang], course; dat. pl. wintra gangum, 633; geára gongum, 648; wyrda gangum, 1256.

gangan, red. vb., go; imperative gangaþ nú (snúde), go now (quickly), 313, 372, 406.

gár, m., spear; gáras lixtan, the spears glittered, 23, 125; gáras . . . forð onsendan, send forth . . . spears, 118.

gárþracu, f., storm of spears, battle; æt gárþræce, 1186.

gárþríst, bold with the spear, 204.

gást, m. (1) ghost, spirit (as principle of life); his gást onsende, gave up the ghost, 480; gáste gegearwod, supplied with spirit, 889. (2) spirit, soul; gáste minum, 471. (3) pl. spirits (demons) (of Christ); se gásta helm, 176; (of God), gásta géocend, 682, 1077, — scyppend, 791, — weard, 1022; fram unclænum . . . gástum, from unclean spirits (i.e. demons), 302; géomre gástas, 182. (4) the spirit, spirit of God, Holy Ghost; hálig gást, 936, 1145; frófre gást, 1037, 1106; þurh gástes gife, 199, 1058, 1157; gástes mihtum, 1070, 1100; þurh dryhtnes gást, 352.

gástgerýne, n., spirit's secret, spiritual mystery; gástgerýnum, 189, 1148.

gásthálig, holy in spirit, endowed with the Holy Ghost, 562.

gástléas, without spirit, soulless, dead; gingne gástléasne, 875.

gástsunu, m., spiritual son; godes gástsunu, God's spiritual son (Christ), 673.

gê ... gê, both ... and, 965, 966; whether ... or, 629, 631.

gê, prn.; 2d pers. pl. ye, you, 290, 293, 294, and often.

geáclian, wv. II., frighten, excite, disquiet ; egsan geáclad, by fear disquieted, 57 ; egesan geáclod, 1129.

geâcnian = ge-êacnian, become pregnant, fructify ; wæstmum geácnod, 841.

geador, adv., together, 26, 889.

geagnewide, m., contradiction, answer; grimne geagnewide, angry contradiction, 525; génewidas gléawe, wise answers, 594.

geagninga, adv., directly, completely, perfectly, 673.

geâr, n., year, 7; geára hwyrftum, 1; geára gongum, 648; æfter geárum, 1265.

geâra, adv., formerly, of yore, 1266.

geârdagas, m. pl., days of the year, days of life, 1267 ; days of yore (geârdagum, 290, 835).

geare, (gere, gearu, gearwe.) adv., readily, clearly, well, accurately, exactly, fully, completely, 167, 300, 419, 531, 648, 719; gere, 860; gearwe, 1246; (gearu, 1045?); comp. geawor, 946; superl. gearwast, 328.

geárolîce, adv., readily, fully, thoroughly, 288.

gearu, ready, 85, 222, 605, 1029, 1045 (?) ; pl. gearwe, 23, 227, 555.

gearusnotter, very wise, skilled ; with gen. gidda gearosnotor, 418 ; with dat. giddum gearusnottorne, 586.

gearwe, s. geare.

gearwian, wv. II., make ready, prepare one's self, 1000.

geâsne, with gen., poor in, destitute of ; gôda geâsne, 924.

geatolic, adorned, splendid, stately; geatolic gûðscrûd, splendid battle dress, 258 ; geatolic gûðcwén, stately queen of battle, 331.

gebann, n., commission, order, behest ; þurh heard gebann, by strict behest, 557.

gebǽro, n. pl., conduct, demeanor (beornes gebǽro. 710) ; actions, deeds (þéoda gebǽru, 659).

gebêodan, sv. II., bid, command, direct, 276, 1007.

gebîdan, sv. I., wait, 865.

gebindan, sv. III., bind; p.p. sǽle gebunden, 772; bitrum gebunden, 1245.

geblissian, wv. II., rejoice, make glad, delight ; p.p. geblissod, 840, 876, 990, 1126.

gebrec, n., breaking, crash, noise ; borda gebrec, crash of shields, 114.

gebringan (s. bringan), gebrôht, [614].

gebyrde, by birth, innate, natural ; him gebyrde is, it is innate in him, 593.

gecêosan, sv. II., choose, select ; pret. sg. gecéas, 1039, 1166 ; p.p. gecorenne, 1059 ; tô gecéosanne (gerund), 607.

geclǽnsian. wv. II., cleanse, 678; p.p. geclênsod, 1035, 1311.

gecnâwan, red. vb., know, recognize ; pret. sg. gecnéow, 1140; pret. sg. opt. gecnéowe, 708 ; p.p. gecnáwen, 808.

gecost, tried, proved; bill gecost, tried sword. 257; héape gecoste, with a tried band, 269 ; guman gecoste, 1186.

gecweðan, sv. V., speak ; pret. sg. gecwæð (formula) þæt word geewæð, this word he spake, 338, 344, 440, 939, 1191.

geewême, pleasing, dear, 1050.

geeȝðan, wv. I., announce, to make known, 409, 588, 861; opt. pres. geeȝðe, 690; imperative, þonne þu snúde geeȝð, then speak out quickly, 446; gerund, tô geeȝ-ȝanne, 533; show, reveal, 595; opt. pres. geeyðe, 1091; p.p. geeȝðed, 816, 1050; geeȝðde . . . wundor, showed a miracle (i.e. worked a miracle), 866.

geeynd, f., nature; manna ge-cynd, nature of men, human nature, 735.

geeyrran, wv. I., turn [Ger. kehren], change; nama wæs ge-cyrred, the name was changed, 1061; geogoð is geeyrred, youth is .passed, 1205.

gedafenlic, becoming, suitable, proper, 1168.

gedôn, (S. 429), do, apply; tô hwan hio þa næglas . . . gedôn meahte, to what purpose she might apply these nails, 1158; show; gedô nú . . . forð béacen þin, show forth now thy sign, 784.

gedryht, f., multitude, host, 27, 737, 1290.

gedwola, m., error, heresy, 311, 371, 1041, 1119.

gedȳrslan, wv. II., honor, glorify; gedȳrsod, [451].

geearnian, wv. II., earn, deserve, 526.

geefnan, wv. I., accomplish, execute; hio geefnde swá, she executed it thus, 1015.

gefær, n., journey, warlike expedition, army, 68.

gefaran, sv. VI., go, depart, depart hence, die; gefærenne man, 872.

gefæstnian, wv. II., fasten, make fast : p.p. gefæstnod, 1068.

gefêa, m., joy, 195; gefêan, 870, 949, 980.

gefeallan, red. vb., fall; p.p. gefeallen, 651.

gefeoht, n., fight, combat, battle; þurh gefeoht, 646; æt gefeohte, in battle, 1184.

gefêon, sv. V. (1), rejoice, be delighted; contracted participle,(S. 373); ferhð gefêonde, the soul rejoicing, 174, 991; pret. pl. leode ge-fægon, the people were delighted, 1116. (2) rejoice at, glory in (with gen. of object of joy); weorces ge-feat, rejoiced at the work, 110, 849; ewên siðes gefeah, the queen gloried in the voyage, 247.

geferan, wv. I., fare, come, go; úp geferan, ascend, 736; feorran geferede, those come from afar, 993.

gefetian, wv. II., fetch, bring, 1053; gefetigean, 1161.

gefie, n., fraud, deceit; mid fæcne gefice, with delusive deceit, 577.

gefiit, n., contention, strife; ge-fiitu ræran, raise strife, 443; gefiitu rærdon, joined strife, 954.

gefrætwian, wv. II., fret, adorn; p.p. gefrætwad, 743.

gefrêge, known, 968.

gefremman, wv. I., do, perform, commit; gif wé . . . bôte gefrem-maþ, if we do repentance, 575; feala . . . wundra gefremede, 363 (cf. 779, 912); oft gê dyslice dǽd gefremedon, 386; þe wé gefremedon, which we committed. 402 (cf. 415, 818); effect (fram blindnesse bôte gefremede, 298); grant (miltse ge-fremede, 501).

gefriegan, sv. V., learn by inquiry, learn; p.p. gefrigen, 155; gefrægon, [1116].

gefrignan, sv. III., find out by asking, learn; pret. pl. gefrugnon, 172; gefrugnen, 1014.

gefullæstan, wv. I., help, 1151.

gefulwian, wv. II., baptize; p.p. gefulwad, 1014.

gefylgan, wv. I., follow, persist in (with dat.); gif gê þissum léase leng gefylgað, if you persist in this lie longer, 576.

gefyllan, wv. I., fill (opt. sg. gefylle, 680; p.p. gefylled, 452, 1143); finish, fulfil (opt. sg. gefylle, 1084; pret. sg. gefylde, 1071; p.p. gefylled, 1131, 1135).

gefȳsan, wv. I., hasten, incite, set in motion; flodas gefȳsde, 1270; with gen. be ready for; siðes gefȳsde, [22], 260.

gegearwian, wv. II., make ready, equip (p.p. gegearwod, 47); equip, supply (gäste gegearwod, provided with spirit, 889).

geglengan, wv. I., adorn, decorate; golde geglenged, 90.

gehæftan, wv. I., chain, hold captive, torture; hungre gehæfted, tortured by hunger, 613.

geheaðrian, wv. II., confine; in nêdcleofan nearwe geheaðrod, confined in its narrow prison, 1276.

gehealdan, red. vb., hold, observe; ond þæt forð gehéold, and observed it (i.e. Christianity) from that time forth, 192.

gehðu, f., care, grief, sorrow; acc. gehðu, 609; on gehðu, 667; dat. pl. gehðum, 322, [531].

gehigd, f., thought; heortan gehigdum, with the heart's thoughts, 1224.

gehladan, sv. VI., load; pret. pl. gehlôdon, 234.

gehlêða, m., companion, comrade; holtes gehlêða, the wood's companion, 113.

gehwâ, prn., each, every (with following gen.); gen. worda gehwæs, 569; dat. sg. daga, niða, beorna, manna gehwâm, 358, 465, 1187, 1229; acc. on healfa gehwæne, (548); dat. sg. fem. in ceastra gehwære, 973 (s. note 548).

gehwæðer, prn., each of two, either, both; gehwæðres wâ, woe in either event, 628; bega gehwæðres, in both respects, 964.

gehwær, adv., everywhere, [518], 1183.

gehweorfan, sv. III., turn; sé ðe tô bôte gehwearf, who turned to repentance, 1126.

gehwylc, prn. (with gen.), each; tǽcna gehwylces, 319 (cf. 423, 910, 1030, 1156, 1310); gumena gehwylcum, 278; scylda gehwylcre, 1313; féonda gehwylcne, 1179; þinga gehwylc, 409 (cf. 645, 1317); ânra gehwylc = each, 1287 (S. 347): (without following substantive), gehwylcne, 598: (as adj.), dǽdra gehwylcra, of all deeds, 1283.

gehȳdan, wv. I., hide, conceal; p.p. gehȳdde, 832; gehȳded, 1002.

gehȳnan, wv. I., bring low, humiliate, afflict, weaken, 923; hungre gehȳned, weakened by hunger, 720.

gehȳran, wv. I., hear, perceive, learn (by hearsay), 333, 364, 442, 511, 660, 709, 957, 1002, 1282; hear = hearken unto; swâ ðû gehȳrdest þone hálgan wer, as Thou heardest that holy man, 785.

gehyrstan, wv. I., adorn, decorate; golde gehyrsted, 331.

gehyrwan, wv. I, neglect; word gehyrwan, 221.

geiewan, geŷwan, wv. I., show; pret. geŷwdest, 787; geŷwde, 488; p.p. geŷwed, 74, 183; geiewed, 102. [**geléecan,** 43; translated by Kemble, move.]

geléedan, wv. I., lead, conduct; hine . . . ûp geléeddon of carcerne, they led him up out of prison, 714.

geléestan, wv. I., accomplish, carry out, perform, do (Ger. leisten); tô geléestenne, 1166; geléeste, 1197; exercise, practice, 1208.

geléafa, m., belief, faith, 491, 966, 1036, 1137.

geléafful, faithful, 960; geléaffull, 1048.

geléodan, red. vb., grow, increase; geloden under léafum, grown under leaves, 1227.

gelettan, wv. I., hinder; geletest láð werod, thou shalt hinder the hated crowd, 94.

gelic, like; englum gelice, like the angels, 1320; superl. adv. winde geliccost, very like the wind, 1272.

geliðan, sv. I., go, reach (syþþan tô hŷðe . . . geliden héefdon, after they had attained to the harbor (reached the harbor), 219); go, pass away, vanish (lifwynne geliden, vanished with the joy of living, 1269).

gelimpan, sv. III., happen (swâ hit gelamp, 271, 1155); befall, happen to, 441; succeed, be successful, 963.

gelŷfan, wv. I., believe, 518, 796.

gemang, n., troop, crowd; on gemang, among, etc.; on chénra gemang, into the hosts of the pure (i.e. among the pure), 96; on féonda gemang, in the midst of the enemies, 108 (cf. 118).

gemengan, wv. I., mix, mingle, contaminate; mâne gemengde, 1296.

gemêtan, wv. I., meet, find; p.p. gemeted, 871, 1013, 1225.

gemetgian, wv. II., moderate, temper; him gemetgaþ call éldes léoma, He tempers for them entirely the fire's glare, 1293.

gemôt, n., meeting, assembly; on gemôt, 279.

gemyltan, wv. I., melt; gemylted, 1312.

gemynd, n. f., memory, mind; on gemynd, in memory, 644; in gemynd comaþ, they come into mind, 1303; þe on gemynd nime, who taketh in mind (i.e. remembers), 1233; on gemynd begéat, He poured it into my mind, 1248.

gemynde, mindful; gemynde ymb, mindful of, 1004.

gemyndig, mindful, heedful (with ymb), 213; (with gen), 266, 819, 902, 940.

gên, adv., again, once again, 373, 925; moreover, furthermore, 1218; still, now, 1063, 1078, 1080, 1092.

gênewide, s. geagn-.

geneahhe, adv. enough, sufficiently, in the highest degree, very, 1065, 1158.

genêgan, wv. I., address; wordum genêgan, 385.

genemnan, wv. I., name; þára . . . sint . . . syx genemned, of these six are named, 741.

generian, wv. I., save; pret. generede, 163; generedon, 132; free, deliver (ond fram unclêenum eft generede déaðla gâstum, and he often delivered from the unclean spirits of devils, 301).

geniðla, m., enemy, enmity, hostility; oncyrran geniðlan, avert the enmity, 610; fram hungres geniðlan, by the hostile attacks of hunger, 701.

geniman, sv. IV., take; pret. sg. genam, 599.

gêoc, f., help, assistance, consolation; tó gêoce, 1139, 1247.

gêocend, helper (of God); gásta gêocend, 682; (also of Christ), 1077.

geofen, n., sea; ymb geofenes staeð, about the sea-coast, 227; ofer geofenes strêam, over the sea's current, 1201.

geogoð, f., youth; on geogoðe, in youth, 638; geogoð is gecyrred, youth is past, 1265.

geogoðhâd, m., period of youth, youth; geogoðhádes glæm, the joy of youth, 1267.

geolorand, m., yellow border, shield, 118.

gêomor, sad, saddened, 627; gêomrum, 922; pl. gêomre, 182, 322.

gêomormôd, sad at heart, sorrowful in mind; gêomormóde, 413, 555.

geond, prep. (with acc.), through, throughout, beyond; geond middangeard, 16, 1177 (cf. 278, 784, 969).

geopenigean, wv. II., open, reveal, disclose, 1102; pres. opt. geopenie, reveal, 792; p.p. geopenad, opened, 1231.

georn, zealous; georn on móde, zealous in spirit, 268.

georne, adv., zealously, eagerly, earnestly, 199, 216, 322, 413, 471, 600, 1157, 1171; exactly, accurately, 1163.

geornian, wv. II., desire, [1260].

geornlîce, adv., zealously, 1097, 1148.

gêotan, sv. II., pour; p.p. goten, 1133.

geræde, n., hæleða gerædum, for mediation with the men, (Grein, Pompe), 1054; hæleða gerædum, by the interposition of men (durch der Helden Anstiften, Grein), 1108 (veranstaltung, vermittlung?, Zupitza).

gereccean, wv. I., report, narrate, 649.

gerestan, wv. I., rest; ond geresteð nó, and resteth nevermore, 1083.

gerûm, n., room; on gerûm, away, apart, 320.

gerŷman, wv. I., make room, prolong, extend; tidum gerŷmde, extended with time (?), 1249.

gerŷne, n., secret; dryhtnes gerŷno, the secret of the Lord, 280; þæt gerŷne rihte, that true secret, 566; wryda geryno, secret of events, 589, 813.

gesælig, blessed, saved (Ger. selig), 956.

gesamnian, wv. II., assemble; p.p. gesamnod, 26, 282.

gesceâdan, red. vb., separate, decide; hild wæs gesceáden, the battle was decided, 149. (Cf. N. E. shed in watershed.)

gesceaft, f., creation (samod calle gesceaft, likewise all creation, 729; (of heaven), 1089; creature, 729 (?); callra gesceafta, of all creatures, 894); what is created, object (of the cross), þurh þá . . . gesceaft, 183, 1032.

gesceap, n., creature, object (of the cross); þurg þæt beorhte gesceap, 799.

gescrîfan, sv. I., prescribe, determine, decree; wyrd gescrâf, the Fate decreed, 1047.

gesceyrdan, wv. I., injure, destroy; heap wæs gesceyrded, the multitude was destroyed, 141.

gesceyrtan, wv. I., shorten, lessen, 141 (?).

gesêcan, wv. I., seek; dôm gesêceð, He seeketh judgment (i.e. comes to pass judgment), 1280; pret. gesôhte, 230, 255, 270.

geseegan, geseeggan, wv. I., say, speak, proclaim; geseeggan, speak, 168; geseegan, proclaim, announce, 985.

gesêðan, wv. I., verify, prove, 582.

geseft, softened, mild, pleasant; superl. geseftost, most pleasant, 1295.

gesêon, sv. V., see, 1308; gesion, 243; pres. pl. gesêoð, 1121; pret. sg. geseah, 88, 100; geseh, 842; pret. pl. gesâegon, 68; gesâwon, 1111; pret. sq. opt. gesêge, 75; p.p. gesegen, shown (?), 71 (S. 391.2).

gesettan, wv. I., set, place, put, destine, determine, [614]; tô þegnunge þinre gesettest, Thou predestinedst (them) to Thy service, 739; þæt hê gesette on sacerhad ... Judas, that he should establish Judas in the priesthood, 1055.

gesihð, s. gesyhð.

gesîon, s. gesêon.

gesittan, sv. V., sit, sit down; gesæton, they sat down. 868.

gespon, n., plaiting, etc., web, twist; wîra gespon, twist of wires (nails), 1135.

gesprecan, sv. V., speak; pret. sg. opt. gespræce, 667; p.p. gesprecenra, 1285.

gesteald, n., dwelling, mansion; êcra gestealda, the eternal mansions, 802.

gesund [Ger. gesund], sound, healthy, happy, prosperous; gesundne sîð, a prosperous voyage, 997.

gesweorcan, sv. III., darken, grow dark; rodor eal gesweare, the whole heavens grew dark, 856.

geswerigan, sv. VI., swear; ic þæt geswerige þurh sunu meotodes, this I swear by the Son of the Creator, 686.

geswîcan, sv. I., omit, forsake, cease from (with gen.); þæs unrihtes eft geswicaþ, we cease again from this unrighteousness, 516.

geswiðrian, wv. II., lessen, diminish, weaken; p.p. geswiðrod, 698, 918; geswiðrad, 1264.

gesyhð, f., sight, view, appearance, a vision; þurh þá fægeran gesyhð, on account of this joyful vision, 98; æt þære gesyhðe, at this sight, 965; on gesyhðe, in a vision, 184; in sight, visible, 346; in sight, 847; on gesihðe, before his eyes, in sight, 614.

gesyllan. wv. I., give, 1284.

gesŷne, visible, evident, clear; þá wæs gesŷne, 144, 264.

getâecan, wv. I., show, reveal (2d p. sg. pret. getâehtesð, 1075), impart; pret. opt. getâehte, 601.

getellan, wv. I., tell, count; geteled rimes, 2; geteled rime, 634.

getengan, wv. I., devote, dedicate; hine ... sylfne getengde ... in godes þeowdôm, and devoted himself to the service of God, 200.

getenge, resting on, near, adjacent; sunde getenge, resting on the sea, 228; grunde getenge (lying on the ground), near the surface, 1114.

getimbrian, wv. I. and II., build, erect; getimbrede, 1010.

getrȳwe, true, faithful; Criste getrȳwe, 1035.

getȳd, taught, skilled, practised; cræftum getȳde, skilled in arts, 1018.

getȳnan, wv. I., shut in, enclose, bury, getȳnde, 921; getȳned, 722.

geþanc, m., thought; on geþance, 267, 807; geþanc, 1239; geþonca, 1286; geþancum, 312.

geþeaht, f., reflection, consideration, counsel; þurh snyttro geþeaht, through the counsel of wisdom, 1060; næfre ic þā geþeahte . . . sēcan wolde, I was never willing to visit the conferences, etc., 468; knowledge; rûmran geþeaht, more extended knowledge, 1241.

geþencean, wv. I., think, consider, think of; snyttro geþenceþ weras wisfæste, in prudence think of your wisest men, 313.

geþinge, n., fate; bidan beorna geþinges, await the fate of the men, 253.

geþôht, m., thought; þæt wæs þrêalic geþôht, that was a horrible thought, 426.

geþolian, wv. II., endure, suffer, 1292.

geþone, s. geþanc.

geþrêan, wv. III. (S. 416, n. 4); torture, torment, oppress; egesan geþrêade, with fear oppressed, 321.

geþrêatian, wv. II. persecute; hungre geþrêatod, persecuted with hunger, 695.

geþrec, n., rush; beorna geþrec, 114.

geþringan, sv. III., overcome, devastate, 40.

geþrôwian, wv. II., endure, bear, suffer; pret. sg. geþrôwade, 519, 563; geþrôwode, 859; pret. pl. geþrôwdon, 855.

gewadan, sv. VI., go, advance, press in; sefa dêop gewôd, the mind pressed in to great depth, 1190.

gewǣlan, wv. I., torture, pain; sorgum gewǣled, pained by sorrows, 1244.

geweald, n., might, power [Ger. gewalt]; þurh fingra geweald, through the fingers' power, 120; dôma geweald, power over the wills, 726; on þǣre cwêne gewealdum, in the power of this queen, 610.

gewendan, wv. I., wend, turn; gewended tô wuldre, turned toward heaven, 1047; gewende tô wǣdle, turns to poverty, 617.

geweorðan, sv. III., be, become, happen, occur, 456, 611; pres. cûþ þæt gewyrðeð, this will become known, 1192; swige gewyrðeð, it becomes still, 1275; on gesihðe . . . geweorðað, they become visible, are before his eyes, 614; pret. sg. gewearð, happened, occurred, 632, 641; became, was, 923; pret. pl. gewurdon, were, 1288; p.p. hu is þæt geworden, how has that happened? 643; wæs him frôfra mǣst geworden in worlde, to them the greatest of consolations was come in the world, 994.

geweorðian, wv. II., distinguish, honor; wigge geweorðod, distinguished in battle, 150 (cf. 823, 1193 [1196]); in þrȳnesse þrymme geweorðad, honored in the glory of the Trinity, 177.

gewerian, wv. I., cover over,

clothe; hilderincas hyrstum gewerede, the knights in armor clad, 263.

gewîtan, sv. I., go; pret. gewât . . . hâm, he went home, 148; go away, vanish, 1272, 1277; gewât, 94.

gewitt, n., wits, understanding, mind; wisdômes gewitt, understanding of wisdom, 357, 1190 (cf. 459, 938).

gewlencan, wv. I., adorn, decorate, bedeck; wirum gewlenced, bedecked with metal wires, 1264.

gewrit, n., writ, scripture, book; gewritu herwdon, you neglected the Scriptures, 387; on gewritu setton, put in writing (i.e. record), 654, 658; nom. pl. gewritu, 674; prt. pl. on gewritum, in writing, 827, 1256.

gewunian, wv. II., dwell in, inhabit; siððan frôfre gást wíc gewunode, after the Spirit of consolation inhabited the dwelling, 1038.

gewyrcan, wv. I., work, construct, 104; create (þû geworhtest, Thou createdst, 727, 738); commit (þéah wê ðbylgð . . . gewyrcen, though we commit transgression, 513).

gewyrd, f., event, occurrence, 647.

geðwan, s. geîewan.

gidd, n., song, speech; gidda gearosnotor, skilled in speech, 418 (cf. [531 ¹], 586) (s. gearusnotter).

gif, if (with ind.), 435, 459, 514, 533, 576, 1004; (with opt.), 441, 542, 621, 773, 777, 782, 789, 857.

gifan, sv. V., give (gifað, 360); grant (geaf, 365).

gifu, f., gift, present, benefit, grace, favor, 265; acc. godspelles

gife, 176 (cf. 596, 1144); gife, 182, 967, 1033, 1201, 1247; þurh gástes gife, 199, 1058, 1157.

gildan, sv. III., yield, return, repay; ne geald hê yfel yfele, he did not return evil for evil, 493.

gim, m., gem; gimmas lixtan, the gems glistened, 90.

gîman, wv. I., care for, be careful of, pay attention to, observe (with gen.); hlâfes ne gíme, and take no notice of the loaf, 616.

gimcyn, n., kind of gems, precious stones; gimcynnum, 1024.

gîna, yet, still, 1070.

ging, young, 353, 464, 875; (comp. gingra, 159).

gio, once, 436.

girwan, wv. I., prepare, erect; girwan godes tempel, to build a temple of God, 1022.

gîsel, m., hostage; tô gisle, as a hostage, 600.

glæd, bright, gleaming, glad; þê glædra, the gladder, 956.

glædmôd, glad at heart, 1096.

glǽm, m., gleam, splendor, joy; ûr wæs géara geogoðhádes glǽm, in the days of yore the buffalo was the joy of youth, 1265.

glêaw, skilled, sagacious, wise, 594, 638, 807, 1163, 1212; superl. þà glêawestan, the wisest, 536.

glêawhðdig, wise-in-mind, 935.

glêawlîce, adv., prudently, wisely, 189.

glêawnes, f., wisdom, prudence; glêawnesse þurhgoten, impregnated with wisdom, 962.

glêd, f., heat, fire, flames (Ger. glut); in glêda gripe, in the grip of the flames, 1302.

gnornian, wv. II., be sorrowful, moan, bemoan; ŷr gnornode nŷdgefera, the bow bemoaned its companion in need, 1260.

gnornsorg, f., sadness, sorrow; gnornsorge wæg, he bore his sorrow, 655; gnornsorga mæst, the greatest of sorrows, 977.

gnyrn, f., sadness, 1139; wrong, blemish; eallra gnyrna léas, free from all blemishes, 422.

gnyrnwräᵉc, f., revenge for wrong; nales gnyrnwræcum, in nowise with revenge for wrong, 359.

god, m., God, 4, etc.; gen. godes, 109, etc.; dat. gode, 965, 1135; acc. god, 209, etc.

gôd, good; gen. pl. gôdra, 637; substantive good; gôda geâsne, poor in goods, 924.

godbearn, n., God's Son, Christ, 719.

godcund, godlike, divine; godcunde gife, 1033.

gôddênd, pl., benefactors, 359.

godgimmas, m., pl., heavenly jewels (gottes gemmen, sterne des himmels, Gm.), (jewels, Kemble), [1114].

godspel, n., gospel; godspelles gife, 170.

gold, n., gold; swâ smæᵗe gold, as purified gold, 1309; æplede gold, appled gold, 1260 (s. note, 1260); instr. golde, 90, 331, 1024.

goldgim, m., goldgem; goldgimmas, 1114.

goldhoma, m., garment ornamented with gold; unter goldhoman, among the gold-bespangled (garments), 992.

goldhord, n., gold hoard, treasure of gold, treasure, 791.

goldwine, gold distributing friend, ruler, king (of Constantine), 201.

gomen, n., game, rejoicing, joy, pleasure, 1265.

gong, s. gang.

gram, hostile; on gramra gemang, in the midst of the hostile, 118; gramum gûðgeláᵉcan, against the hostile warriors, 42.

grâp, f., grasp, clutch; grâpum gryrefæst, terribly firm in grasp, 760.

grêot, m., grit, sand, earth; grêote begrauene, covered with sand, 835.

grim, grim, fierce, angry; grimme geagnewide, angry contradiction, 525.

grîma, m., helmet; gylden grima, 125.

grîmhelm, mark-helm, helmet, (with visor), 258.

gring, f. n. (?) slaughter, downfall; herga gring, fall of the masses, 114.

gringan, sv. III., fall, perish; hæðene grungon, the heathens fell, 126. (For gring and grinnan, compare cring and cringan.)

gripe, m., gripe, grip, grasp; in gléda gripe, in the flames' grip, 1302.

grund, m., ground, bottom; grunde getenge, near the surface (or on the ground?), 1114; in wylmes grunde, on the bottom of the waves of fire, 1299; earth (ofer sidne grund, throughout the wide earth, 1289); bottom, abyss (in sûsla grund, into the abyss of tortures, 944).

gryrefæst, terribly firm, 760.

gûð, f., battle, combat, 23, [43].

gûðcwên, queen of battle (of Helen), 254, 331.

gûðgeláᵉca, warrior; gramum

gūðgelǽcan, against the hostile warriors, 43.

gūðheard, brave in battle (of Constantine), 204.

gūðrōf, renowned in battle, renowned, 273.

gūðscrūd, n., battle-dress; geatolic gūðscrūd, 258.

gūðweard, ward of battle, leader, prince; gūðweard gumena, 14.

guma, m., man (human being), 464, 531; pl. guman, 561, 1186; gen. pl. gumena, 14, 201, 254, 278, 638, 1096, 1203.

gumrīce, n., kingdom of men, kingdom; on þām gumrice, 1221.

gylden, golden, 125.

gylt, m., guilt, sin; minra gylta, of my guilty actions, sins, 817.

II.

habban, wv. III., anv. (1) have, hold, possess, 621; 3d p. sg. ind. hafað, 825; pres. opt. sg. hæbbe, 594; opt. pl. hæbben, 316, 408; pret. ind. sg. hæfde, 63, 1253; pret. pl. hæfdon, 49, 381. (2) auxiliary vb., have; 1st p. sg. ind. hafu, 808 (S. 416 1); 3d p. sg. hafað, 910; opt. pres. sg. hæbbe, 288; pret. sg. ind. hæfde, 224, 412, 1130, 1254; pret. pl. hæfdon, 155, 249, 369, 415, 870, 998.

hād, m., rank, class; þara on hāde sint . . . syx genemned, of those in this class six are named, 749; shape, form (on weres hāde, in the form of a man, 72; in cildes hād, in the form of a child, 72, 336, 776; þurh lēohtne hād, in a glorious manner, 1246 [s. note, 1246]) (N. E. suffix hood).

hǽder, bright, clear (Ger. heiter); hædrum stefnum, with clear voices, 748.

hǽðen, heathen, 126, 1076.

hæft, m., bondage, imprisonment, 703.

hæftnēd, f., necessity of captivity, bondage, thraldom; of hæftnēde, 297.

hǽl, f., hail, health; Elenan hǽl ābēodan, to bid Helen hail, 1003.

hæleð, m., man, hero, warrior, 511, 640, 936; acc. sg. hæleð, 538; nom. acc. pl. hæleð (S. 281 2), 273, 1006, 1297; gen. pl. hæleða, 73, 156, 188, 852, 1054, 1108, 1204; dat. pl. hæleðum, 661, 671, 679, 700, 1012, 1273.

hǽland, m., healer, Saviour (Ger. heiland), (of God), 726; (of Christ), 800, 862, 912, 920, 1063.

hālig, holy (attributive), 218, 625, 679, 740, 751, 843, 885, 936, 976, 1087, 1145, 1195; f. hālige rime, 333, 1169 (cf. 720, 1012, 1224); n. þæt hālige trēo, 107, 128, 429, 442, 701, 841; m. se hālga god, 751; dat. tō þǽre hālgan byrig, 1006, 1054, 1201; acc. m. þone hālgan wer, 785; acc. f. þurh þā hālgan gesceaft, 1032; acc. n. hālig, 758; acc. pl. þurh hālige bēc, 364, 670, 853; (substantive), se hālga, 1094; þæs hālgan, 86; on þone hālgan, 457; hāligra, 821; hālgum, 988.

hǽlo, f., health, healing, cure, 1216.

hām, m., home; in þām engan hām, in that narrow home (i.e. hell), 921; acc. hām, home, 143, 148.

hand, f., hand; mid bǽm handum, with both hands, 805 (cf. 843); handa sendan, lay hands (on), 457.

handgeswing, n., swing of the

hånds, combat; heard handgeswing, 115.

bǣs, f., behest; þurh þæs hålgan hæs, at the behest of this holy one, 86.

håt, hot, 628, 1133; in håtne wylm, 1297; superl. håttost, 579.

håtan, red. vb. (1) call, name (hê wæs . . . be naman håten, he was called by name, 505; be naman håteð, 756). (2) bid, order, enjoin, command; pret. sg. heht, 42, 79, 99, 105, 129, 153, 276, 691, 863, 877, 999, 1003, 1007, 1023, 1051, 1101, 1198, 1202; hêt, 214; pret. sg. opt. hehte, 509; imperative, håt, 1173.

hê, he, 9, 13, etc.; she, hêo, 570, 1136; hio, 268, 325, 420, 568, 569, 571, 598, 710; it, hit, 170, 271, etc.; gen., his, his, 147, 162; her, hiere, 222; hire, 1200; dat., him, him, 18, 72, etc.; her, hire, 223, 567, etc.; acc., him, hine, 14, 200, etc.; it, hit, 350, 702; pl. nom. and acc., they and them, hie, 48, 175, etc.; hêo, 116, 254, etc.; hio, 166, 324, etc.; gen. pl., their, hiera, 360; hira, 174, 359; dat. pl., them, him, 173, 182, etc.

heaðofremmende, giving battle, fighting, 130.

heaðowelm, m. (war-wave), fierce flame; hottost heaðowelma, 579; of þām heaðuwylme, 1305.

hêafodwylm, m., tears; håt hêafodwylm, 1133.

hêah, high, on hêanne bêam, 424; ofer hêanne holm, beyond the high sea, 983; superl. hihst (197?).

hêahengel, m., archangel, 751.

hêahmǣgen, m., high strength, mighty power; godes hêahmǣgen, 464 (cf. 753).

healdan, red. vb., hold; rîce healdan, to hold dominion, 449;

hold, keep, preserve, observe; opt. sg. pres. þæt dû dryhtnes word healde, 1169; pret. sg. hê wǣre wið þec . . . hêold, he kept his faith in (toward) thee, 824; pret. pl. hêoldon . . . hæleða rǣdas, 156; hold, defend, keep (lifes trêo . . . hâlig healdan, to keep the tree of life undefiled, 758).

healf, f., side; on healfa gehwǣne, 548 (s. note, 548); on twâ halfa, 955; on twâ healfe, 1180.

healfcwic, half-quick, half-alive, half-dead, 133.

healsian, wv. II., adjure; ic ðow healsie þurh heofona god, 699.

healt, halt, 1215.

hêan, abject, poor, miserable, 1216; depressed, 701.

hêanne, s. hêah, hêan.

hêannes, f., height; on hêannesse, on high, 1125.

hêap, m., heap, troop, multitude, army, 141, 269, 549, 1206.

heard, hard; on heardum hige, in my hard heart, 809; comp. stane heardran, harder than stones, 565; hard, cruel, terrible (heardre hilde, with cruel battle, 83); heard hundgeswing, hard combat, 115; strict, imperative (þurh heard gebann, by imperative order, 557); hard (to bear), severe, intolerable (witum heardum, with intolerable tortures, 180; cf. 704).

hearde, adv., fiercely, very; hearde . . . corre, very angry, 400.

heardecg, hard of edge, sharp-edged, 758.

hearding, m., bold man, hero; heardingas, 25, 130.

hearm, m., harm, injury; feala mê hearma gefremede, he did me . . . many injuries, 912.

hearmloca, m., place of affliction, prison; under hearmlocan, 695.

hebban, sv. VI., raise, lift, 107; pret. pl. hôfon, 25; p.p. hafen, 123, 890.

heht, s. hâtan.

hel, f., hell; helle duru, 1230.

helan, sv. IV., cover, hide, conceal; leng helan, 703, 706.

helledêofol, m., devil of hell, 901.

hellegrund, m., abyss of hell, 1305.

hellesceada, m., hellish enemy, devil; þone hellesceaþan, 957.

helm, m., helmet, protector (of Constantine), 148, 223; (of Christ), 176, 475.

help, f., help; tô helpe, 679, 1012; acc. helpe, 1032.

hêo, n., hue, form; þurh mennisc hêo, in human form, 6.

heofen, heofon, 728, heofun, 753, m. (1) heaven, 728, 753; heofones, 1230; heofona, 699; heofonum, 188, 527; heofenum, 801. (2) heavens (heofenum, 83, 976; heofonum, 101).

heofoncyning (cining), m., King of Heaven, 170, 367, 748.

heofonlic, heavenly, 740, 1145.

heofonrîce, n., kingdom of heaven; heofonrices weard, 197, 445, 718; heofonrices god, 1125; heofonrices hyht, 629; in heofonrice, 621.

heofonsteorra, m., star of heaven; swylce heofonsteorran, 1113.

heolstor, n., darkness, concealment, 1082, 1113.

heolstorhof, n., dark dwelling; under heolstorhofu (of hell), 764.

heorte, f., heart; gen. sg. heortan, 1224; dat. sg. æt heortan, 628.

heorucumbul, n., standard of war, ensign, 107.

heorudrêorig, sword-gory, bloody, 1215.

heorugrim, savagely, fierce; hetend heorugrimme, dire enemies, 119.

hêr, adv., here; bûtan hêr nûða, except here now, 661.

here, m., army, multitude, troops; 65; gen. sg. herges, 143; heriges, 205; dat. sg. herge, 52; acc. sg. here, 58; gen. pl. heria, 101; herga, 115, 210; heriga, 148; dat. pl. hergum, 32, 41, 110, 180; herigum, 406.

herebyrne, f., war corselet, [22].

herecumbol, n., battle-standard, ensign, 25 (?).

herefeld, m., battle-field, field; on herefelda, 126; ofer herefeldas, 269.

heremægen, n., warlike force, multitude; for þâm heremægene, 170.

heremeðel, n., assembly of the people, assembly; tô þâm heremeðle, 550.

hererêswa, m., warrior, leader of the army; him hererêswan, to him the leader of the army (of Constantine), 995.

heresîð, m., warlike expedition, 133.

heretêma, m., army-leader; âhæfen ... tô heretêman, raised to leader of the forces, 10.

hereweorc, n., army-work, battle; þæs hereweorces, 666.

hereþrêat, m., army's troop, cohort; on þâm hereþrêate, 265.

herg, s. here.

hergan, herian, wv. I., praise, adore; (with reference to God), god hergendra, 1097; god hergendum, 1221; (with reference to Christ), ðe þone åhangnan cyning heriad, 453; sunu wealdendes ... heredon, 893.

herla, s. here.

herigean, wv. III. (?), despise; ic þå rôde ne þearf hleatre herigean, I dare not despise this cross with the laughter of scorn, 920.

herwan, wv. I., neglect, scorn, despise; ac hie hyrwdon mê, but they despised me, 355; ond gewritu herwdon, and the scriptures neglected, 387.

hete, m., hate; þurh hete, 24.

hetend, pl., haters, enemies; wið hetendum, against the enemies, 18; hetend heorugrimme, dire enemies, 119. (Cf. hettend.)

Hierusalem, 273, Jerusalem, 1056; Jerusalem (s. note, 273).

hige, s. hyge.

higefrôfor, f., consolation for the heart, heart-consolation, 355.

higegléaw, of wise mind, prudent; gehýraðð, higegléawe, hålige rûne, hear, O ye of wise minds, the holy secret, 333.

higeþanc, m., thought of the mind; higeþancum, 156.

hild, f., battle, fight, combat, 18, [22]; dat. tô hilde, 32, 49, 52, 65; instr. hilde, 83.

hildedêor, daring in battle, brave in battle, 936.

hildegesa, m., terror of battle; hildegesa stôd, terror of battle spread, 113.

hildemecg, m., warrior, [22].

hildenædre, battle-adder, warsnake, missile; hildenædran, arrows (?), 119; spears, 141.

hilderinc, m., warrior, hero; hilderincas hyrstum gewerede, battle-knights in armor clad, 263.

hildeserce f., battle-sark, coat of mail, 234.

hildfruma, m., battle-prince (of Constantine), 10, 101.

hîwbeorht, bright of hue, beautiful, brilliant, 73.

hlâf, m., loaf, bread, 613; hlâfes, 616.

hlæfdige, f., lady, 400; hlæfdige mîn, 656 (of Helen).

hlâford, m., lord (of Constantine), 265, 475, 983.

hleahtor, m., laughter of scorn; hleatre, 920.

hlêapan, red. vb., leap, run, 54 (s. note, 54).

hlêo, m., protection; under swegles hlêo, under the protection of heaven, 507; wið hundres hlêo, as a protection against hunger, 616; protector, shield; (of Constantine), æðelinga hlêo, 99; wigena, 150; (of Judas), eorla, 1074.

hlêoðrian, wv. II., (utter sounds), speak, 901.

hlêor, n., cheek, 1099, 1133.

hlihan (hlihhan), sv. VI., laugh, laugh for joy, rejoice; hlihende hyge, the heart rejoicing, 995.

[hlôwan, red. vb., low, roar, blow loudly; hlêowon hornboran, the trumpeters blew loudly, 54.] (See hleapan.)

hlûd, loud, 1273.

hlûde, adv., loudly, 110, 406.

hlýt, m., lot, portion, throng; mid håligra hlýte, with the throng of the holy, 821.

hnâg, debased, deplorable; wênde him tráge hnágre, feared the deplorable evil, 668.

hnesce, soft, 615.

hof, n., court-yard, house, dwelling (Ger. hof); tô hofe, to court, 557; fram þám engan hofe, out of this narrow dwelling (Judas' prison), 712; in þám réonian hofe, in this sad spot (of the burial place of the crosses), 834.

holm, m., rounded height (cf. N. 983) [230]; ofer hêanne holm, over the high sea, 983.

holmþracu, f., tossing of the sea, restless sea, 728.

holt, n., forest, wood; holtes gehlêða, 113. (N.E. holt.)

hôn, red. vb., hang, crucify; pret. pl. hengon, 424; p.p. hangen, 852.

hord, n., hoard, treasure; hord under hrûsan, 1092.

horh, filth, defilement; instr. horu, 297 (S. 242. 2).

hornbora, m., hornbearer, trumpeter; hornboran, 54.

horu, s. horh.

hospewide, m., contemptuous words, insulting, scornful speech, 522.

hrâ, n., body, 579; body without life, corpse, 885.

hraðe, adv., quickly, straightway, promptly, 76, 406, 669, 710.

hrædlîce, adv., quickly, 1087.

Hrêðas, same as Hrêðgotan.

hrêðer, m. (?), the inside, soul, 1145.

hreðerloca, m., inclosure of the interior, breast; hreðerlocan onspéon, opened his bosom, 86.

Hrêðgotan, the renowned Goths, 20.

hrefen, m., raven, 52; hrefn, 110.

hrêmig, rejoicing, exulting (with instr.); hûðe hrêmig, exulting in booty, 149; blissum hrêmig, exulting with joy, 1138.

[hreodian, 1239 (zittern, Leo).]

hrêof, rough, leprous; hrêofe, 1215.

hrêosan, sv. II., fall, 764.

hring, m., ring, sound; wôpes hring, sound of weeping, 1132.

hringedstefna, m., ringed-prow (vessels with prows provided with rings for making them fast to the land); hringstefnan, 248.

hrôðer, m., joy, consolation, delight; tô hrôðer, 10, 1100.

hrôf, m., roof; ofer wolcna hrôf, upon the roof of the clouds, 89.

hrôpan, red. vb., call, proclaim, make proclamation; hrêopan friecan, 54, 550.

hrôr, strong, brave; hrôrra tô hilde, of the brave in battle, 65.

hrûse, f., earth; under hrûsan, 218, 625, 843, 1092.

hû, adv., how (in dir. interr.), 456, 611, 632, 643; (in indir. interr.), 176, 179, 185, 335, 367, 474, 512, 561, 954, 960, 997.

hûð, f., plunder, booty; hûðe hrêmig, 149.

Hûgas, pl., proper name, (21?).

Hûnas, pl., Huns, [21]; gen. pl. Hûna, 20, 32, 41, 49, 58, 128, 143.

hund, n., hundred; tû hund, 2; d, = fif hund, 379; ee, = tû hund, 634.

hungor, m., hunger; hungres, 616, 701; dat. hungre, 703; instr. hungre, 613, 687, 695, 720.

hûru, adv., verily, certainly, 1045, 1150.

hûs, n., house, frame; þæt fæge hûs, that doomed frame, 881; þurh þæt fæcne hûs, on account of this uncertain human body (*i.e.* frame), 1237.

hwæðre, adv., however, yet; hwæðre . . . nyste, yet he did not know, 719.

hwan (from hwâ); tô hwan, to what (purpose), 1158.

hwǽr, interr. adv., where (in indir. interr.), 205, 217, 429, 563, 624, 675, 720, 1103.

hwæt (from hwâ), n., what (in indir. interr.); hwæt se god wǽre, 161; hwæt sio syn wære, 414; þurh hwæt, etc., 400; (in indir. interr., with gen.), hwæt . . . þǽs, 532, 608, 1165; hwæt þæs wǽre dryhtnes willa, 1160; hwæt þǽr eallra wæs on manrîme morðorslehtes, dareðlâcendra dêadra gefeallen, 649; (in dir. interr.), hwæt is þis, 903; (interjection), forsôoth! indeed! how! etc., 293, 334, [357], 364, 397, 670, 853, 920.

hwæt (sharp), bold, brave; hwate wǽras, 22.

hwætêadig, rich in courage, very brave; se hwætêadig, the brave man, 1195.

hwætmôd, bold in mind, courageous; hæleð hwætmôde, 1006.

hwîl, f., while, time; sume hwile, somewhile (?), 479; acc. hwile nû, now for a while, 582, 625; dat. pl. hwilum, sometimes, once [1252].

hwît, white, 73.

hwonne, adv., when, until; bîdan . . . hwonne, to wait . . . until, 254.

hwôpan, red. vb. (whoop), threaten with; acc. pers. and dat. of thing, þê elþêodige egesan hwôpan, the enemies threaten thee with terror, 82.

hwurfe [629], excederet (Grimm).

hwyle, prn., which, what; on hwyleum þâra bêama, 851; on hwylene, 862.

hwyrft, m., course; dat. pl. geâra hwyrftum, in the course of years, 1.

hycgan, wv. III., think, hope, [629].

hŷdan, wv. I., hide, conceal; p.p. hŷded, 218; hŷdde, 1108.

hŷð, f., harbor, haven; tô hŷðe, 258.

hyder, adv., hither; sume hyder, sume þyder, 548.

hyge, m., mind, heart, soul; hige onhyrded, the soul strengthened, 841; hlihende hyge, the rejoicing heart, 995; min hige, 1082; dat. sg. on heardum hige, in my hard heart, 809; on hyge, in thy heart, 1160; acc. sg. hyge, 685, 1094.

hygegeômor, of sad heart, mournful, 1216; bigegeômre, 1297.

hygerûn, f., heart's secret; hygerûne ne mâð, he did not keep back the secret of his heart, 1099.

hyht, m., hope, joy; acc. sg. heofonrices hyht (629?); hyht untwêonde, an unwavering hope, 798; gen. pl. hyhta hihst, the highest (of) joy(s), 197.

hyhtful, full of joy; ic þurh Iûdas ǽr hyhtful gewearð, 923.

hyhtgifa, giver of joy (of Christ); hæleða hyhtgifa, the mens' Giver of joy, 852.

hŷnð, or hŷnðo, oppression, affliction, misery; in hŷnðum, 210.

hŷran, wv. I. (1) hear, learn [1st p. pret. sg. hyrde, 240; pret. pl. hyrdon, 538, 572, 670, 853]. (2) hear, hearken, obey (with dat.) [heofoncyninge hŷran sceoldon, should hearken to the King of Heaven, 367; pret. sg. 2d p. þām ðū hýrdest ǣr, whom thou formerly obeyedst, 934; pret. pl. lārum ne hýrdon, they did not obey the teachings, 839 (cf. 1210)].

hyrde, m. (-herd), keeper, guardian (Ger. hirt); þrymmes hyrde, 348, 859.

hyrst, f., armor; hyrstum gewerede, 263.

byrwan, s. herwan.

hyse, m., youth, young man, son; hyse lēofesta, dearest son, 523.

I.

ic, prn., I, 240, 288, 319, and often.

ican, wv. I., eke, increase; iceð ealdne nið, increases the old hate, 905.

ides, f., woman, wife, queen (of Helen), 405; dat. idese, 229; acc. sg. idese, 241.

Ierusalem, s. Hierusalem.

ilca, prn. (with def. art.), the same; þurh þā ilcan gesceaft, 183; þæt ilce, 436.

ilde, s. elde.

in, prep. (1) with dat. in (in rīce, 9; in þrýnesse þrymme, 177; in fýrðe, 196; in hynðum, 210 [cf. 391, 412, 425, 484, and often]); upon (þone mǣran dæg . . . in ðām, that glorious day . . . upon which, 1224); on, upon (in cynestōle, on the throne, 330; in beorge, upon the mountain, 578). (2) (with acc.) in, into (in middangeard, 6, 775; in godes þēowdōm, 201, etc., 274, 305, 693, 765, 775, 931, 913, 944, 1026, 1089, 1205, 1287, 1297, 1299, 1302, 1303, 1305; in cildes hād (ā)cenned, 336, 776; in lēoht cymen,

to come to light: [temporal] in woruld weorulda, in the world of worlds [i.e. in eternity], 452; in hira lifes tid, during their lifetime (s. note, 1209), 1209).

in, adv., in (bil in dufan, plunged the sword in, 122); in, into (ēodon . . . in on þā ceastre, they went [within] into the city, 846).

inbryrdan, s. onbryrdan.

ingemynd, f., n., inward thought, ardent thought, 1253.

ingemynde, impressed; on ferhð-sefan ingemynde, impressed upon the minds, 896.

ingeþanc, m., inner thought, earnest thought; feores ingeþanc, 680.

innoð, inner parts, breast; æðelne innoð, the noble breast, 1146.

innan, adv., within (on innan); prep. with dat. within, in (burgum on innan, within the cities, 1057).

instæpes, adv., on the spot, immediately, 127.

inwit, n., iniquity; þurh inwit, through wickedness, 207.

inwitþanc, m., wicked thought; inwitþancum wrōht webbedan, wove crime with wicked thoughts, 308.

inwrēon, s. onwreon.

Ioseph, Joseph; bān Iosephes, Joseph's bones, 788.

is, 3d p. sg. pres. is, 426, 465, 512, 553, 591, 593, 633, 636, 643, 703, 750-752, 771, 822, 903, 906, 917, 918, 1123, 1168, 1204, 1265.

Israhēlas, pl. Israelites; gen. pl. Israhēla, 338, 361, 433, 800.

Iūdas, (1) Judas Iscariot, 922; (2) Judas (afterwards Cyriacus), 418, 586, 600, 609, 627, 655, 667, 682, 807, 860, 875, 924, 935, 1033, 1050 (undeclined).

Iûdêas, pl. Jews; gen. pl. Iûdêa, 206, 268, 837; dat. pl. Iûdêum, 216, 328, 977, 1203; acc. Iudeas, 278.

îwan, wv. I., show [842].

K.

kalendas, pl., calends, first day of the Roman month; on maias kalendas, on the calends of May, 1229 (s. note, 1229).

L.

lâ, interj., lo! behold! forsooth! 903.

lâc, n., gift, present; acc. lâc, 1137; dat. tô lâce, as a present, 1200.

lâcan, red. vb., spring, jump; (of flames) flicker, flare (lâcende lig, flaring flame, 580, 1111); fly (lâcende fêond, flying enemy [of devil], 900).

lâð, loathsome, loathed, hated; geletest lâð werod, thou shalt hinder the hated crowd, 92; gen. pl. lâðra lindwered, the shield-bearing band of the loathed, 142; dat. pl. lâðum on lâste, behind the loathed ones, 32; superl. wyrda lâðost, the most detested of occurrences, 978.

lêdan, wv. I., lead, 241, 691; lead, hold (sê ðe foran lêdeð bridels on blancan, who holds in front the bridle on the white horse, 1184); spread (wide lêded, spread far, 969).

laðian, wv. II., invite, summon; 3d p. sg. pres. laðað, 551; p.p. laðode, 383; laðod, 556.

lâðlic, loathsome, hateful; lâðlic wîte, hated punishment, 520.

lago, m., lake, sea, ocean, name of the rune for l (ᚱ), 1269.

lagofæsten, n., water-fastness, sea; ofer lagofæsten, 249; ofer lagufæsten, 1017.

lagostrêam, m., water-stream, (of Danube) river; on lagostrêame, 137.

lama, m., a lame person; pl. laman, the lame, 1214.

land, n., land; acc. land, 270 (on Creca land, 256, 262, 999); land (earth) (landes frætwe, ornament of the land, 1271).

lêne, lent, transitory, 1271.

lang, long, 432.

lange, adv., long, 602, 723, 793, 1119; comp. leng, 576, 702, 706, 907.

lâr, f. (lore), teaching, instruction, doctrine (acc. lâre, 335, 368, 388, 432, 929; dat. pl. lârum, 839, 1210); instruction, advice, information (lâre, 1166, 1246; dat. sg. tô lâre, 286); advice, instigation (dat. pl. Sawles larum, at the instigation of Saul, 497).

lêran, wv. I., teach (Ger. lehren), instruct (pret. sg. lêrde, 529:) p.p. lêrde, 173, 191; exhort, urge (1st p. sg. pres. lêre, 522; lêran, 1206).

lârsmið, m., teacher; þurh lârsmiðas, 203.

lês, adv., less; (conj.) þý lês, lest; (with opt.) þý lês tóworpen sîen, lest there be destroyed, etc., 430.

lêssa, comp., less; werod lêsse, less men, 48.

lâst, m., trace, track (cf. shoe-last); on lâste, = behind; lâðum on lâste, 30.

lêstan, wv. I., perform, carry out, follow; lâre lêstan, to follow the teaching, 368.

lǽtan, red. vb., let, allow, cause; imper. lǽt mec . . . wunigan, let me dwell, etc., 819; pret. sg. leort ðā tācen forð . . . ūp ēðigean, He caused the sign to ascend, 1105; pret. pl. léton . . . scriðan, they let . . . stride, 235; céolas léton æt sǽfearoðe . . . bidan, they let the ship await at the seashore, etc., 250.

late, adv., late, 708.

lǻttēow, m., leader; lifes lǻttiow, 620, 899; gen. sg. lǻttēowes, 1210.

lēaf, n., leaf, foliage; under lēafum, 1227.

leahtor, m., reproach, sin; leahtra fruman lārum, to the teachings of the source of sins, 839.

leahtorlēas, sinless, 1209.

lēan, n., reward, gift; wigges lēan, a warrior's reward, 825.

lēas, loose, free (with gen.), 422, 497, 778; free, deprived, robbed (with gen.) (dugnða lēas, bereft of joy, 693; dōmes lēasne, robbed of happiness, 945), loose, false (lēase lēodhatan, the false haters of men, 1300).

lēas, n., falsehood, lying, 680; dat. sg. lēase, 576.

lēasing, f., lie; lēasunga, 689; mid lēasingum, 1123.

lēasspell, n., false news, [580].

lef, weak, feeble, 1214.

lēgen, flaming, fiery; lēgene sweorde, with fiery sword, 757.

leger, n. (cf. lair), lying-place, bed, couch; in legere, in its bed, 602; legere fǽst, 723; lic legere fǽst, the body fast on its couch (i.e. dead), 883.

leneten, m., spring (lent), 1227 (s. note, 1227).

leng, s. lange.

lēod, f. pl., men, people; leode, 20, 128, 163, 208, 1111; leoda, 181, 285; leodum, 666, 723.

lēodfruma, m., prince of the people (of Constantine), 191.

lēodgebyrga, people's protector (of Constantine), (11), 203; lēodgebyrgean (of representative), Jews 536.

lēodhata, m., hater of the people; lēase lēodhatan, the false haters of men, 1300.

lēodhwæt, very valiant, [11].

lēodmæg, relation of the same people, one of the people, people's companion; lēodmǽga, 880.

lēoðrūn, f., song-secret, secret instruction; þurh lēoðrūne, 522.

lēoðucræft, m., art of poetry; lēoðcrǽft onlēac, opened up the art of poetry, 1251.

lēof, dear, valued, 1036, 1048; wk. nom. m. lēofa, 511; neut. lēofre, = pleasant, 666; gen. pl. lēofra, 1206; superl. leofesta, 523.

leofað, s. lifgan.

lēoflic, lovely; lēoflic wif, 286.

lēofspell, n., dear news; lēofspell manig, many a message of love, 1017.

lēoht, bright, light, illuminating, beautiful, 163; lēohtne gelēafan, 491; þurh lēohtne hād, 1246; mid þá lēohtan gedryht, 737; lēohte gelēafan, 1137.

leoht, light; him wæs leoht sefa, his heart was light, 173.

lēoht, n., light, 7, 94, 1045 (?); (of Christ) calles lēohtes lēoht, 486; acc. lēoht, 298, 307, 1123; instr. lēohte, 734; gen. pl. lēohta, 948.

lēohte, adv., brightly, clearly, 92, 966, 1116.

lēoma, m., ray of light, light,

glare; éldes léoma, fire's glare, 1294.

leomu, s. lim.

leornian, wv. II., learn; pret. pl. leornedon, 397.

leornungcræft, m., learning, 380.

leort, s. lætan, 1105.

lesan, sv. V., collect; wundrum læs, I collected (it) wonderfully, 1238.

libban, wv. I., live; lifdon, 311.

líc, n., body; life belidenes líc, body robbed of life (corpse), 877; líc legere fæst, body fast on the couch (corpse), 883.

licgan, sv. V., lie, [921].

líchoma, m., body (home of the soul); in lichoman, in the fleshly tabernacle, 737.

líf, n., life, 526, 606; gen. sg. lifes, 137, [518], 520, 664, 700, 757, 793, 899, 1027, 1209; dat. sg. life, 575, 878; acc. sg. líf, 305, 622, 1046.

lífdæg, m., day of life; gif þé fæt gelimpe on lifdagum, if this happen to thee in the days of thy life, 441.

líffruma, m., author of life (of Christ), 335.

lifgan, wv. II., live; leofaδ, 450; lifgende, alive, 486.

lífweard, m., lifewarden, guardian of life (of Christ), 1036.

lífwyn, f., joy of life; lifwynne, with the joy of living, 1209.

líg, m., fire, flame; læcende lig, 580, 1111; lige befæsled, 1300.

lígewalu, f., fiery torment; fram ligewale, from the torture of fire, 296.

lige, m., lie, 575; acc. lige, 307; dat. on lige, 666.

ligescaru, n., lying cunning;

ligescearwum, with lying deceptions, 208.

ligesynnig, sinning by lies, lying; ligesynnig . . . féond, 899.

lim, n., limb; pl. leomu; leomu célodon, the limbs were cold, 883.

limséoc, limb-sick, lame, 1214.

lindgeborga, m., protector armed with a shield, [11].

lindhwæt, valiant with the shield; se lindhwata léodgebyrga, the protector of the people, valiant with the shield, (11).

lindwered, n., troops armed with shields; shield-bearing band, 142.

lindwîgend, m., shield-warrior; héape gecoste lindwigendra, with a chosen band of shield-bearing warriors, 270.

líxan, wv. I., shine, glitter, glisten; pret. pl. gâras lixtan, 23, 125; gimmas lixtan, 90; næglas . . . lixton, 1116.

loc, n., lock; locum belúcan, to lock up with locks, 1027.

loca, m., imprisonment, snare; of locan déofla, from the devil's snares, 181.

lôcian, wv. II., look; pret. lôcade, 87.

lof, m., praise (with obj. gen.); Crîstes lof, praise of Christ, 212; heofonciaininges lof, 748; lof, 890.

lofian, wv. II., praise; lofiaδ, 453.

lúcan, sv. II., lock, enclose, set in gold; sinegim locen, 264.

lufe, f., love; lufan dryhtnes, 918, 1206; for lufan, for the love of, for the sake of; for dryhtnes lufan, for the Lord's sake, 491; for sawla lufan, for the love of souls, 564.

lufian, wv. II., love; swâ þîn môd lufaþ, as thy heart desireth, 597.

lufu, f., love; fyrhät lufu, ardent love, 937.

lungre, adv., soon; forthwith, 30, 368.

lust, m., pleasure, joy (Ger. lust) (cf. lust); on luste, = rejoiced,138; with joy, 261; lustrum,* willingly, 702; with pleasure, 1251.

lyft, m., f., air (Ger. luft); under lyfte, 1271; geond lyft, 734; on lyft, 900.

lyftläcende, floating in the air, 796.

lysan, wv., loose, release; lysan . . . of häftnéde, to release from bondage, 296.

lyt, little, few; (with gen.) härfdle wigena tó lyt, he had too few warriors, 63.

lytel, little; on swä lyttum fäce, in such a little while, 960; ymb lytel fäce, 272, 383; adv. nû lytle ær, now a little before, 604.

lythwôn, little, but few; lythwôn becwom Hûna herges häm, but few of the army of the Huns reached home, 142.

M.

mâ (s. mâra, comp. from micel), more, 634; more, hereafter, 817; more, longer, 431.

maðellan, wv. II., speak, harangue; pret. sg. maþelode, 332, 604, 685, 807; maþelade, 401, 573, 627, 642, 655.

mâðum, m., treasure, object of value; þeah he . . . maðmas þege, though he received the treasures, 1259.

mæg, f., kinsman, relation; cä-seres mæg, 330, 669.

magan, pret. pres. can, be able;

ic mæg, 632, 635, 702, 705; ðû mealht, 511; hê mæg, 448, 466, 588, 611, 735, 770; pl. magon, 582, 583, 1291; opt. mæge, 677, 1178; pret. sg. mealhte, 33, 160, 243, 609, 860, 1159; pret. pl. mealhton, 166, 324, 477, 979.

mægen, n., strength, power, might, 608; instr. mægene, 1223; acc. mægn, 408; gen. pl. mægena, 347, 810; troop, multitude, army, 55, 61, 138, 233, 283, 1293; acc., 242.

mægeneyning, m., mighty king, 1218.

mægenþrym, m., mighty strength, great glory; mycle mægenþrymme, with very great glory, 735.

maias, May; on maias kalendas, 1229.

mæl, n., time; ær fäela mæla, a long time before, 987 (s. note, 987).

mælan, wv. I., speak; wordum mælde, 351; wordum mældon, 537.

man, n., man, person, 467; mannes, 660; man, 872; gen. pl. manna, 326, 735, 923, 1229, 1312; dat. pl. mannum, 16, 626; indef. prn., one, 358, 711, 755.

mân, n., wickedness, crime; mâne gemengde, 1296; þurh morðres mân, 626; gen. pl. mâna gehwylc, 1317.

mânfréa, m., criminal lord; morðres mânfréa, the wicked prince of murder (i.e. devil), 912.

mânfremmende, sin-committing; sâwla . . . mânfremmende, sin-committing souls, 907.

maneg, many (attrib.), 231, 258, 1017; monige, 499; manegum, 15; (subst.) manegum, 501; manigum, 970, 1176.

manrîm, n., number of men; on manrîme, 650.

mânweore, sinful; mê . . . swâ manweorcum,tome . . . sosinful,812.

mânþêaw, m., sinful custom; ond mânþêawum mínum folgaþ, and follows my sinful usages, 930.

manþêaw, m., man's habit, custom, 930 (?).

mærð, f., glory; mærðum ond mihtum, with glory and power, 15; mærðum,with glory,gloriously,871.

mære, bright, glorious, 970 (gen. sg. þære mæran byrig, 864 ; acc. sg. ymb þæt mære trêo, 214; þurh þâ mæran word, 990; þurh þâ mæran miht, 1242; ymb þâ mêran wyrd, 1064; superl. mærost bêama, 1013, 1225); known, well known, 1177; well known, renowned (mihtum mære, renowned in power, 340; þone mæran dæg, 1223).

Mâria, Mary; mid Mârian, 1233; þurh Mârian, 775.

mæst (superl. from micel), most, greatest (with gen.), 31, 35, 196, 977, 984, 993; pl. mæste, 274; (attrib.), mæste-snyttro, 381, 408.

mê, me, to me (dat.), 163, 164, 317, 375, 409, 462, 679, 812, 912, 1074; me (acc.), 361, 700, 920; mec, 469, 528, 819, 910, 1078.

meaht, meahte, s. magan.

mear. s. mearh.

mearcpæð, n., mark-path, path running through the marks, 233 (see note, 233).

mearh, m., horse (cf. mare), 55, 1193; dat. meare, 1176.

mec, s. mê.

mêðe, weary, tired (mêðe ond metelêas, 612, 698), miserable (mê swâ mêðum, to me so miserable, 812).

meðel, n., council, assembly (on meðle, 546, 593), speech (to God), prayer (on meðle, in prayer, 786).

meðelhêgende, holding conclave, deliberating, 279.

meðelstede, m., place of assembly, council-chamber; on meðelstede, 554.

medoheal, f., mead-hall; in medohealle, 1259.

melda, m., informer, betrayer; þæs morðes meldan, betrayers of the murder, 428.

mengan, wv. I., mingle; mengan ongunnon, mingled, confounded, 306.

mengo, f., many, multitude; dat. mengo, 377, 596; mengu, 225; menigo, 871.

mennisc, human; þurh mennisc, hêo, in human form, 6.

meotod, m., Creator, 366; meotud, 1040; metud, 819; gen. sg. meotodes,686, 986; meotudes, 461, 474, 564; metudes, 1313.

merestræt, f., sea-street, seaway, 242.

metan, sv. V., mete, measure, traverse; þær him eh fore milpaðas mæt, where the horse once traversed with him the mile-paths, 1263.

mêtan, wv. I., meet, find; pret. sg. mêtte, 833; pret. pl. mêtton, 116; p.p. mêted, 986.

metelêas, without food; mêðe ond metelêas, 612, 698.

metud, s. meotod.

micel, great; mycel, 426, 646; þurh þâ myclan miht, 507; instr. mycle mægenþrymme, 755; dat. pl. ôfstum myclum, with great haste, 44, 102, 1000; myclum, adv., greatly, 876.

mid, prep. (1) with dat. or instr.,

with, 105, 377, 577, 622, 707, 714, 712, 805, 821, 843, 814, 854, 865, 1025, 1067, 1123; *among*, 328, 407, [451], 1203; mid Marian, 1233. (2) with instr. mid þýs béaene, 92; mid þý, 1178; *among* (mid þý folce, 891). (3) with acc., *with* (mid þá æðelan ewén, 275; mid horn, 297; mid sigeewén, 998; mid þá léohtan gedryht, into the presence of the brilliant hosts, 737).

miðan, sv. l., conceal, keep secret; pret. sg. wælrúne ne máð, he did not conceal the battle secret, 28; hygerúne ne máð, he did not keep back the secret of his heart, 1099.

middangeard, m. (middle world), world, earth; gen. sg. middangeardes, 810; acc. in middangeard, 6, 775; geond ——, 16, 1177, ofer ——, 434, 918.

middel, m., middle; in þám midle þréad, punished in the middle (of the purgatorial fire), 1296; on þone middel, 864.

midl, n., bit of a bridle, 1176, 1193.

miht, f., might, power; dat. sg. mihte, 584, 1163; acc. sg. miht, 295, 310, 558, 597, 727, 1242; gen. pl. mihta, 337, 366, 786, 819, 1043; dat. pl. mihtum, 15, 340, 1070, 1100.

mihtig, mighty, 680, 1068; se mihtiga cyning, 942.

milde, mild, gracious, 1043, 1317.

milpæð, mile-path; milpaðas mæt, 1263.

milts, f., mercy, 501.

mín, prn. (gen. of ic), of me; mín on þá swiðran, on the right of me, 347.

mín, poss. prn., my, mine, 163, 319, 436, etc.

mód, n., mood, spirit, soul, heart, 597, 990, 1061; gen. sg. módes snyttro, 551; on módes þeaht, 1242; dat. móde, 268, 629 (?), 1223.

módblind, blind in heart, 306.

móderæft, m., mood-craft, power of mind, 408.

módewânig, sad at heart, sorrowful, 377.

módeg, s. módig.

módgemynd, f., n., memory; þurh módgemynd, 389; heart, 840.

módgeþanc, m., thought of the heart, inmost thought; módgeþanc minne eunnon, you know my inmost thought, 535.

módig, spirited, proud, brave, 1263; módigra mægen, 138, 1293; mearh under módegum, midlum geweorðod, among the courageous, the horse adorned with the bit, 1193.

modor, f., mother, 214, 340.

módsefa, m., mind, heart; on módsefan, 876.

módsorg, f., heart-sorrow; módsorge wæg . . . cyning, grief of heart experienced the king, 61.

molde, earth, mould; mearh moldan træd, the horse trod the earth, 55.

moldweg, m., way upon the earth, earth; on moldwege, 467.

monig, s. maneg.

monigfeald, manifold; swâ monigfeald, such manifold things, 641.

morðor, n., murder, violent death, deadly sin; morðres, 428, 626, 942.

morðorhof, n., place of punishment (murder-court); of þám morðorhofe (of hell), 1303.

morðorslelit, m., slaughter; morðorslehtes, 650.

morgenspel, n., morning news; mære morgenspel, the happy news of morning, 970.

môrland, n., moorland, 612.

môtan, pret. pres., may, be allowed, etc.; 3d p. sg. môt, 916; pl. môton, 906, 1307, 1315; opt. môten, 433; pret. pl. môston, 175, 1005.

Moyses, Moses, 283, 337; dat. Moyse, 366; acc. Moyses, 786.

mûð, m., month; þurh æniges mannes mûð, 660; þurh þæs dêman mûð, 1283.

mund, f., hand; mundum þinum, with Thy hands, 730.

mycel, s. micel.

myndgian, wv., II. remember; wê þæs hereweorces . . . myndgiaþ, we remember this work of the army, 657.

myngian, wv. II., remind; mec þæra nægla . . . fyrwet myngaþ, desire of knowledge reminds me of these nails, 1079.

myrgan, wv. I., be merry, "rejoice," (Kemble), [244].

N.

næfre, adv., never, 388, 468, 538, 650, 778.

nâgan, pret. pres, not have; pret. pl. nâhton foreþancas, they had not forethought, 356.

nægel, m., nail; pl. n. and a. næglas, 1109, 1115, 1158, 1173; gen. pl. nægla, 108, 1078; dat. pl. næglum, 1065, 1103, 1128.

nales, adv., not at all, by no means, 359, 470, 1253; nalles, 818, 1134.

nama, m., name, 418, 437, 530, 586, 750, 1061; naman, 465, 503; be naman, by name, 74, 505, 756.

nænig, m., no one, none, 505.

nære = ne wære, was not; þæs twêo nære, of this there was no doubt, 171; gif hê þin nære sunu, if he were not Thy son, 777.

næs = ne wæs, was not; næs; næs . . . gâd, 991.

næs, m., ness (naze), headland, promontory; under nêolum niðer næsse, under the steep descending cliff, 832.

nât = ne wât, not know; þæt ic nât, which I do not know, 640.

nâthwyle, indef. prn. (I know not which), some, some one or other, 73.

Nazareð, Nazareth, 913; in Nazareð, 913.

ne (adv.), not (non), 28, 62, 81, 166, 219, etc.

nê (conj.), and not, nor (nec), 167, 221, 240, 399, 524, 567, 684, 860; nê . . . nê, neither . . . nor, 572.

neah, adv., enough, sufficiently, continually; neah myndgaþ, we remember continually, 657.

nêah, near; superl. nihst, nearest, last, [197].

nêah, adv., near; êgstrêame neah, 66.

nêan, from near, near by, nearly, [657].

nearo, f., narrowness, restraint, oppression, embarrassment (niwan on nearwe, in this new embarrassment, 1103; nihtes nearwe, in the oppression at night, 1240 ?), narrow room, prison (of nearwe, 711), hiding-place, concealment (of nearwe, 1115).

nearolic, narrow, oppressive; niða nearolicra, oppressive enmity, 913.

nearuscaru, f., secret cunning, intrigue; þurh nearuscaru, 1109.

nearusorg, f., crushing sorrow; nearusorg dreah, suffered the crushing sorrow, 1261.

nearwe, adv., narrowly, exactly, 1158, 1276.

neat, n., neat-cattle, ox, etc.; þa weregan neat, 357.

neawest, f., vicinity, neighborhood; on neaweste, 67, 874.

ned, s. nyd.

negan, wv. I., approach, address; wordum negan, 287, 559.

nemnan, wv. I., name; pret. nemde, 78, 1060; p.p. nemned, 1195.

neoðan, adv., beneath, 1115.

neol, steep, deep; under neolum niðer næsse, under the steep-descending naze, 832.

neolnes, depth, abyss; in neolnesse nyðer bescufeð, hurleth down into the depth, 943.

neorxnawang, m., paradise, 756 (s. note, 756).

neosan, wv. I. (with gen.), visit, go to; burga neosan, 152.

neowe, s. niwe.

nergend, nerigend (saving), saviour, deliverer (of God), 503, 1086 (nerigend), 1173; (of Christ), 461, 465, 799, 1065 (nerigend), 1078.

nesan, sv. V., endure, survive, 1004 (s. note, 1004).

nesan = neosan, wv. I., visit, [1004].

nið, m., man, person; pl. gen. niða, 465, 503, 1086.

nið, strife, violence, enmity, hostile acts; acc. hie wið godes bearn nið ahofun, they stirred up strife against the Son of God, 838; ealdne nið, old feud, 905; gen. pl. niða

nearolicra, oppressive acts of hostility, 913.

niðer, adv., nether, downward, down, 832; nyðer, 943.

niðheard, brave in strife, 195.

nigoða, ninth; wæs þa nigoðe tid, it was the ninth hour, 874; oð þa nigoðan tid, until, etc., 870.

nihst, s. neah.

niht, f., night; pl. þreo niht, 483; .VII. nihta fyrst, 694; butan .VI. nihtum, 1228; adv. gen. nihtes, by night (cf. Ger. nachts), 198, 1240.

nihthelm, m., helmet of night, darkness; nihthelm toglad, the helmet of night fell apart, 78 (s. note, 78).

nihtlang, lasting the night; nihtlange fyrst, for the space of the night, 67.

niman, sv. IV., take; þæt he þone stan nime, that he should take the stone, 615; þe on gemynd nime, who takes in mind, remembers, 1233; take away, snatch away; tionleg nimeð, the destructive flame snatcheth away, etc., 1279; ær þec swylt nime, ere death snatch thee away, 447 (cf. 676).

niod, f., eagerness, zeal, purpose, [629].

nis = ne is, is not, 911.

niwe, new, 195; niwan stefne, 1061, 1128; niwan on nearwe, 1103; neowne gefean, 870.

niwigan, wv. II., renew, 941.

no, adv., never, not at all, by no means, 780, 838, 1083, 1302.

noldon = ne woldon, did not wish, 566.

nu, adv., now, 313, 372, 388, 406, 426, etc.; (strengthened), naþa, butan þec (her) naþa, 539, 661; (conj.), inasmuch as, since, now that, 534, 635, 702, 815, 908, 1171.

nûþâ, s. **nû**.

nȳdcleofa, m., prison, dungeon; of nȳdcleofan, 711; in nédcleofan, 1276.

nȳðer, s. **nîðer**.

nȳdgeféra, m., companion in (time of) need; ȳr gnornode nȳdgeféra, the bow bemoaned its companion in need, 1201.

nȳdþearf, f., need, necessity; for nȳdþearfe, out of necessity, 657.

nysse = ne wisse, **nyste** = ne wiste (S. 420), did not know, 1240, 719.

nyton = ne witon, do not know, 401.

O.

ôð, prep. with acc. (temporal), until, 139, 312, 590, 870; ôð þæt, until then, 1257; conj., until, 866, 886.

oððe, or, 74, 159, 508, 634, 975, 1114.

ôðer, prn., other, 506; æfter ôðrum, 233; ôðerne, 540, 928.

ôðfæsten, wv. I., inflict upon; him . . . déað ôðfæsten, to inflict death upon him, 477.

œðil = éðel, (1260?).

ôðȳwan, wv. I., show, appear; pret. ôðȳwde, appeared, 163.

of, prep. with dat. (instr.), of, out of, from (separation), 75, 181, 186, 187, 282, 295, 297, 303, 440, 482, 700, 711, 715, 736, 762, 780, 794, 803, 845, 1226, 1303, 1305, (source), 915, 1023, 1087, 1113, 1115.

ofen, m., oven, furnace; þurh ofnes fȳr, through the fire of the furnace, 1311.

ofer, prep. with dat., over; ofer þâm æðelestan engelcynne, 733; with acc., over, 31, 118, 158, 233, 237, 244, 249, 255, 269, 385, 881, 918, 981, 983, 996, 997, 1017, 1133, 1135, 1201; over, upon, 89, 239, 434, 1289; ofer riht godes, against the truth of God, 372; ofer þæt, after that, 432, 448.

ofermægen, n., over-might, superiority, greater number, 64.

oferswîðan, wv. I., overcome, 1178; oferswiðesð, 93; oferswiðedne, 958.

oferwealdend, m., highest lord, sovereign (of Christ); se ricesða ealles ofer wealdend, the mightiest Sovereign of all, 1236.

oferþearf, f., great need; for oferþearfe ilda cynnes, on account of the great need of mankind, 521.

ofost, f., haste; ofstum myclum, with great haste, 44, 102, 1000.

ofstlîce, adv., hastily, with haste, 225, 713, 1197.

oft, adv., often, 238, 301, 386, 471, 513, 1141, 1213, 1253.

on, prep. with dat. (instr.), on, 37, 59, 101, 232, etc.; in (on rîme, in number, 284 [cf. 650]); on, upon, 126, 133, 241, 242, 253, etc.; in (circumstantial), 28, 36, 53, 67, 69, 70, etc.; among, 754, 820 (on gesylðe [s. gesylð]; on .xx. fôtmælum feor, at a distance of twenty feet, 830); in (temporal), 105, 398, 441, 528, 571, 638, 639, 960, 1288; with acc., on, 179, 206, 250, etc.; upon, 84, 117, 717, etc.; to, in, into, 96, 134, 262, 291, etc. (on willsið, for the journey, 223; on healfa gehwæne, on every side, 548 [cf. 955, 1180]; on unriht, wrongly, 582; [temporal], in his dagana tid, during the period of his days, 193; on þone scofeðan dæg, on the seventh day, 697; on þá æðelan tíd, in that glorious day, 787; on þá sliðan tíd, at that dreadful hour, 857; on maias kalendas, on the calends of May, 1229, [cf. innan and gemang]).

onǽlan, wv. I., set fire to, inflame, burn; ádc onǽled, burnt by the fire, 951.

onbindan, sv. III., unbind, loose; báncofan onband, unbound my body, 1250 (s. note, 1250).

onbregdan, sv. III., start up; hé of slǽpe onbrægd, he started up out of his sleep, 75.

onbryrdan, wv. I., excite, inspire; p.p. onbryrded, 1095; inbryrded, 842, 1046.

oncnáwan, red. vb., know, perceive, recognize, acknowledge, [229], 362, 395; pret. oncnéow, 966.

oncnáwe, "cognitus," (Gm.), oncnǽwe, "declared" (K.), [229]. Does this word occur anywhere?

oncor, m., anchor; oncrum fæste, made fast with anchors, 252.

oncweðan, sv. V., answer, 324; pret. oncwæð, 573, 669, 682, 935, 1167.

oncýðig, [sorrowful, 725] (cf. uncýðig).

oncyrran, wv. I., turn, change (naman oncyrde, changed his name, 503); turn away, avert (oncyrran rex geniðlan, avert the enmity of the ruler, 610.

ond (so written, 931, 977, 984, 1210, — otherwise abbreviated), and (never written and, Zupitza).

ondrǽdan, red. v., fear; ne ondrǽd þú ðé, do not fear, 81.

onfón, red. vb., receive, take, with acc., gen., dat. (instr.); pret. sg. fulwihte onféng, 192; swengas, 238; fulwihtes bæð, 490, 1033; þám nǽglum, 1128; pret. pl. láre on féngon, 335.

ongeán (ongén), prep. with dat., against (ongean gramum, 43; hire ongén þingode, spoke to her, 609, 667 [post positive]).

onginnan, sv. III., begin, with inf. (often best translated by the historical aorist of the inf.); pret. sg. ongan, 157, 198, 225, 283, 384, 558, 570, 696, 828, 850, 901, 1068, 1094, 1148, 1156, 1164, 1205; pret. pl. ongunnon, 303, 306, 311; with acc., begin, institute, 468.

ongitan, sv. V., understand, perceive, recognize (ongitaþ, 359); impera. ongit, 464; p.p. ongiten, 288.

onhyldan, wv. I., bow; hleor onhylde, he bowed his face (lit., cheek), 1099.

onhyrdan, wv. I., strengthened, encouraged; hige onhyrded þurh þæt hálige tréo, 811.

onhyrtan, wv. I., "animare, recreare" (Gm.), [841].

onléon, sv. I., lend, grant; dat. pers. and gen. rei, ǽr mé láre onlag, before he granted me instruction, 1246.

onlíce, adv., like, 99.

onlúcan, sv. II., unlock, open; léoðucræft onléac, opened up the art of poetry, 1251.

onmédla, m., haughtiness, pride, glory; ald onmédla, 1266.

onscunian, wv. II., shun, fear, detest, despise; onscunedon þine sciran scrippend eallra, 370.

onsendan, wv. I., send (forð onsendan, 120; þine béne onsend, send up thy prayer, 1089); send away, give up (on galgan his gâst onsende, He gave up His ghost on the cross, 480).

onsîon, s. **onsŷn**.

onspannan, red. v., unspan, unloose, open; hrêðerlocan onspêon, he opened his bosom, 86.

onsŷn, f., sight, face, countenance; fore onsŷne êces dêman, before the face of the Eternal Judge, 746; ic ne wende æfre tó aldre onsion mine, I never turned my face to life (i.e. earthly things), 349.

ontŷnan, wv. I., open; pret. ontŷnde, 1249; p.p. ontŷned, 1230.

onwindan, sv. III., unwind, loosen, open; brêostlocan onwand, opened the bosom's enclosure, 1250.

onwrêon, sv. I. and II., uncover, discover, disclose, reveal, 589, 674; pret. sg. onwrâh, 1243; pret. opt. onwrige, 1072; p.p. onwrigen, 1124, 1254; with, 1072 (cf. inwrige, 813).

open, open, known; open caldgewin, a known battle in olden times, 647.

ôr, [1266] (Leo, "geld").

orenǽwe, evident, well known, 229.

ord, m., point, point of a spear, spear (bord ond ord, 1187; bordum ond ordum, 235); beginning (fram [dæges] orde, 140, 590; æfter orde, 1155); first, chief, prince (of Christ) (æðelinga ord, 393).

ôwiht, aught, something; ôwiht swylces, anything at all of this sort, 571.

P.

Paulus, Paul; sanctus Paulus, 504.

plegean, pres. sv. V. (S. 391. 1), pret. wv. II., move rapidly, play, prance (sæmearh plegean, the seahorse prance, 245); to move (the hands) rapidly, clap, applaud (hê mid bæm handum . . . ûpweard plegade, he clapped with both hands toward heaven, 806).

R.

râd, f., ride, expedition, journey; tó râde, for a journey, 982.

rêd, m., counsel, advice (rede) (hæleða rêdas, the counsels of men, 156); foresight (rêdes þearf, need of foresight, 553); power, might (min is geswiðrod rêd under roderum, my dominion under heaven is diminished, 919); advantage, weal (begra rêdum, for the weal of both, 1009).

rêdan, red. vb., advise, counsel; swâ hire gâsta weard reord of roderum, as the Guardian of spirits counselled her from heaven, 1023.

raðe = **hraðe**.

rêdgeþeaht, f., counsel, consultation, deliberation, 1052, 1162.

rador, s. **rodor**.

rêdþeahtende, taking counsel, sagacious, wise, 449, 869.

rand, m., border (of shield); þonne rand dynede, then the shield made a noise, 50.

rǽran, wv. I. (rear), promote, stir up, enkindle; gellitu rǽran, 443; sæce rǽran, 941; gellitu rǽrdon, 951.

rêc, m., smoke, 795, 804.

reccan, wv. I., explain, expound, narrate, 281, 284; opt. pres. reccen, 553.

rêniend, m., arranger, [880].

reodian, wv. II., pass through a sieve, sift; geþane reodode, sifted the thought, 1239.

rêonig, rêoni, sad, 1083; in þam rêonian hofe, in that sad court, 834.

rêonigmôd, sad-hearted, down-hearted, 320.

r e o r d b e r e n d, endowed with speech, man; reordberenda, 1282.

reordian, wv. II., speak, say; reordode, 405, 417, 463, 1073 [speisen, Gm., 1239].

rêotan, sv. II., weep, mourn; rêonig rêoteð, mourneth in sadness, 1083.

rex (Lat.), king, ruler (of God), 1042; (of Helen), 610 (!).

rîce, n., might, power, dominion, 13, 449, 917; supremacy, victory, 147 (rîces ne wênde, he did not hope for victory, 62); kingdom, empire, 1231 (rîces, 59, 820; in rîce, 9; acc. rîce, 40, 631).

rîce, powerful, mighty; sio rîce cwên, 411; superl. se rîcesða calles oferwealdend, the most powerful Sovereign of everything, 1235.

rîcene, adv., instantly, at once, 607, 623, 982, 1162.

rîesian, wv. II., be mighty, rule, 434; þæt rîcsie sê, that He rule, 774.

rîdan, sv. I., ride; pret. pl. ridon, they rode, 50.

riht, right, true, 13; þurh rihte þû, 281.

riht, n., right (ofer riht godes, against the right of God, 372); that which is right, true judgment, truth (rihtes wêmend, the discloser of truth, 880; rihte, 390, 663; ryhte, 369; riht, 601, 1241; seeall . . . riht gehŷran dêda gehwylera, shall hear judgment for all deeds, 1282); right, possession (rihta gehwylces,

of every right, 910; ûnige rihte, with any possession, 917).

rihte, adv., rightly, exactly, truthfully, 553, 566; ryhte, 1075.

rîm, n., number (geteled rimes, 2; geteled rîme, 634); the number told (on rime, 284; rîm, 635).

rîmtalu, f., number; on rimtale rîces þines, in the number of Thy kingdom, 820.

rinc, m., man, warrior, hero; pl. rincas, 46.

rôd, f., rood, cross, 219, 624, 720, 887, (973), 1012, 1224; gen. rôde, 147, 856, 1235; dat. rôde, 103, 206, 482, 601, 774, 1067, (1241); acc. rôde, 631, 919, 1023, 1075; gen. pl. rôda, 834, 869, 880.

roder, s. **rodor**.

rodor, m., heaven (rodora [radora] waldend, 206, 482, 1067; cyning on roderum, 460, 1075; fæder on roderum, 1151; of roderum, 762, 1023); heavens (rodor eal gesweare, 856; under radores ryne, 795; under radorum, 13, 46, 147, 631, 804, 919, 1235.

rodorcyning, m., King of heaven (of Christ); rodorcyninges bêam, 887; rôd . . . radorcyninges, 624.

rôf, strong, valiant, renowned, 50.

Rôm, f., Rome; Rôme bisceop, bishop of Rome, 1052.

Rômware, pl., Romans, 46; gen. Rômwara, 9, 40, 59, 62, 129; Rômwarena, 982.

rûm, roomy, wide, extensive; rûmran geþeaht, more extended knowledge, 1241.

rûn, f., mystery, secret (rune) (hâlige rûne, 333, 1169; enge rûne, 1262); (secret) council (êodon þâ fram rûne, 411; tô rûne, 1162).

ryht, ryhte, s. riht, rihte.
ryne, m., expanse; under radores
ryne, under the expanse of the
heavens, 795.

S.

sǽ, m., f., sea, ocean, 240; sǽs
sidne fæðm, the sea's wide expanse,
729.

sæc, f., contest; æt sæcce, 1178,
1183, [1257].

sacan, sv. VI., contend, [1181].

sacerdhâd, m., priesthood; on
sacerdhâd, 1055.

Sachîus, Sachias, 437.

sacu, f., contest, strife, war; þis
is singal sacu, this is constant strife,
906; sæce, 1031; sæce rǽran, to stir
up strife, 941.

sǽfearoð, m., sea-coast; æt sǽfearoðe sande bewrecene, in the
sand-whipped sea-coast, 251.

sægde, s. secgan.

* sagian, wv. II., say, tell; saga,
623, 857.

sǽl, m., f., happiness : on sǽlum
= happy, 194.

sǽlan, wv. I., tie, bind, make
fast with ropes (Ger. seilen); sǽlde,
228.

sǽlð, f., good fortune, prosperity,
[1244].

Salomôn, Solomon; gen. Salomônes, 343.

salor, n. (?), hall, room, royal
hall; tô salore, 382, 552.

same, adv., similarly; swâ some,
= similarly, in like manner, 653,
1066, 1278; swâ same, 1207, 1284.

sǽmearh, m., sea-horse, ship,
245; pl. sǽmearas, 228.

samnian, wv. II., collect, assemble, gather; mægen samnode, 55;

werod samnode, 60; werod samnodan, 19.

samod, adv., together, simulta-
neously, (614), [629], 729, 889;
somed, 95.

sâmwîslîce, adv., semi-wisely,
half-wittedly, foolishly, [293].

sanctus (Lat.), saint; sanctus
Paulus, 504.

sand, n., sand (shore), 251.

sǽne (with gen.), slow, slack,
negligent; þæs siðfates sǽne, neg-
lectful of this journey, 220.

sang, m., song; earu sang âhôf,
the eagle raised his song(= screech),
29; wulf sang âhôf, the wolf raised
his song(= howl), 112; sang âhôfon,
they raised a song, 868.

sâr, n., (sore), pain, sorrow; acc.
sâr, 941; dat. pl. sârum, 479, 697, 933.

sâwl, f., soul, 890; gen. pl. sâwla,
461, 564, 799, 906, 1172.

sâwllêas, soulless, lifeless; sâwl-
lêasne, 877.

Sawlus, Saul; Sawles lârum, at
the instigation of Saul, 497.

secacan, sv. IV., shake, move
rapidly, escape, vanish; p.p. sceacen, 633.

sceâdan, red. vb., divide, separate, decide, rule; pret. sceâd, 709.

sceaða, m., scather, injurious
enemy; (of devils), scyldwyrcende
sceaðan, the sin-committing foes,
762.

sceal, s. sculan.

scealc, m., slave, servant, subject; scealcas ne gǽldon, the sub-
jects did not delay, 692.

sceamu, f., shame; sceame, 470.

sceât, m., corner, lap, bosom;
under womma sceâtum, in the bosom
of sins, 583; (Grein), latebra, latibulum.

scêawian, wv. II., (show), see,
behold; pret. sg. sceáwode, 345;
sceáwedon, 58.

sceððan, sv. VI. and wv. I.,
scathe, injure, oppress; ćow sćo
wergðu forðan sceðþeð scyldfullum, for that reason this punishment oppresses you laden with
guilt, 310, [709?].
[scênan? wv. I., "in die höhe
heben (zeigen, scheinen machen),
aber auch rütteln, schütteln"
(Grimm), (151)].

sceolde, s. sculan.

sceolu, f., school, troop, (shoal),
multitude, 763; árléasra sceolu,
the throng of the godless, 836,
1301.

scînan, sv. I., shine, gleam;
scinaþ, 743, 1319; scinende, 1115.

scippend, m., creator, 370; scyppend, 791.

scirian, wv. I., arrange in parts,
determine; hira dǽl scired, 1232.

scîr, sheer, bright, clear, pure,
310, 370.

scrîðan, sv. I., stride, move; ofer
fifelwǽg . . . scriðan . . . brimþisan, (they let) the rusher over
the sea (= ships) stride (= move)
over the sea, 237.

scrifan, sv. I., determine, rule,
[709].

scûfan, sv. II., push, throw;
scûfan scyldigne . . . indrȳgne sćað,
to throw the guilty one in the dry
well, 692.

sculan, pret. pres., should, ought;
2d p. sg. scealt, 673; 3d p. sg. sceal,
545; pl. sceolon, 756; pret. sg.
sceolde, 764, 1049; pret. pl. sceoldon, 367, 982; (with omission of
infinitive), sceol, 1192; opt. pres.
scyle, 896; sceoldon, 838; (para-

phrase of future), scealt cwylmed
weorðan, thou shalt be tortured to
death, 687; sceall . . . drêogan,
951; sceol . . . áwended weorðan,
580; sceal . . . þrowian, 768; sceall
. . . weorðan, 1176; sceall . . .
gebȳran, 1281; pl. sculon . . .
drêogan, 210.

scûr, m., shower; flâna scûras,
showers of arrows, 117.

scyld, f., debt, obligation, crime,
sin (Ger. schuld); gen. pl. scylda,
470, 1313.

scyldful, f., full of guilt, laden
with guilt; ćow . . . scyldfallum,
310.

scyldig, guilty; scyldigne, 692.

scyldwyrcende, sin-committing,
762.

scyndan, wv. I., hurry, hasten;
lungre scynde, hastened hurriedly,
30.

scyppend, s. scippend.

sê, prn. demonstrative, m., 465,
928, 1195; (f. sio, sćo); n. þæt, 426,
456, 1050, etc.; gen. m. n. þæs, 39,
60, 86, etc.; (adverbial), so (intensive), 704; (conj.), for that reason,
therefore, 210, 768; that, because,
812, 823, 963; gen. f. þǽre, 293, 610,
etc.; dat. m. n. þâm, 70, 133, 146;
dat. f. þǽre, 324, 545; acc. m. þanc,
294; þone, 243, 302, etc.; acc. f. þâ,
98, 183, 274, etc.; acc. n. þæt, 107,
117, 128; instr. m. n. þȳ, 185, 485,
891, 1178; (before comparatives),
the — þȳ bliþra, 96; þȳ fæstlicor, 797;
þê sorgléasra, 97; þê sêl, 796; þê
gearwor, 946; (conj.), þȳ lǽs, in
order that . . . not, that . . . not,
lest, 430; pl. nom. acc. þâ, 153, 160,
etc.; gen. þâra, 285; þâra, 450, 470,
740, etc.; dat. þâm, 277, 754, etc.

Prn. rel., m., sê, 213, 545, 1196; sê

þe, 303, 774, 913, etc.; f. sio, 709; n. þæt, 101; gen. m. n. þæs, 1251; (conj.), þæs þe, since, after (temporal), 4, 68; since, because, 957, 1140, 1317; dat. m. n. þâm, 421, 444, etc.; acc. m. þone, 423; acc. f. þâ, 398, 1235; pl. nom. acc. þâ, 172, 317, etc.; þâ þe, 154, 280, etc.; gen. þâera, þâra þe, 508, 818, etc. (with sing. predicate), 975, 1226; dat. þâm. 354, 1067. *Art. def.*, m., se, 11, 42, 76, 87, etc.; (with vocative), hæled min se léofa, 511; f. sio, 254, 378, 384, etc.; séo, 266, 309, 558, etc.; n. þæt, 94, 272, etc.

séa, m., well, cistern; in drýgne séa, into the dry cistern, 693.

scaro, s. searu.

searu, n., plot, deceit; þurh feondes searu, 721.

searucræft, scaro, m., artistic skill, art; scarocræftum, 1026; [artifice, treachery, 721].

searuþanc, m., ingenious thought, shrewdness, sagacity; searoþancum, in wise thoughts, 414; snottor scaruþancum, wise in sage thoughts, 1190.

sêcan (sêcean), wv. I., seek, look for, inquire, 216, 420, (sécean), 1149, 1157; sécaþ, 1180; pret. pl. sôhton, 322, 411, 474; person, from whom something is sought, with dat. and tô (post positive); þe ic him tô séce, 319, 410; him tô sôhte, 325, 568; seek, visit, 469, 598, (sécean) 983.

secg, m., man, warrior, (1257); pl. secgas, 47, (secggas) 260, 552, 998, 1001; secga, 97, 271.

secgan, wv. I., say, inform, tell, (secggan) 160, 317, 376, 567, 574; secgaþ, 674; pret. sægdest, 665; sægde, 366, 437; sægdon, 190, 588, 1117.

sefa, m., mind, heart, 173, 627, 956, 1190; on sefan, 382, 474, 532, 1149, 1165; þurh sidne sefan, through expanded mind, 376.

segn, m., token, field-ensign, banner (of cross), 124; (Lat. signum).

sêl, good (only in superl.); sêlest, 532, 1170; sêlost, 1165; âr sêlesta, 1088; sêlestan, 1019; (with following gen.), sêlust, 527; sêlest, 975, 1028; sêleste, 1202.

sêl, adv., comp. better; þê sêl, the better, 796; superl. sêlest, 374; sêlost, 1158.

self, s. sylf.

sellan, wv. I., give, grant; pret. sg. scalde, 182, 1171; p.p. seald, 527.

semninga, adv., immediately, forthwith, 1110, 1275.

sendan, wv. I., send; sende, 931; pret. sende, 1200; þæt on þone hâlgan handa sendan ... fæderas ússe, that our fathers lay hands on this holy one, 457.

scosan, s. siŏŏan.

seofeŏa, seventh; on þone seofeŏan dæg, on the seventh day, 697; seofon, seven; VII., (694).

seolf, s. sylf.

seolfren, (silvern), made of silver; in seolfren fæt, in a silver casket, 1026.

sêon, sv. V., see; pret. pl. sâegon.

sconoŏdôm, m., synodal resolution, assembly's conclusions; sconoŏdômas, 552.

seppan, or sêpan? wv. I., teach, instruct; septe sôŏewidum, taught with true speeches, 530.

seraphin, seraphim; þe man seraphin be naman hâteŏ, 755.

settan, wv. I., set, put (on gewritu setton, put in writing, 654,

658); set, put, place (heo hie on enéow sette, she put them on her knee, 1136; gesundne sið settan, make a prosperous voyage, 1005); count, reckon (þæt hé him þá wéaðárd to wræce ne sette, that he might not reckon this evil deed for vengeance against them, 495; sárum settan, persecute with pains, 479).

sib, s. syb.

síd, wide, extended, large; ofer sid weorod, among the large crowd, 158; ofer sidne grund, over the wide earth, 1289; sǽs sidne fæðm, the ocean's wide expanse, 729; þurh sídne sefan, through expanded mind, 376.

síde, far; síde ond wide, far and wide, 277.

sidweg, m., wide way, great distance; of sidwegum, 282.

síð, m., journey, voyage, expedition; síðes, 247, 260, 1219; síðe, 1001; síð, 111, 243, 997, 1005.

síð, adv., comp., later, afterwards; ǽr oððe síð, 74 (cf. 975); síð né ǽr, 240 (cf. 572).

síðdagas, pl. m., later days, later time; on síðdagum, 639.

síððan, syððan (sioððan, 1147), adv. dem., after that, afterwards, later, 271, [439], 481, 483, 504, 507, 518, 636, 639, 677, 926, 1028, 1060, 1147, 1302, 1315; rel. conj., since, when, as soon as, after, 17, 57, 116, 230, 248, 502, 842, 914, 1002, 1016, 1037, 1051.

síðfæt, m., journey, voyage, 229; þæs síðfates sǽne, negligent of this expedition, 220.

síðian, wv. II., journey, go; [siðigean, 1107]; siðode, 95.

***síðmægen,** n., [Grein, 26].

síðwerod, n., [Körner, 26].

síe, pres. opt. of subst. verb (S. 427), 542, 675, 773, 789, 799, 810, 817, 893, 1229; pl. sien, 430.

sige, m., victory, 144, (1181).

sigebéacen, n., beacon of victory, victory's sign (of the cross), 888; be þám sigebéacne, 108, 1257; sélest sigebéacna, 975.

sigebéam, m., tree of victory, cross; þæs sigebéames, 905; be þám sigebéame, 420, 444, 665, 861; gen. pl. sélest sigebéama, 1028; acc. pl. sigebéamas, 847.

sigebearn, n., child of victory, victorious son; (of Christ) sigebearn godes, 481, 863, 1147.

sigecwén, f., victorious queen (of Helen), 260, 998.

sigeléan, n., reward of victory; sélust sigeléana, the best of the rewards of victory, 527.

sigeléoð, n., lay of victory, song of victory, 124.

sigeróf, famous for victory, strong in victory; sigeróf cyning, 158 (cf. 437); secgas sigerófe, 41; sigeróf, the renowned in victory, 868; sigerófum, 71, 190.

sigespéd, f., victory, fortune in arms, 1172.

sigor, m., victory; gen. sg., sigores tácen, 85, 104, 1121; acc. sigor æt sæcce, 1183; gen. pl. sigora dryhten, 346 (cf. 488, 732, 1140, 1308).

sigorbéacen, n., sign of victory (of cross), 985.

sigorcynn, n., victorious race; victorious beings (of angels), 755.

sigorléan, n., reward of victory; sigorléan in swegle, reward of victory in heaven, 623.

Siluester, Silvester; fram Siluestre, by Silvester, 190.

sîn, his, [438].

sinc, n., treasure, riches, gold; sinces brytta, dispenser of treasure, 194.

sinegim, m., valuable gem, jewel, 264.

sineweorðung, gift of treasure, gift; him Elene forgeaf sineweor-ðunga, Helen granted him gifts, 1219.

sindon, 1081; sint, 740, 744, 826; syndon, 754; synt, 605, 742, 1267; pl. pres. indic. of subst. verb.

sindrêam, m., everlasting joy; in sindrêame, 741.

singal, continual; þis is singal sacu, 906.

singallice, adv., continuously, 747.

singan, sv. III., sing, (sound); singaþ, 747; sang, 337, 1189; sungon, 561; p.p. sungen, 1154; bȳman sungon, the trumpeters sounded, 109.

sint, s. sindon.

siomian, wv. II., tarry, linger; siomode in sorgum .vii. nihta fyrst, lingered in sorrow for the space of seven nights, 694.

sionoð, m., synod, assembly; tó sionoðe, 154.

sittan, sv. V., sit; þû sylf sitest, Thou Thyself sittest, 732.

six, s. syx.

slæp, m., sleep; on slæpe = asleep, 69; of slæpe, out of sleep, 75.

slîðe, cruel, dire, dreadful; on þâ slîðan tîd, at that dire hour, 857.

smæte, pure (of gold); swâ smæte gold, as pure gold, 1309.

smêagan, wv. II., search into, reflect; georne smêadon, reflected earnestly, 413.

snoter, prudent, wise; snottor searuþancum, skilled in wise thoughts, 1190; super. þâm snote-restum, 277.

snûde, adv., quickly, swiftly, 154, 313, 446.

snyrgan, wv. I., hurry, hasten, 244.

snyttro, f., shrewdness, sagacity, wisdom, 154, 293, 313, 374, 382, 407, 544, 551, 938, 959, 1060, 1172.

sôð, sooth, true, 444, 461, 488, 504, 888, 1122; þone sôðan sunu wealdendes, 892; sôðra . . . wundra, 778.

sôð, n., sooth, truth; dat. sôðe, 390, 663; wið sôðe, 307; acc. sôð, 395, 588, 690, 708, 1140; tô sôðe, in truth, truthfully, 160, 574; þurh sôð, in truth, verily, 808.

sôðcwide, m., true speech; septe sôðcwidum, taught in true speeches, 530.

sôðcyning, m., true king, 444.

sôðfæst, fast in truth, true; sôð-fæste, 1289; sôðfæstra leoht, 7.

sôðfæstnes, f., state of being grounded in truth, truthfulness, piety, justice; sôðfæstnesse sécean, to seek piety, 1149.

sôðlice, adv., truthfully, 317, 665; in truth, indeed, 799; indeed, verily, 200, 577.

sôðwundor, n., true miracle; sôðwundor godes, 1122.

some, s. same.

somed, s. samod.

sôna, adv., soon, forthwith, 47, 85, 222, 514, 713, 888, 1031.

sorg, f., sorrow, grief; dat. sg. sorge, 922, 1031; dat. pl. sorgum, 694, 1244.

sorgian, wv. II., sorrow; sorgað, 1082.

sorglêas, without sorrow, free from care; þê sorgléasra, the freer from care, 97.

spâld = spâdl, spâtl, n., spittle, 300.

spêd, f., speed (Godspeed), success, good fortune; hê âh æt wigge spêd, he had success in battle; mihta spêd, fulness of powers, 366.

spêowan, wv. I., spew, spit; spéowdon, 297.

spild, m., destruction, annihilation; þurh dêofles spild, through the devil's destruction, 1119.

spôwan, red. vb., with instr., have success, be successful; ne môt ênige nû rihte spowan, I cannot now be successful with any right, 917.

sprecan, sv. V., speak; pret. sg. spræc, 332, 401, 725.

stæð, n., beach, shore (Ger. gestade), bank (of river), of Danube, 38, 60; ymb geofones stæð, 227, (cf. 230).

staðelian, wv. II., found, fix, establish, make steadfast; opt. pres. staðelien, 427; ind. pres. staðelige, 797; staðolian, 1094.

stân, m., stone, 613; acc. 615; stâne, pl., 565; instr. pl. stânum, 492, 509.

stânclif, n., crag, cliff; æfter stânclifum, behind the cliffs, 135.

standan, sv. VI., stand; standaþ, 577; pret. pl. stôdon, 227, 232; stand forth, spread (hildegesa stôd, fear of battle spread, 113).

stângefôg, n., stone-fitting, stone-laying; stângefôgum, 1021.

stângripe, m., handful of stones, (Grim); dat. pl. stângreopum, 824.

stânhllð, n., rocky slope, cliff; under stânhleoðum, 653.

stærcedfyrhð, strong-minded, brave, 38.

stêam, m., steam, vapor, smoke; stêam ûp âras, the smoke arose, 803.

stearc, stark, stiff, stiff-necked, hard-headed; stearce, 565; streac ond hnesce, hard and soft, 615.

stede, m., stead, place, locality, region; stede ... ymb Danúbie, the region round the Danube, 135.

stedewang, m., field; æfter stedewange, on the field, 675, (cf. 1021).

stefn, f., voice; hædrum stefnum, 748; clênum stefnum, 750.

stefn, m., time (in multiplication); niwan stefne, anew, again, 1061, 1128.

stênan, wv. I., decorate with stones (gems), 151.

Stephanus, Stephen, 492, 509, 824.

steppan, sv. VI., step, advance, storm; stópon stiðhidige, the courageous stormed, 121; stópon ... stiðhycgende, the steadfast in mind advanced, 716.

stiðhidig, of determined mind, stout-hearted, courageous, 121.

stiðhycgende, stout-minded, steadfast in mind, 683, 716.

stôw, f., stow, place, spot, 675; dat. stôwe, 716, 803; acc. stôwe, 653, 683.

strang, strong, severe; tô ðan strang, so severe, 703.

streac, s. stearc.

strêam, m., stream, current; ofer geofenes strêam, over the sea's current, 1201.

strûdan, sv. II., spoil, rob, plunder; êhta strûdeð, despoils my possessions, 905.

stund, f., period, time (Ger.

stunde); dat. sg. stunde, at that time, 724; dat. pl. stundum, awhile (?), 121; stundum, from time to time, time and again, 232.

sum, indef. prn., some one, some; sume hwile, some while, 479; sume ... sume, some ... others, 131, 132, 133, 136, 518.

sumer, m., summer; ær sumeres cyme, before the advent of summer, 1228.

sund, m., swimming, sound, sea; sunde getenge, made fast on the sea, 228; sunde bewreccne, sea-whipped, (251).

sundor, adv., apart, aside, asunder, 407, 603, 1019.

sundorwîs, especially wise; sægdon hine sundorwisne, they called him especially wise, 588.

sunne, f., sun; sunnan beorhtra, brighter than the sun, 1110.

sunu, m., son (of Christ); sunu meotudes, 461, 474, 564, 686, (cf. 592, 778, 892, 1318); voc. sunu, 447; gen. suna, 222; dat. suna, 1200.

sûsl, n., misery, torture, torment; sûsle gebunden, bound in torment, 772; sûslum beþrungen, oppressed by miseries, 950; in sûsla grund, into the abyss of tortures, 944.

swâ, adv., so (intensive), so (in this manner), 153, 306, 325, 350, etc.; swâ þéah, and yet, nevertheless, 500; as, 87, 100, 190, 207, etc. (swâ brimo faðmaþ, as far as the sea (extends) embraces, 972; swâ = as soon as, 128; swâ ... ne, without, although ... not, 340.

swâmîau, wv. II., become obscure, vanish, [629].

swǽs, beloved, own; mîn swǽs sunu, 447; mîn swǽs fæder, 517.

sweart, black, dark, superl. in þâ sweartestan ... witebrôgan, into the blackest ... of the torturing terrors, 931.

swefan, sv. V., sleep; pret. sg. swæf, 70.

swefen, m., sleep, dream, vision; swefnes woma, noise of a dream, 71 (s. note, 71).

swegl, n., heaven; under swegles hléo, 507; under swegle, 75; in swegle, 623; on swegle, 755.

swelling, m. or f. (?), swelling, swelling sail; under swellingum, under swelling sails, 245.

sweng, m., stroke, blow; ýða swengas, blows of the waves, 239.

s w e o r d, n., sword; légene sweorde, with fiery sword, 757.

sweordgeniðla, m., sworded foe, foe armed with a sword, 1181.

sweot, n., band, multitude, troop, [26]; for sweotum, before the troops, 124.

sweotole, adv., visibly, clearly, plainly, 26, 168, 861.

sweotollîce, adv., clearly, 690.

swîcan, sv. I., fail, fall short, become untrue, [293].

swîð, strong; comp. swiðra; séo swiðre, = the strong (hand), the right (hand); mîn on þâ swiðran, on my right hand, 347.

swîðe, adv., very, strongly, severely, fiercely; tô swiðe, too fiercely, 663; swâ swiðe, so strongly, 940; super. swiðost, = most, very much; twéon swiðost, very much in doubt, 668 (cf. 1103).

swîge, still, silent, 1275.

swilt, s. swylt.

swinsian, wv. II., sound, resound; sǽ swinsade, the sea resounded, 240.

swonrâd, f., swan-road, sea; ofer swonrâde, over the sea, 997.

swylc, such, of this sort (owiht swylces, anything of this kind, 571); such as, whoever (swylce . . . Hûna cyning . . . mcahte âbannan, such as the king of the Huns might order, etc., 32).

swylce, adv., likewise, in the same manner, 3, 1033; like, resembling, as (swylce rêc, as smoke, 804; swylce heofensteorran, like the stars of heaven, 1113).

swylt, m., death, 447; swilt, 677.

syb, sib, f., peace; gen. sybbe, 446, 1315; dat. sybbe, 598; acc. sybbe, 1183; relationship, love, 1207; (Ger. sippe), [26].

syððan, s. siððan.

sylf, prn., self; sylf, 303, 466, 732, 855, 1280; sylfa, [439]; gen. f. hiere sylfre, 222; dat. m. n. sylfum, 69, 184, 1295; acc. m. sylfne, 200, 209; gen. pl. sylfra, 1207; acc. pl. sylfe, 1001; — seolf, 708, 808; seolfum, 985; seolfne, 488, 603; pl. seolfe, 1121; gen. f. hire selfre, 1200.

symle, adv., always, continually, 469, 915, 1216.

Sŷmon, Simon, 530.

syn, f., sin, 414; gen. sg. synne, 772; gen. pl. synna, 497, 514, 778, 940, 958, 1318; dat. pl. synnum, 677, 1244, 1309.

syndon, s. sindon.

synful, sinful; synfulle, those laden with sin, 1295.

synnig, sinful, 956.

synt, s. sindon.

synwyrcende, sin-committing, 395, 944.

syx, six, 741; mid syxum . . .

fiðrum, with six wings, 742; butan .vi. nihtum, 1228.

syxta, sixth; syxte geár, sixth year, 7.

T.

tǽcan, wv. I., show, point out; tǽhte, 631.

tâcen, n., token, mark, sign, 171 (sigores tâcen, 85, 184, 1121; tâcen, 104, 1105; tâcna torhtost, the brightest of signs, 164); sign, wonder, miracle (tâcna gehwylces, of every wonder, 319; tâcnum cŷðan, declare in signs, 854; alra tâcna gehwylc, each of the old heroic deeds, 645).

tĕar, m., tear; tĕaras fĕollon, the tears fell, 1134.

tellan, wv. I., count, reckon, consider, believe; þone ic . . . fæstne talde, whom I believed made fast, etc., 909.

tempel, n., temple; tempel dryhtnes, 1010; godes tempel, 1022; tô godes temple, 1058.

tĕona, m., injury, insult, vexation; tô tĕonan, as a vexation, 988.

tid, f., tide, time, period (on his dagana tid, throughout the period of his days, 193; on þá æðelan tid, in that glorious day, 787; in hira lifes tid, in her lifetime, 1209; feala tîda, many times [lit., much of times], 1044; tidum gerŷmde, prolonged [my time] with time [?], 1249); hour (on þá slîðan tid, at this dreadful hour, 857; oð þá nigoðan tid, until the ninth hour, 870; nigoðe tid, ninth hour, 874).

til, good; swâ tiles, swâ trâges, whether good or evil, 325.

tîonlêg, m., destructive flame, 1279.

tîr, m., glory, 164 (s. note, 164); tire getâenod (decore insignitum, Gm.), stamped with Thy glory, 754.

tîrêadig, glorious, rich in glory, renowned; tirêadig cyning, 104; tirêadig cwên, 605; tirêadig, 955.

tô, prep. (1) with dat. (to whom?), to, 604, 1073, 1100, 1318; (wherefore? to what?) to, etc., 10, etc.; (often best translated by ["as" and] apposition), tô hrôðer, a joy, 16; tô wræce, a vengeance, 17 (cf. 23, 34, 45, 48, etc.) (whither?), 32, 52, 83, 216, etc.; (after sêcan), of, from, 319, 325, 410, 568; (temporal), for, in (tô widan feore, in eternity, 211, 1321; tô sôðe, s. sôð; tô hwan, to what [purpose], 1158; with inflected inf. [Lat. gerund], tô gecýðanne, 533; tô gecêosanne, 607; tô gelæstenne, 1166). (2) with gen., tô þæs, = to such a degree, so; tô þæs heard, so intolerable, 704 (cf. tô þan, = so, 703).

tô, adv., too; tô lyt, 63; tô swiðe, 663; tô late, 708; (adv. of direction), þær hie tô sægon, while they looked on (cf. Ger. zusehen), 1105.

tôgênes, adv., in return, in reply, 167, 536.

tôglîdan, sv. I., fall apart; swâ lago tôglideð, as the sea separates, 1269; nihthelm tôglâd, the helmet of night fell apart (i.e. darkness vanished), 78.

tohte, f., fight, battle; tohtan sêcaþ, such battle, 1180.

torht, bright, luminous; super. tâcna torhtost, the brightest of signs, 164.

torht, n., brightness, clearness; torht ontýnde, 1149.

torn, offence, anger, grief; nalles for torne, by no means on account of grief, 1131.

torngeniðla, m., wrath-provoking enemy; torngeniðlan, 568, 1306.

tôsomne, adv., together, 1202.

tôweorpan, sv. III., throw apart, break in pieces, destroy; p.p. tôworpen, 430.

tôwrecan, sv. V., drive apart, scatter; wurdon heardingas wide tôwrecene, the heroes were driven wide asunder, 131.

trâg, evil; swâ tiles, swâ trâges, 955.

trâg, f., evil; wênde him trâge bnâgre, he feared the deplorable evil, 668.

tredan, sv. V., tread; trydeð, traverses, 612; pret. mearh moldan træd, the horse trod the earth, 55.

trêo, n., tree (lifes trêo, tree of life [in Paradise], 757); tree, tree of the cross (rôde trêo, 147, 206, 856), cross, 89, 107, 128, 165, 214, (trio), 429, 442, 531, 701, 706, 828, 841, 867, 1027; trêow, 664; gen. trêowes, 1252.

Trôiâna, pl., Trojans, 645.

trymman, wv. I., strengthen, encourage; hine god trymede, him did God make strong, 14; fêðan trymedon coredcestum, 35 (?) (s. note, 35).

tû, s. twegen.

tûhund, two hundred, 2; .cc., 634.

turfhaga, m., turf-covering, turf sod; under turfhagen, 830.

twâ, s. twêgen.

twegen, m., two, 854; f. twâ, 880, 955, 1180; n. tû, 605 (cf. 754); dat. twâm, þâm twâm dælum, to these two parts, 1306.

twentig, twenty; .xx., 830.

twêo, m., doubt (*twoness*), 171; twêon swiðost, very much in doubt, 668.

twéogan, twêon, wv. II., doubt, [668].

tyht, m., motion; on tyhte, in motion, 53.

Þ.

Þâ, adv., there, then, 7, 25, 42, 69, 94, etc.; rel. conj., inasmuch as, as, since, when, 1, 172, 294, 389, 709, etc.

Þa, s. sê.

Þaflan, wv. II., consent to, allow, suffer to come to pass, 668.

Þâm, s. sê.

Þan, adv., tô Þan, = so; tô Þan strang, so severe, 703; [wiððan, 926]; (cf. ærÞan, forÞan, siððan).

Þanc, m., thought, grace, thanks; siê ðê . . . Þanc bûtan ende, to Thee be thanks without end, 811 (cf. 893).

Þancian, wv. II., thank; gode Þancode, she thanked God, 962, 1139.

Þanc, s. sê.

Þanon, adv., thence, 143, 148; from that time, 318.

Þâr, adv., there, 41, 81, 114, etc.; where (rel.), 329, etc.; Þâr hê on corðre swæf, *as he slept there* in the crowd, 70; Þâr hie tô sâgon, as they looked on, 1105; Þâr . . . ne, unless, 839, [979].

Þâra, Þêra, Þâre, s. sê.

Þâs, s. Þes.

Þæs, s. sê.

Þæt, s. sê.

Þæt, conj., that, 9, 144, 170, 175, etc.; Þæt þe, that, 59 (?); that, in order that, 324, 375, 409, 428, 552,

677, 679, 1055; that, so that, 15, 36 (!), 209, 501, 580, 830, 933.

Þê, rel. prn., (*alone*) who, which (noun and acc.), 160, 163, 183, 298, 319, etc.; (*with dem.*), s. sê; (*with pers. prn.*), Þê Þis his bêacen wæs, whose sign this was, 162; Þû ðê âhst doma geweald, Thou, who hast power over wills, 726; conj., that, 985; ðê dryhten âr âhangen wæs, where the Lord was hanged, 717.

Þê, s. sê and Þû.

Þêah, conj., yet, 500; although, 48, 82, 174, 362, 393, 479, 509, 513, 707, 824, 1118, [1122], 1259.

Þeaht, f., thought; on môdes Þeaht, in the mind's thought, 1242.

Þeahtian, wv. II., think, deliberate, reflect; Þeahtedon, 547.

Þearf, f., need; nû is Þearf mycel, now there is much need (that), etc., 426; is ðow râdes Þearf, (there is need to you), you have need of foresight, 553.

Þearf, s. Þurfan.

Þearl, strong, severe, violent; Þrèanŷd . . . Þearl, violent, terrible necessity, 704.

Þêaw, m., custom, habit, usage; dat. pl. cristenum Þêawum, Christian usages, 1211.

Þee, s. Þû.

Þegn, m., servant, man, warrior; Þegn ôðerne, 540; Þegna Þrêate, 151; Þegna hêap, 549; disciple, (ond his Þegnum hine . . . seolfne geŷwde, and showed himself to his disciples, 487).

Þegnung, f., service, ministration; tô Þegnunge Þinre, 739; Þâ Þegnunge, 745.

Þencan, wv. I., think; pret. pl. Þôhton, 549; consider, intend, wish,

(lýsan þóhte of hæftnéde, wished to release (you) from bondage, 296).
þéod, f., people, nation, 468; dat. on þysse þéode, 539; ofer þæt Ebréa þéod, 448; pl., men, people, gen. þéoda, 185, 421, 659, 781.
þéodan, wv. I., add, commit, [403]. [ple, 1156.
þéodcwén, f., queen of the peo-þéoden, m., king (of Christ), 487, 563, 777, 858; (of Constantine), þéodnes, 207.
þeodenbealu (acc. to Wülker), added injury, extraordinary injury, 403. [þéodscipe, 1167.
þéodscipe, m., discipline; þurh þéon, wv. (S. 408, 8), commit; þéodon, [403].
þéos, s. þes.
þéostor, þýstor, n., or þéostru, þýstru, f., darkness; léoht wið þýstrum, light with darkness, 307; þéostrum forþylmed, shrouded in darkness, 707.
þéostorcofa, m., dark space; in þéostorcofan, 833.
þéostorloca, m., dark lock-up, dark prison; under þéostorlocan, 485.
þéostre, dark; þéostrum geþan-cum, with dark thoughts, 312.
þéowdóm, m., service; in godes þéowdóm, 201.
þéownéd, f., servitude, slavery; þéownéd þolian, endure the slave's necessity, 770.
þerscan, sv. III., thrash, beat; þirsceð, 358.
þes, prn. (adj. and subs.), this; m. þes, 703, 704; f. þéos, 468, 533, 551, etc.; n. þis, 162, 435, 903, etc.; dat. (m), n. þissum, 576; f. þysse, 402, 539, 643; acc. m. þysne, 312; n. þis, 630, 659; instr (m.), n. þýs, 92; pl. nom. and acc. þás, 749,

1173; gen. þyssa, 858; dat. þyssum, 700.
þlegan, sv. V., receive; pret. sg. þege, 1259.
þín, pers. prn., thy, thine, 489, 510, 597, etc.; s. þû.
þincan, s. þyncan.
þing, n., thing; þinga gehwylc, 409, (cf. 1156); tó þinge, as a fact (?), 608.
þinggemearce, n., characteriza-tion of a thing, determination of time, time; gen. (adv.) þingge-mearces, according to time (as one counts time), 3.
þlugian, wv. II., intercede for (with dat.); ac his eald féondum þingode þrohtherd, but patiently he made intercession for his embittered enemies, 494; speak, made a speech, (him ... wið þingode, spoke to him, 77); Judas hire ongén þingode, Judas replied to her, 609, 667.
þis, þis-, s. þes.
þolian, wv. II., suffer, endure, 770.
þone, s. sé.
þonne, adv., then, 446, 489, 526, 931, 1286; conj., when, if, 50, 473, 618, 1178, 1179, 1185, 1273, 1280; than, (after comp.) læsse ... þonne, 48; ænlicra þonne, 74; furðurþonne, 388; (with implied comp.), þæt wæs fér mycel, open ealdgewin þonne þéos wðcle gewyrd, that was a great danger, the known battle of olden times, (older, or greater?) than this noble event, 647.
þracu, f., onrush, storm, conflict, battle; þræce, to the contest, 45; wið þéoda þræce, against the attack of the people, 185.
þrág, f., time; þrágum, at times, sometimes, 1239, [608].

þræcheard, strong in battle, valiant in combat, 123.

þrægan, wv. I., run; þrægde, 1263.

þréa, m. f., threat, oppression, might; þréam forþryceed, with might oppressed, 1277.

þréalic, terrible, horrible; þæt wæs þréalic geþóht, that was a horrible conception, 426.

þréagan, wv. III., reprove, punish; p.p. in ðám nidle þréad, punished in the middle, 1296.

þréanéd, f., dire necessity; þréanýd, 704; þréanédlum, 884.

þréat, m., crowd, troop, multitude; dat. (instr.), þreate, 51, 326, 329; þegna þréate, 151; folca þ., 215; wigena þ., 217; gumena þ., 254, 1096; secga þ., 271; wera þ., 537; beorna þ., 873; for þyslicne þréat, before such a crowd, 546.

þréo, three, 2, 285, 483, 869, 1286; .III., 833, 847; gen. þréora, 858.

þreodian, wv. II., think over, reflect upon, consider; pret. sg. þreodude, 1239; pret. pl. þrydedon, 549.

þridda, third, 855, 1298; sio þridde, 884; þý þriddan dæge, 185 (cf. 485).

þringan, sv. III., throng, press, hasten; pret. pl. þrungon, 123, 329.

þríste, bold, determined, confident, 267; audacious, 1286.

þríste, adv., boldly, confidently, 409, (1167).

þritig, þrittig, thirty; .xxx., 3.

þroht, m., torture, 704.

þrohtherd, strong in enduring torture, patient, 494.

þrosm, m., smoke; þrosme beþehte, covered with smoke, 1298.

þrówian, wv. II., suffer, endure, 769; þrówode, 421.

þrýðbord, n., strong shield, 151.

þrydian, s. þreodian.

þrym, m., glory, majesty (of God), the Most Glorious; callra þrymma þrym, the Glory of all glories, 486, 519; allra cyninga þrym, the Most Glorious of all kings, 816, (cf. 1090); þrymmes hyrde, Guardian of glory, 348, 859; þrymme, with glory (= glorious), 745; in þrynesse þrymme, in the majesty of the trinity, 177; on þrymme, in majesty, 329.

þrymcyning, m., glorious king, king of glory, 494.

þrymlíce, adv., gloriously, 781.

þrymsittende, throned in glory; ðe ... þrymsittendum, to Thee throned in glory, etc., 811.

þrýnes, f., threeness, trinity; in þrynesse þrymme, 177.

þú, pers. prn., thou, 81, 83, 84, etc.; þú þe, Thou who, 726; þú (alone) (Thou) who, 727, 730, 732; gen. þin, sé éhteð þin, who will persecute thee, 928; dat. þé, 79, 81, 82, 441, etc.; acc. þec 403, 447, 539, 676, 823, 931; þé, 522, 789, 814, etc.

þúf, m., banner, 123.

þurfan, pret. pres., need; ne þearft ðú ... sár niwigan, thou needst not renew the sorrow, 940; need, may, dare (?), ic þá róde ne þearf hleahtre herigean, this cross I dare not despise with the laughter of scorn, 919 (?); cf. þorfte, 1104.

þurh, prep. with acc., through, causal (occasion, agent, means, instrument), 120, 147, 158, 165, 172, 183, 199, 281, 289, etc., 459, 626, 646, 808, 1106; at, because of, on account of, 86, 98, 400, 1167, 1301;

(manner), in, with, 6, 685; by, for the sake of (þurg þæt beorhte gesceap, etc., by that bright object [I will pray], 790; ic þæt geswerige þurh sunu meotodes, that I swear by the Son of the Creator, 686; ic cow healsie þurh heofona god, I adjure you by the God of heaven, 699).

þurhdrîfan, sv. I., shove through, penetrate, imbue; mid dysige þurhdrifen, imbued with folly, 707.

þurhgêotan, sv. II., pour through, fill, imbue, saturate; gleawnesse þurhgoten, impregnated with knowledge, 902.

þurhwadan, sv. VI., go through, bore, pierce; þe . . . fêt þurhwôdon, (of the nails) which pierced the feet, etc., 1066.

þus, adv., thus, so, 180, 400, 528, 1120, 1237.

þûsend, n., thousand; m., 285, 326. þŷ, s. sê.

þyder, adv., thither, on that side, 548.

þyncan, wv. I., seem, appear; pret. sg. þuhte, 72; sêlost þûhte, 1165; opt. pres. sêlest þince, 532; seem good, dô swâ þê þynce, do as seems good to thee, 541.

þys, s. þes.

þyslic, thuslike, such a; for þyslicne þreat, before such a crowd, 546; (adv.), in this manner, thus, 540.

þysne, þyssa, þysse, þyssum, s. þes.

þŷst, s. þeost.

U.

ûðweota, m., wise man, philosopher, scribe; ûðweotan, 473.

ûhta, m., or ûhte, n. (S. 280. 1),

dawn of morning; on ûhtan, at dawn, 105.

ûhtsang, m., song at dawn, [29].

unâseegendlîe, unutterable, 466.

unbrêce, indestructible, everlasting; æðelum unbrêce, in its properties endless, (1029).

unclêne, unclean; fram unclênum . . . gâstum, 301.

uncûð, unknown; uncûðe wyrd, unknown occurrence, 1102.

uncŷðig, ignorant, 961; clues oncŷðig, unacquainted with power, powerless, 725.

undearninga, adv., openly, unreservedly, 405; undearnunga, 620.

under, prep. (with dat.), under, 13, 46, 75, 147, 245, 507, etc.; under (deep in), 218, 485, 625, 653, 695, 832, 843, 1092; (with acc.), under, 44, 764.

ungelîce, adv., unlike, differently, unequally, 1307.

unhwîlen, without limit of time, eternal; drêam unhwilen, 1232.

unlifgende, lifeless, 879.

unlŷtel, not a little, much, great; mægen unlŷtel, not a little crowd, 283; folc unlŷtel, not a little folk, 872.

[unne, f., permission, favor, [1246].]

unoferswîðeð, unvanquished, invincible, 1188.

unriht, wrong, false; unrihte æ, unrighteous law, 1042.

unriht, n., wrong, injustice, sin; unrihtes, 472, 516; on unriht, 582.

unrîme, numberless, unnumbered; unrime mægen, 61.

unseyldig (Ger. unschuldig), guiltless, innocent; unscyldigne, (423), 496.

unscynde, not injuring, blameless, glorious; dôm unscyndne, 365; gife unscynde, 1201, 1247.

[unscôe,unsick,1247; Ettmüller.] unsláw, unslow, stirring, active, 202.

unsnyttro, f., unwisdom, folly; unsnyttro, in folly, 1285; unsnyttrum, foolishly, 947.

unsôfte, adv., unsoftly, with difficulty; sume unsófte aldor generedon, some saved life with difficulty, 132.

untrâglîce,adv.,without reserve, without hesitation, 410.

untwêonde, undoubting, unwavering; hyht untwêondne, unwavering hope, 798.

unweaxen, not grown up, young; mec . . . unweaxenne, 529.

unwîslîce, adv., unwisely, 293.

ûp, adv. (direction), up, upwards, 87, 95, 353, 700, 712, 714, 717, 736, 794, 803, 879, 1107, 1226.

uppan, prep. (with dat. or acc. postpositive), over; him ûppan, over him, 886.

uppe, adv., up, above; uppe = on high, 52; [im schwange, 1266, according to Dietrich].

ûprador, m., upper heaven, firmament, 731.

ûpweard, adv., upward, toward heaven, 806.

ûr, m., aurochs, name of the rune for u.

ûrigfeðera, dewy-winged, 29; ûrigfeðra earu, 111.

ûs, pers. prn., dat. us, 400, 637; acc. ûsic, us, 533.

ûsse, pl., our; fæderas ûsse, 425, 458.

ût, adv., out; beran ût þræce rincas under roderum, to lead out to combat the heroes under heaven, 45.

W.

wâ, adv., woe; ond gehwædres wâ, and in either event woe (?), 628.

wadan, sv. VI., wade, go, advance; wadan wægflotan, wave floaters press on, 246.

wæðan, wv. I., hunt, roam around; wæðed be wolcnum, darts over (past) the clouds, 1274.

wædl, f., poverty, want; gewende tô wædle, betakes himself to want, 617.

wæg, m., wave; wæges welm, the wave's motion, 230.

wægflota, m., wave-float, ship; pl. wægflotan, 246.

wæghengest, m., wave-horse, ship (Ger. hengst); wæghengestas, 236.

wald, s. weald.

wælfel, greedy for corpses, ghoulish, 53.

wælhlence, f., battle-link, coat of mail; pl. wælhlencan, 24.

wælhrêow, wild in battle, unrestrained, cruel; wælhrêowra wig, the battle of the cruel, 112.

wælrest. f., death-rest, bed of slaughter, grave's quiet; wunode wælreste, rested in the quiet of the grave.

wælrûm, f., battle-secret; wælrûne ne mâð, he did not conceal the battle-secret, 28.

wan, wan, wanting color, dark, black (of the raven), 53.

wang, m., field; nê þæs wanges wiht, nor anything of this field, 684.

wangstede. m., point of the field, locality, field; of Sâm wangstede, 794; on Sâm wangstede, 1104.

wannhâl, unhealthy, weak; wraðu wannhâlum, help for the sick, 1030.

wansælig, unhappy, miserable; weras wonsælige, 478; werum wansæligum, 978.

wæpen, n., weapon, 1189; wæpen âhôf, took up arms, 17; wæpnum, 48.

wæpenþracu, f., storm of weapons, conflict; acc. wæpenþræce, 106.

wær, fidelity (wær wið þec, fidelity toward Thee, 823); favor, protection (wære bêodan, announce protection, 80).

wærlic, cautious, prudent; worda wærlicra, of prudent words, 544.

wæstm, m. f. n., growth, fruit; wæstmum gêacnod, fructified with fruit, 341.

wât, s. witan.

wæter, n., water; ymb þæs wæteres wylm, around this water's stream, 39 (cf. 60).

wê, pers. prn., we, 364, 397, 399, 401, 402, etc.

wêadêd, f., woful deed, evil deed, 495.

weald, m. (Ger. wald), forest · on wealde, 28.

wealdan, red. vb., rule, possess; with instr. duguðum wealdan, 450; with gen. þæs ðu . . . wealdest, this Thou controllest, 761; walde . . . wuldres on heofenum, possesses glory in heaven, 801.

wealdend, wielder, guider, ruler, lord, king (of God), 4, 80, 391, 512; (waldend), 732, 752, 773, 781, 789(?),851,892,1043,1085,1090(?); (of Christ) (waldend), 206, 337, 347; (waldend), 421, 482, 1067.

weallan, red. vb., well up, boil, move (of waves), agitate; weallende gewitt þurh wigan snyttro, mind agitated (lit. moving) by the warrior's wisdom, 938.

weard, m., warden, watch, guardian, protector; (of God), 84, 197, 1022, 1101, 1316; (of Christ), 338, 445, 718; (of Constantine), 153; ceastre weardas, the guardians of the city, 384.

weardian, wv. II;, guard, protect, take possession of, inhabit; stede weardedon ymb Danûbie, they took possession of the region around the Danube, 135; hreðer weardode, inhabited the bosom, 1145.

wearhtreafu, n. pl., home of the damned, hell; of ðam wearhtreafum, 927.

weaxan, sv. VI., wax, grow, increase; pret. sg. wêox, 12, 914, [547].

webbian, wv. II., weave, project; inwitþancum wrôht webbedan, with wicked thoughts wove crime, 309.

weccan, wv. I., wake, [106].

wed, n., pledge, security, extenuation; wed gesyllan, to give pledge (?), 1284.

wêdan, wv. I., rage; wêdende, 1274.

wefan, sv. V., weave; worderæft wæf, I wove skill of words, 1238.

weg, m., way; weg to wuldre, way to heaven, 1150.

wegan, sv. V., carry, bear; môdsorge wæg . . . cyning, the king experienced sorrow of heart, 61; gnornsorge wæg, he bore sorrow, 655.

welm, s. wylm.

wêmend, adviser, discloser; rihtes wêmend, revealer of right, 880.

wên, f., hope, name of the rune w; wên is geswiðrad, hope is departed, 1264.

wêna, m., expectation; dêaðes on wênan, in expectation of death, 584.

wênan, wv. I. (with gen.), hope for, expect; wênan, 1104; pret. sg. wende, 62, [348]; wendon, 478, [880]; wende him tráge hnágre, he feared the deplorable evil, 668.

wendan, wv. 1., wend, turn; þæt hie hit for worulde wendan ne meahton, that they might not avert this before the world, 979; pret. sg. wende (348); wende hine of worulde, he turned himself from the world, 440.

wendelsǽ, m., boundary sea; boundary of the sea; æt wendelsǽ, 231.

weorc, n., work; hrefn weorces gefeah, the raven rejoiced at the work, 110; cwên weorces gefeah, 849; synna weorc, 1318; weorcum fáh, besmirched by deeds, 1243.

weorðan, sv. III., with p.p. (forming passive or circumlocution for pret.), 581, 688; pret. sg. weard, 5, 9, 69, 102, 178, 183, 638, 776, 804, 989, 1035, 1050; pret. sg. opt. wurde, 336, 429, 961, 976; (without p.p.), be, become, happen, occur (weorðan, 220, 1049, 1177; wyrðeð, 575; weorðen, 428; wearð, 15, 41, 501, 1036, 1042; wurdon, 130, 584, 1278; wurde, 401).

weorðian, wv. II., hold worthy, honor; pret. sg. weorðode, 1137; pret. pl. weorðodon, 831; pret. pl. opt. weorðeden, 1222; p.p. weorðod, 1196.

weorpan, sv. III., throw, cast; p.p. worpene, 1304.

weorod, troop, legion, band, folk, multitude, 158; dat. sg. weorode, 844; gen. pl. weoroda, 752, 815, 897; dat. pl. weorodum, 351, 782, 867 (cf. weorud, 1117; weorude, 1281; weoruda, 223, 681); wereda, 1085; werod, 19, 48, 53, 60, 94; werodes, 38; werode, [217], 230; weroda, 789, 1150 (?).

weoruld, s. woruld.

wer, m., man, person, 508; weres, 72, 341, 959, 967, 1038; wer, 785; weras, 22, 287, 314, 478, 547, 559; wera, 304, 475, 537, 543, 596; werum, 236, 978, 1222.

wered, s. weorod.

wergan, wv. 1., condemn, curse, despise; þú gé wergdon þanc, for you despised him, 294.

wergð(u), f., curse, condemnation, punishment, 309; of wergðe, 295; wergðu dréogan, suffer punishment, 211, 952.

wêrig, weary, unhappy, miserable; sio wêrge secolu, the miserable throng, 763; þá wéregan néat, 357; wêrge wræcmæcggas, unhappy men of misfortune, 387.

werod, s. weorod.

werodlêst, f., want of men; for werodlêste, for want of men, 63.

werþêod, f., men-folk, folk, people; on þysse werþêode, 649; geond þá werþêode, 969; werþêodum, 17.

wesan, sv. V., be; wæs, 1, 7, 11, 13, etc.; wêron, 22, 25, 46, etc.

westan, adv., from the west, 1016.

wêsten, m. n., waste, desert, wilderness; on wéstenne, 611.

wîc, n., dwelling; wic gewunode, inhabited the dwelling, 1038 (cf. wic beheold, 1144).

wicg, n., horse; sê þæt wicg byrð, who directs (?) that horse, 1190.

wîcian, wv. II., dwell, encamp; pret. sg. here wicode, the army encamped, 65 (cf. wicedon).

wîd, wide, broad, expanded; tô widan feore, for extended time, = in eternity, forever, 211, 1321; on widan feore, in extended time (*i.e.* during the long period of the world's existence); widan fyrhð, during long life, = eternally, 761 (cf. 801).

wîde, widely, 131, 969; side ond wide, far and wide, 277.

wîð, prep. (with gen.). (1) against; wið hungres hlêo, protection against hunger, 616. (2) (with dat.), against, 18, 64, 165, 185, 416, 525, 837, [926], 1182, 1188 (him . . . wið þingode, he spoke to him, 77); with, 307, 308. (3) (with acc.), against, toward, 403, 513 (wære wið þec, fidelity toward thee, 823, 927?).

wiðercyr, m. (Ger. wiederkehr), return, 926.

wiðerhycgende, hostile-minded, hostile, 952.

wiðersæc, n (?)., hostility, opposition; wiðersæc fremedon, they offered contradiction, 569.

wiðhycgan, wv. I., scorn; beteran wiðhycge, (that) he scorn the better, 618.

w i ð r ê o t a n, sv. II., contend against, resist; gê þam ryhte wiðroten hæfdon, you had withstood the right, 369.

wiðsacan, sv. VI., oppose, contend against, renounce, scorn, abandon; (with dat), wiðsæcest sôðe ond rihte, 663; pret. sg. þinum wiðsôc aldordôme, 767; þam wyrsan wiðsôc, 1040; pret. pl. wiðsôcon sôðe ond rihte, 390; (with acc.), wiðsæcest þone âhangan cyning, 933; pres.

opt. þâ wiste wiðsæce, 617; pret. pl. þæt wê wiðsocun ær, 1122 (?).

wiðweorpan, sv. III., reject; wiðwurpon, 294.

wîf, n., wife, woman, 223, 286, 508; wifes, 1132; werum ond wifum, 236, 1222.

wîg, m. n., war, battle, 131; wîges wôma, noise of war, 19; acc. wig, 112; wigges lêan, 825; dat. (instr.) wigge, 48, 150, 1182, 1189, 1196.

wiga, m., warrior; gen. sg. þurh wigan snyttro, 938; pl. wigan, 246; gen. pl. wigena, 63, 150, 153, 217, (wigona), 344, 1090.

wîgend, m., warrior, 106; wîgende, 984.

wîgg, s. wîg.

wîgspêd, f., success of war, victory, 165.

wîgþracu, f., storm of war, attack; æfter wigþræce, after the battle-storm, 430; þâ wigþræce, 658.

wiht, f. n., wight, whit, anything; nê þæs wanges wiht, nor anything of this field, 684.

wilfægen, of elated will, glad, 828.

wilgifa, m., granter of desires, giver of joy; (of Constantine), þæs wilgifan word, 221; (of Christ), weoroda willgifa, 815; (of God), hira willgifan wundor, 1112.

willa, m., will, wish, desire, joy, 773, 789, 963, 1136, 1160; dryhtne tô willan, for the Lord's sake, 193 (cf. 678, 1011); acc. willan, 267, 681, 1071, 1085, 1132, 1153; willum gefylled, filled with joy, 452 (cf. 1252).

willan, anv. (S. 428), will, wish (often forming future, but with idea of volition); 1st p. sg. wille,

574, 700, 814; 2d p. sg. opt. wille, 608, 621; 3d p. sg. opt. wile, 420; pret. sg. wolde, 219, 469; pret. pl. woldon, 40, 361, 394, 971; wolde ic, þæt ðu funde, I would that thou wouldst find (them), 1080; hú wolde þæt geweorðan, how could this happen! 456.

willgifa, s. wilgifa.

willhrêðig, glad-hearted (because of a fulfilled wish), exultant, 1117.

willsîð, m., desired journey; on willsîð, for the longed-for journey, 223.

willspel, n., desired news, good tidings, glad message; æt þám willspelle, at this good news, 994; wilspella mæst, this greatest coveted news, 984.

wind, m., wind; winde geliccost, 1272.

winemæg, m., friendly man, friend; winemagas, 1016.

winnan, sv. III., fight, contend 1181 (s. note, 1181).

winter, m., winter (year); .xxx. . . . wintra, thirty (of) winters, 4; wintra gangum, in the course of years, 633.

wintergerîm, n., number of years, 654.

wîr, m., wire; ofer wira gespon, 1135; wirum gewlenced, 1264.

wîs, wise, learned, 592; super. þá wisestan, 153, 169, 323.

wîsdôm, m., wisdom, 1243; gen. sg. wisdômes, 357, 543, 596, 939, 1144, 1191; acc. 334, 674.

wîse, f., wise, manner, circumstance; þá wisan, 684.

wîsfæst, very wise; weras wisfæste, 314.

wist, f., substance, food, 617.

wiste, s. witan.

wita, m., wise man, councillor; witan snyttro, wisdom of a wise man, 544.

witan, pret. pres., know (wit, wot); ic wát, 419, 815; pl. witon, 644; pret. sg. wiste, 860, 1203; pret. pl. wiston, 459; imperative, wite, 946.

wîtan, sv. I., reproach; þe him sio cwén wite, (with) which the queen reproached them, 416.

wîte, n., punishment, torture (of hell), hell; láðlic wite, 520; in wita forwyrd, 765 (cf. 1030); heardum witum, 180; in witum, 771.

wîtebrôga, m., torturing terror; þá wyrrestan witebrôgan, the worst torturing terrors, 932.

wîtedôm, m., prophecy, prediction, 1153.

wîtga, m., prophet, 351, 1189; gen. sg. witan sunu, the son of a prophet, 592; pl. witgan, 561; gen. witgena, 280, 334, 394.

wlanc, proud, stately; wlanc manig, many a proud one, 231.

wlîtan, sv. I., see, look; wlát ofer ealle, he glanced over all, 385.

wlite, m., appearance, form, beautiful form, beauty; on wlite, 1319.

wliteg, s. wlitig.

wlitescŷne, beautiful in appearance, 72.

wlitig, beautiful, 77; þæt wlitige treo, 165; super. wlitegaste, 749; wliti wuldres treo, 89.

wôð, f., voice, tone, song; wôða wlitegaste, the most beautiful of songs, 749.

wolcen, n. (welkin), cloud; pl. ofer wolcna hróf, upon the roof of the clouds, 89; under wolcnum, 1272; be wolcnum, 1274.

wolde, s. **willan**.

wom, m. n., spot, blemish, sin; under womma sceatum, 583 (cf. 1310).

womful, full of blemishes, sinful; womfulle synwyrcende sceaðan, the bespotted, sin-committing enemies, 761.

womsceaða, sin-besmirched enemy, 1299.

wôma, m., noise; wiges wôma, 19; swefnes wôma, noise of a dream, vision, 71.

wonhŷdig, heedless, foolish; wonhŷdige, 763.

wonsǽlig, s. **wan**.

wôp, m., weeping; wôpes hring, sound of weeping, 1132.

word, n., word; gen. sg. wordes, 314, 419; instr. worde, 946; acc. word, 221, 334, (338), 344, 394, 440, 547, 582, 724, 749, 771, 939, 990, 1003, 1072, 1108, 1191; gen. pl. worda, 544, 569, 1284; dat. (instr.) wordum, 169, 287, 351, 385, 529, 537, 559, 589, 803, 1319; wordum ond bordum, 24.

wordcræft, m., wordcraft, art of speech; wordcræftes wis, 592; poetic art (wordcræft, 1238).

wordcwide, m., speech; wrixledan wordcwidum weras, the men exchanged thoughts in speech, 547.

wordgerŷne, n., verbal secret, secret (hidden in words); þurh witgena wordgerŷno, through the prophets' secret in words, 289, (cf. 323).

world, s. **woruld**.

worn, m., multitude, number, (304 ?), 633.

worpian, wv. II., throw, throw

at, pelt; stânum worpod, pelted with stones, 492; stângreopum worpod, 825.

woruld, f., world; world, 1277; on worulde, 561; of . . ., 440; in . . ., 994, 1153, (worlde) 1252; fram . . ., 1142; acc. on woruld, into the world, 508; in woruld weorulda, in the world of worlds (*i.e.* in eternity), 452; for worulde, before the world, (*i.e.* before humanity), 4, [304], 979.

woruldgedâl, n.; separation from the world, death; tô woruldgedâle, 581.

woruldrîce, n., kingdom of the world; on woruldrice, 456, (cf. 779); in worldrice, 1049.

woruldstund, f., life in the world; æfter woruldstundum, throughout my sojourn upon earth, 363.

wrǽc (?), s. **wracu**.

wrǽcmæcgg, m., miserable man, man of misfortune; wêrge wrǽcmæcggas, unhappy men of misfortune, 387.

wracu (or **wræc** ?), f., revenge, punishment; tô wræce, a vengeance, 17, (cf. 495).

wrâð, perverse, perverted; þurh wrâð gewitt, 459; wroth, angry, hostile (wið wrâðum, against the hostile, 165; wrâð wið wrâðum, hostile against hostile, 1182).

wrâðe, adv., perversely, 294.

wraðu, f., support, help, 1030; þær ðû wraðe findest, where thou wilt find help, 84, [294].

wrǽtlîce, adv., wonderfully, splendidly, artistically; super. wrǽtlicost, 1020.

wrecan, sv. V., drive, press forward; stundum wrǽcon, they pressed forward a while, 121, 232.

wreccan, wv. I., awake, 106.

wrêon, sv. I. and II., cover, conceal; pret. pl. wrigon, 583.

wríðan, sv. I., wreathe, twist; wriðene wælhlencan netted (?), coats of mail, 24.

wrixlan, wv. I., exchange, change, (547), 759.

wrôht, m. f., accusation, crime, 309.

wrôhtstæf, m., crime; þurh wrôhtstafas, through crimes, 926.

wuldor, n., glory; wuldres, 752, 801; wuldre, 1135; wuldor, 813; wuldres miht, might of glory, glorious might, 295, 727; wuldres trêo (of cross), tree of glory, 89, 828, 867 (cf. 217, 844, 1252); with gen. pl. most glorious (cyninga wuldor, 5, 178, cf. 186); glory, heavenly glory, heaven (wuldres, 77, 84, 738, 1040, 1090; in wuldre, 747, 782, 823; tô wuldre, 1047, 1150); glory (glorification), 893, 1117, 1124.

wuldorcyning, m., King of Glory (of God); wuldorcyninges, 1321; wuldorcyninge, 291, 963, 1304.

wuldorfæst, glorious, (as fast as heaven?); wuldorfæste gife, 967.

wuldorgeofa, m., bestower of glory; weoruda wuldorgeofa (God), the men's Bestower of Glory, 681.

wuldorgifu, f., glorious gift, grace; onwrige wuldorgifum, might reveal it by grace, 1072.

wulf, m., wolf, 28, 112.

wund, f., wound; synna wunde, the wound of sins, 514.

wundor, n., wonder, miracle, 868, 1112, 1122, 1254; pl. wundor, 827, 897; feala . . . wundra, many (of) miracles, 363, 777; wundrum, wonderfully, 1238.

wundorwyrd, f., wonderful event; ymb wundorwyrd, 1071.

wundriau, wv. II., marvel, wonder; wundrade ymb þæs weres snyttro, she marvelled at the wisdom of this man, 959.

wunîgan, wv. II., dwell, be, 821, (remain), 908; pres. opt. wunige, 624; pret. sg. wunodest, 950; wunode, 724, 1028.

wy l m, m., wave, motion (of wave), current, stream; wæges welm, wave's motion, (230); ymb þæs wæteres wylm, beside this water's stream, 39; (of fire), in þæs wylmes grund, 1299; in wylme, 765, 1310; in hâtne wylm, 1207.

wyn, f., joy, bliss; wuldres wynne, bliss of heaven, 1040.

wynbêam, m., tree of delight; (of cross), wuldres wynbêam, 844.

wynsum, winsome; of ðám wangstede wynsumne, from this winsome spot, 794.

wyrcan, wv. I., work; þá hé worhte, which he wrought, 827 (cf. 897); work, build, 1020 (nales seeame worhte gáste mínum, in no wise wrought I this shame to my spirit, 470).

wyrd, f., Weird, fate (hûru, wyrd gescráf, forsooth, Fate decreed, 1047); fate, event, transaction, object (acc. wyrd, 541, 583, 1064, 1102; wyrda, 80, 589, 813, 978, 1124, 1256).

wyrdan, wv. I., destroy; minne . . . folgað wyrdeð, destroyeth my following, 904.

wyrðe, worth, worthy, dear, 291.

wyrresta, the worst; þá wyrrestan witebrôgan, the worst of the torturing terrors, 932.

wyrsa, worse; þám wyrsan wiðsóc, opposed the worse, 1040.

Y.

ȝȣ, f., wave ; ȝȝa swengas, strokes of waves, 239.

ȝȣhof, n., wave-dwelling, ship ; ald ȝȣhofu, old ships, (252).

yfel, n., evil; ne geald hê yfel yfele, he did not return evil for evil, 403; yfela gemyndig, mindful of evils, 902.

yfemest, adv., uppermost; yfemest in þâm âde, 1290.

ylde, s. elde.

yldra, s. eald.

ymb, prep. (with acc.), (loc.), around, about, 50, 66, 260, 869; about, on, near, 39, 136 ; on, 60, 227; (temporal), after, 272, 383; ymb sige, for victory, 1181; about, concerning, in regard to, 214, 442, 534, 541, 560, 664, 959, 1064, 1071. 1255.

ymbhwyrft, m., sphere of earth ; calne ymbhwyrft, 731.

ymbsellan, wv. I., surround, envelop ; þâ ymbsealde synt mid syxum eac fiȝrum, which are also surrounded with six wings, 742.

ymbsittend, besieger ; Hûna ... ymbsittendra âwêr, of the Huns . . . encamped somewhere round about, 33.

ȝppe, evident, known, 435.

ȝr, bow, name of the rune for y ; (according to Rieger) gold, 1260.

yrfe, n., inheritance, heritage ; yrfes brûcaþ, enjoy the heritage, 1320.

yrming, unfortunate man, [1290].

yrmȝu, s. ermȝu.

yrre, (wrong, erring), angry, 573; eorre, 401; þurh eorne hyge, in her angry soul, 685.

OLD AND MIDDLE ENGLISH.

[ANGLO-SAXON.]

Beówulf: An Anglo-Saxon Poem.

(Vol. I. of the Library of Anglo-Saxon Poetry.)

Contains also the Fight at Finnsburh. With Text and Glossary on the basis of Heyne's fourth edition, edited, corrected, and enlarged by JAMES A. HARRISON, Professor of English and Modern Languages, Washington and Lee University, and ROBERT SHARP, Professor of Greek and English, Tulane University of Louisiana. *Third Edition, revised.* 12mo. Cloth. x + 325 pages. Mailing Price, $1.25; Introduction, $1.12.

THIS edition is designed primarily for college classes. It has been recommended by Professors Dowden and Nicoll to their classes in the Universities of Dublin and Glasgow.

F. A. March. *Prof. of Anglo-Saxon, Lafayette College:* The best there is for class use. (*Nov.* 2, 1885.)

Hiram Corson, *Prof. Eng., Cornell Univ.:* Altogether the one best adapted to the wants of American students.

Cædmon's Exodus and Daniel.

(Vol. II. of the Library of Anglo-Saxon Poetry.)

Edited from Grein, with Notes and Glossary, by THEODORE W. HUNT, Professor of Rhetoric and English Language in Princeton College. *Third Edition, revised.* 12mo. Cloth. 121 pages. Mailing Price, 65 cents; Introduction, 60 cents. The Glossary has been much enlarged.

THIS edition is designed mainly for college classes, and includes 589 lines of the *Exodus* and 765 of the *Daniel.*

F. A. March, *Lafayette College:* It is a matter of honest pride to see an American publish a neat and conven- ient edition of it.

Andreas: A Legend of St. Andrew.

(Vol. III. of the Library of Anglo-Saxon Poetry.)

Edited, with Critical Notes, by W. M. BASKERVILL, Professor of English Language and Literature in the Vanderbilt University. Text and Notes, viii – 78 pages. Paper. 25 cents. To be issued soon in Cloth, with Glossary. *See the Announcements.*

GRIMM'S, Grein's, and Kemble's editions have been freely used. The chief canon of criticism followed has been to adhere to the reading of the Ms. wherever it was possible.

T. W. Hunt, *of Princeton College :* | **Modern Language Notes** (*J. W.* It is very neatly issued, and in text *Bright*) *:* The editor's work bears and notes is highly satisfactory. | the stamp of great care and industry

An Old- and Middle-English Reader.

(Zupitza's Alt- und Mittel-Englisches Lesebuch.)

Translated and edited for the Library of Anglo-Saxon Poetry by Prof. G. E. MacLean, Ph.D. (Lips.), of the University of Minnesota. The Text, in paper. vi + 115 pages. The complete volume in the summer of 1888. *See also the Announcements.*

THE Text consists of two parts, — Old-English and Middle-English. It is believed to be exceptionally accurate, the manuscripts having been collated personally by Professor Zupitza. The thirty-four pieces are typical as regards the language in its different stages and the literature. They embrace poetry and prose from the rise of the literature in England through the Middle-English Period, — from Cædmon's *Hymn* to John Lydgate's *Guy of Warwick,* — a period of seven hundred years. The selections are short, and, when possible, entire ; they are arranged chronologically, and at a glance reveal the changes in the language.

A new feature is the printing, in parallel columns, of specimens for the study of the West Saxon, Northumbrian, and Mercian dialects.

The Phonological Investigation of Old English.

Illustrated by a series of fifty problems. By ALBERT S. COOK, Ph.D. (Jena), Professor of the English Language and Literature in the University of California. 12mo. Paper. 26 pages. Mailing Price, 22 cents; for Introduction, 20 cents.

Chaucer's Parlament of Foules.

A revised Text, with Literary and Grammatical Introduction, Notes, and a full Glossary. By T. R. LOUNSBURY, Professor of English in the Sheffield Scientific School of Yale College. 12mo. Cloth. 111 pages. Mailing Price, 55 cents; Introduction, 50 cents.

F. J. Child, *Prof. of English Lit-* ' is so good a book that I am inclined *erature in Harvard University :* It | to slight even better poetry for it.

Carpenter's Anglo-Saxon Grammar and Reader.

By STEPHEN H. CARPENTER, late Professor of Rhetoric and English Literature in the University of Wisconsin. 12mo. Cloth. 218 pages. Mailing Price, 70 cents; Introduction, 60 cents.

Carpenter's English of the XIV. Century.

By STEPHEN H. CARPENTER. 12mo. Cloth. 327 pages. Mailing Price, $1.00; Introduction, 90 cents.

ILLUSTRATED by Notes, Grammatical and Philological, on Chaucer's *Prologue* and *Knight's Tale*, and so forming an excellent introduction to that author.

Beówulf, and The Fight at Finnsburh.

Translated by JAMES M. GARNETT, M.A., LL.D., Professor of the English Language and Literature in the University of Virginia. With Facsimile of the Unique Manuscript in the British Museum, Cotton, Vitellius A XV. *Second Edition, revised.* 12mo. Cloth. 156 pages. Mailing Price, $1.10; Introduction, $1.00. *See Announcements.*

Francis A. March, *Prof. of Comparative Philology, Lafayette College:* This is the best translation so far in our language, and will do honor to American scholarship.

J. Earle, *Prof. of Anglo-Saxon in the University of Oxford, Eng.:* It is a very complete piece of work, bringing the whole subject up to the very front line of its progress.

An Old English Grammar.

By EDUARD SIEVERS, Ph.D., Professor of Germanic Philology in the University of Tübingen ; translated and edited by ALBERT S. COOK, Ph.D. (Jena), Professor of the English Language and Literature in the University of California. Second edition, revised and enlarged. 12mo. Cloth. xx + 273 pages. Mailing Price, $1.25 ; for Introduction, $1.12.

IT is hoped that this version will be found not only to present in English the most approved text-book on the subject, but to present it in a form better adapted for the use of students, and in some respects more in accord with the views of the best authorities.

F. J. Child, *Prof. of Eng., Harvard Univ.:* It is an absolutely masterly book, as would be expected of those who have made it. (*Feb.* 4, 1888.)

C. F. Richardson, *Prof. of Eng.,*

Dartmouth College : No more important work is now accessible to the student of the early grammatical forms of our twelve-hundred-year-old English language. (*Feb.* 28, 1888.)

BOOKS ON ENGLISH LITERATURE.

Copies sent to Teachers for Examination, with a view to Introduction,
on receipt of the Introduction Price given above.

GINN & COMPANY, Publishers,
Boston, New York, and Chicago.